# UNCLE SAM'S KIDS

To Roz and Charlotte
Thanks for Coming to
Gull Cottage —

Enjoy!
Randy Bartlett

# UNCLE SAM's KIDS

## RANDY BARTLETT

First Edition

ISBN-13: 979-8-6491-6156-5

Cover image by A-P-Graphics, created with the use of: 1) Photo of Frankfurt (Wikimedia Commons / Bundesarchiv, B 145 Bild-F005759-0004 / Schlempp / CC-BY-SA 3.0) and 2) Map (Wikimedia Commons / US Library of Congress, Geography & Map Division, ID g6081s.ct004402).

Independently Published

Printed in the United States of America

To my family with much love.
And to Rickie: We were kids, once.

# Part 1
## Danish Summer

# *Doc*

Most people have no idea how different it is growing up in a military family—constantly moving, packing, unpacking, friends and pets reduced to memories, no roots. You make friends quickly because you know you could be saying goodbye at any time, from a few months to, at best, a couple of years. For me, that was never easy. Even now, when someone asks where I'm from, I'm not quite sure what to answer.

"Nowhere, really; my father was in the Navy."

Copenhagen, spring 1956.

This time we moved into a house like no other my family had ever lived in. Owned by the U.S. Navy for its attachés to Denmark (my father being the latest), it was in Taarbaek, a coastal fishing village north of the city. The inside of its two stories of yellow stucco radiated craftsmanship from a bygone era: large rooms, aged hardwood floors, and a water view from nearly every window. Twelve-foot ceilings were the norm except in my attic bedroom, which had one window and a small balcony. On a clear day you could see across miles of gun-metal-blue water to Sweden, a distant mirage appearing and disappearing on the horizon. The best thing about my room, however, was that it was one door away from Elena's bedroom, also in the attic. Not that much older than I—nineteen, maybe—she was the Danish cook and housekeeper Mom hired soon after our arrival. Her shoulder-length, reddish-gold hair, Marilyn Monroe anatomy, and saucy personality kept me in eternal hopes of spectacular future adventures—no matter how farfetched the likelihood of such thoughts ever coming true might be.

Across the cobblestone street out front, the edge of Dyrehaven, Copenhagen's famous deer park, beckoned. I spent hours that summer exploring its forests, ponds, and meadows. Out back, a battered cement sea wall protected our rectangular, manicured lawn with its carefully tended rose beds from the unpredictable seas of the Øresund. My favorite thing about the backyard was a wooden dock that jutted out from the wall, daring swells from the next storm to carry it away. Fishing was my thing, and its weather-beaten planks provided a perfect platform for catching cod and mackerel.

The afternoon I met Doc Gordon I was in my room unpacking household things, recently arrived from the Naval Air Station in Jacksonville, Florida, our previous location. Inside a box marked "personal" with Pa's name on it I found his old Smith & Wesson .38, snugged in its leather shoulder holster—ammo for it, too. During the air wars in the Pacific and later Korea, it was his service revolver, issued to carrier pilots in case they were shot down. He taught me how to use it at the base target range in Jacksonville, so I was already a pretty good shot; but I knew he'd skin me alive if he ever found out what I was about to do with it. Loading the cylinder, I stepped onto the balcony. Nobody was around. Nearby Bellevue Beach, a popular seminude sunbathing spot, was almost empty. Pa was at his office in the Embassy, Mom off satisfying her passion for porcelain at the Royal Copenhagen factory. My younger brother, Curt, was with the son of some Danish piano player I'd never heard of named Victor Børge. Lissa, my little sister, was at her first nursery school. I was pretty sure Elena, the only other person around besides me, was in the kitchen preparing dinner. She wouldn't hear the shot.

I had this problem, you see. A seagull had taken to roosting on the gazebo, splattering it with foul-smelling leftovers from his digested crab and fish meals. This did not go over well with Mom, who liked to sit in the green and brown Victorian house at the far end of the dock to sip an occasional early-morning cup of tea. She complained to Pa at breakfast one morning, and he looked straight at me.

"Andy, I think it would be a great idea if you kept the dock shipshape every day before chow," he said, as if giving an order from the bridge of an aircraft carrier.

"Why can't Elena do it?" I replied, without thinking.

The coffee mug in his hand froze. It was from his early days on the USS Lexington, before it was sunk in World War II. Silence smothered the table. I could feel his eyes scanning the side of my face like radar waves. We all knew my comment had triggered Pa's quick temper.

"Because I asked you to do it," he replied, after a second warning glance from Mom. The sacred mug, with its blue Navy anchor on one side and CV-2 on the other, slowly returned to its place next to his half-eaten scrambled eggs and ham. We all relaxed, especially me. "Elena has plenty of work to do," he continued, "so I'm sure she'll be happy to supply you with a bucket, scrub brush, and hot water. Understood?" From then on, instead of sleeping in, I spent my early-morning hours crawling around on hands and knees, scraping seagull shit. Somehow, that bird had to go.

Revolver in hand, I stood on the balcony that crisp afternoon of my first Scandinavian summer, counting roses while waiting for the seagull to appear. Finishing the red ones, I'd just started on the cream yellow blossoms when the pest arrived, another squirming crab clamped in its beak. Cocking the hammer, I steadied the pistol on the iron balcony railing, sights on my target's head. Exhaling half a breath, I tightened my index finger on the trigger. Suddenly, motion at the edge of my vision—somebody was trotting across the yard. Too late! The revolver kicked, and a fountain of water from the slug's near miss sent the gull flapping for altitude. The intruder grabbed his stomach, jerked forward, and collapsed on the grass beside the roses.

I was in shock. My God! Is he dead? Sirens. Ambulances. Danish police standing around the body, looking at me with the gun in my hand. A terrifying vision of Pa, answering his office phone and jumping to his feet —I started to shake. How did this happen? I couldn't have hit him.

After an eternity (seconds?), the body jumped up grinning, arms raised in surrender.

"Don't shoot, Lone Ranger. I give up. Was that the beginning or the end of the war?"

"What are you doing in my backyard?" I yelled, when I could speak.

"Looking for you, of course."

The French doors to the living room swung open, and

Elena hurried across the grass toward him, her lovely face a mask of worry.

"Elena. My Viking goddess." He swept her backward in his arms, almost to the ground. Braless orbs squeezed against the cotton work blouse she kept partially unbuttoned when Mom wasn't around.

"Stop slobbing my neck," she giggled.

More laughter, and the two of them looked up at me. I hid the pistol behind my back.

"Is something the matter, Elena?" I shouted.

"You do not have to speak so all of Taarbaek village may hear, Andy. I heard a terrible noise and asked Doc what it was, but he does not know. Do you?"

Doc? She knows him?

"Probably a truck backfiring on the Strandvej," I managed. My free hand was white from squeezing the twisted iron balcony railing.

"When I was little, I heard drunken German soldiers shooting. It was like that."

"It did sound like a gunshot, didn't it?" said the boy beside her. He wore a white T-shirt, Levis with rolled up cuffs, sweat socks, and black penny loafers—definitely American.

"Who are you and what do you want?" I yelled, not caring if the neighbors heard me.

"I came over to meet you," he replied. "I'll come up so you can welcome me properly."

"Suit yourself," I answered, without enthusiasm. "Elena can show you inside."

"I already know. Be there in a minute."

I had barely covered Pa's pistol with a couple of fishing magazines before I heard his footsteps racing up the curving attic stairs, three at a time. The door flew open.

"Come in, whoever you are," I said. "Don't bother to knock."

The kid extending his hand to me could have been a Marine drill instructor—trim waist, lean, muscular torso, sandy flattop, rugged face—I was instantly jealous. Why hadn't that Charles Atlas course I sent away for in Florida done anything for my muscles? I followed all his instructions: opened my window every night, inhaling and exhaling deep breaths; stood naked in front of the full-length mirror on the bedroom door, twisting my ice cream-bloated carcass into pretzels of pain. I overdosed on steak and eggs, just like he said. What a waste of commissary grocery tips.

"Frederick Gordon," my visitor said, grinning. "Every-body calls me Doc."

"Andy Barnes. You scared the hell out of me down there. I'm still shaking."

"You're not supposed to shoot people, you know." His gray eyes brimmed with mischief.

"It was your fault," I said, annoyed. "You ran across my line of fire."

"Well," he replied, after an awkward silence, "guess I'll have to forgive your lack of judgment. First time I ever came over to meet somebody and got shot at, that's all." He glanced around, sniffing. "Man, this place stinks. How'd these crates get so moldy?"

"All I know is that our stuff got sent to Germany two months ago by mistake," I replied. "It just arrived. My folks were really pissed."

"Need a hand unpacking?"

For the next hour Doc helped open, sort, and carry boxes that didn't belong in my room downstairs as we swapped stories of our families and where we'd lived. He told me about his pal Jerry Casey, the kid who'd had this same room before me.

"That's Jerr's makeout sofa," Doc said, pointing behind me to a sagging, two-cushion affair in serious need of a one-way trip to the dump. "Used to spend a lot of time on it with Karen, their Danish maid, when his parents were at Embassy parties." I stared at the well-used piece of furniture with new respect, thinking of Elena and me making out on it.

At some point I made a comment about Mom complaining that this move was "worse than Pearl Harbor."

"Like she was there," he laughed.

"She was. So was I."

His eyebrows arched. "Uh-huh. Sure."

"It's true, Doc. I'm not lying. During the attack, our house near Waikiki got blown up by a stray Japanese bomb. It exploded outside my bedroom. Mom wasn't killed because she was standing on the back porch watching the attack. I was in my crib. The whole place was full of smoke, busted rafters, and holes from shrapnel."

"Quite a story. Why should I believe it?" He stood, shaking his head.

Did he think I was feeding him a bunch of bull? Or, worse, lying to him? Was he about to leave? Heart pounding, I took a step toward him. "I'm not making it up. It's the truth. If you don't believe me, bug off. You know the way out."

"Jeez, cool it, man."

Another pause, followed by his infectious grin. "I always heard people with red hair and glasses had terrible tempers. Now I believe it."

"Sorry. It's just that … that lying isn't my thing, and if I feel people are accusing me, I get …." My voice trailed off.

"No hard feelings, Andy. Don't worry about it. I'd never call somebody a liar until I knew him better," he replied, with a smile.

Doc's gaze settled on my guitar case. "You play that thing?"

"No. I play the guitar inside it."

"I stepped into that one, didn't I? How long? Do you sing?"

"A couple of years, and yeah, I sing, but I do it by ear— can't read a note of music."

"Is some lovely creature sobbing for you back in Jacksonville?" he asked, changing the subject.

I thought of Judy. She appeared on our school bus one morning, and I offered her my seat. We had the same study period—the last class of the day—so we used to sneak out and sit together on the football bleachers until the buses arrived. Things were going so well between us, until Pa got his orders to Copenhagen. The night before I left, we went to a movie on the base and spent most of the time in tears. What was she doing now?

"Sort of," I answered. "I knew one that …."

"Just one?"

"Her name was Judy. I took her fishing and she almost tipped the boat over trying to land her first bass."

"Fishing?" Doc said, as though smelling something unpleasant. "You couldn't think of anything better to do with her?"

My face exploded into instant sunburn. "Don't get me wrong. There were lots of neat girls living on the base, but we mostly did stuff together—Teen Club dances, movies, swimming parties—so there wasn't a lot of one-on-one time, if you know what I mean."

"Okay, so you're not much when it comes to girls," he

said, picking up a recently unpacked picture of my cat.

"What was its name?"

"Tum Tum," I replied. Sending her in a crate across the country to my grandmother's had been the most painful part of moving to Denmark. "She liked to roll over and have me scratch her tummy."

My visitor rolled his eyes.

"You're supposed to do that with girls, not cats. Did your fishy girlfriend want her tummy rubbed … when you weren't forcing her to go fishing, that is?"

"Of course not. It's that …."

"Man, you're in worse shape than I thought," he cut in, shaking his head. "Hopeless. Can't tell the difference between fish, cats, and girls. I'm beginning to wonder if I can salvage you."

I was about to tell him he wasn't funny, but he was already talking about Rhein-Main Air Base in Frankfurt, Germany. I was beginning to find his rapid changes of topic irritating.

"Biggest in Germany. It's the one that supplied the Berlin Airlift. My stepdad was involved in that operation," he added, proudly. "You did fly into Rhein-Main, right?" he added, seeing my confusion.

"Not the Barnes family. Mom refuses to set foot in an airplane, so we came by ship."

"Well, you'll see it soon enough, when you fly down there with the rest of us next fall.  You are going to Frankfurt High, aren't you?"

"I have no idea. Pa wants to send me to sea on some Danish cadet training ship."

"You mean the Danmark? The Danish Navy's three-masted square-rigger? Wow! I'd sell my soul to do that. Imagine climbing the mainmast to the crow's nest at dawn and seeing ocean all around." His eyes glittered. I would see that look many times during the coming year.

"Jesus Christ, Doc. You sound like my father." I told him about dinner the night Pa started talking about my becoming a guest naval cadet. There was a vacancy, and the Danes had decided to offer it to the son of a foreign naval attaché.

"He said it was a lifetime opportunity. I got this pep talk about salt air, scrubbing wooden decks, and climbing the rigging. I told him I wasn't sure I wanted to go away from home that long—or sail around the world, for that matter; but he had already submitted the paperwork. He keeps reminding me that my chances are excellent."

Doc looked at me in disbelief. "You don't want to go?"

"I'd rather stay here and take correspondence courses."

"Never," he replied, slapping his palm onto the desk, knocking the magazines off Pa's revolver. "I did those horrible things the first year we lived here—dull, boring, they were terrible. Frankfurt High's much better—it's a real school. So, why are you holed up in your room instead of checking out Danish girls?"

"I … there was nothing else to do, so …."

"What? You're in Denmark, and you say there's nothing to do?"

"We've only been here a short time, and—"

"Let me clue you in, Lone Ranger: you and I—mostly you—are strangers in paradise. This is a fabulous country —wonderful food, friendly people, athletic women." His voice trailed off as he stared into space. "When you get exhausted chasing them, Bakken's almost across the street. You've been to Bakken, haven't you?"

"I've been meaning to go, but—"

He threw up his hands and paced back and forth,

shaking his head.

"This is worse than I thought. He lives across the street from the most exciting place in Copenhagen, and doesn't have a freakin' clue about anything. What am I going to do with him?"

"I've had enough of this," I interrupted. "Why don't you...."

Paying no attention, he proceeded to rave about how great Bakken was, the food, drunks gambling away their paychecks and getting into fights, its fabulous women, and rides "so dangerous they wouldn't be allowed back in the States."

"How did you get the name 'Doc'?" I asked when his lecture was over. "I've never known anyone called 'Doc' before."

"My dad," he answered, "but nobody knows where he got it from."

"You never asked him?"

For the first time, my new friend was slow to respond. A trace of pain crossed his face.

"He was killed when his P-38 was shot down over Holland. I barely remember him."

I looked at the kid next to me. I had never experienced anything worse than one of my cats getting killed by a car. What would my life have been like if Pa hadn't come back? Apart from burns during a kamikaze attack, the only wounds he'd received were cuts on his lip and cheek from pieces of his plane's windshield in one of his dogfights with Japanese Zeros. He smoked, drank, and had a short temper; at times, when I was little, I was afraid of him. But he worked hard at his career, took care of his family, and I knew that, in his way, he loved me.

Doc picked up one of my fishing rods, waving it in

circles over my head.

"Hey, that's my favorite bass rod. I've had it since I was a kid."

"You're still a kid," he replied, pressing my shoulder down. "On your knees.

"I solemnly pledge to do everything in my power to see that the Lone Ranger, here, grows up properly in Denmark," he began. "Furthermore, I will do what I can to prevent him from becoming a social catastrophe at Frankfurt, and you will find I always keep my promises, Mr. Barnes."

"I told you, I'd just as soon take correspondence courses."

His grip tightened. "As I was saying, when he comes to Frankfurt this fall, I promise to provide sage advice regarding matters of love involving members of the opposite sex." A pause. "If you get involved with the same sex, you're on your own."

"I've had enough of this crap," I growled, struggling to get up.

Tapping both shoulders with my bass rod, he released me.

"Arise, Lone Ranger. Tonto, at your service."

"Then the first thing Tonto can do is stop this Lone Ranger garbage," I said, rubbing my knees as I stood up. "Why do you assume I'm going to Frankfurt? And what makes you think I'd like it?"

Rolling his eyes, he plunked down on Jerry Casey's makeout sofa, snatching Pa's .38 off the desk. My stomach tightened.

"Heavy sucker," he commented, waving the revolver as he stepped to the balcony. Beyond the dock, a sailboat heeled over in a puff of wind.

"How much you wanna bet I can put a hole through that Danish flag on its mast?"

"Are you crazy? That gun you're fooling around with is loaded."

"Skip the Boy Scout stuff, Barnes."

I imagined Pa's face, a volcano of fury, erupting as I tried to explain why I'd let some new kid take potshots at Danish sailboats from my bedroom balcony. I made several useless grabs for the revolver.

"Put it down—please, Doc. Look, let's go  out on the end of the dock and … and I'll show you where the Taarbaek nudist camp is, okay?"

"You mean that place half a mile down the shore where the women weigh three hundred pounds, and not one of 'em is under age seventy? Come on, Barnes. Jerry and I rowed down there more than once. Why don't you try it by yourself sometime. You could ask one if she'd like to go fishing with you."

His aim shifted to our wooden backyard table, where the annoying seagull was back, this time  gulping leftover biscuits from dishes on Mom's silver tea tray.

"Doc, no! Everybody in Taarbaek will …."

The .38 jumped in his hand. Instantly, the back of Mom's favorite lawn chair smacked against the tray, sending it skidding across the table top. A chunk of seawall disintegrated as the ricocheting .38 slug whined into the gazebo roof at the end of the dock. Wood splinters fluttered toward the Øresund's lapping wavelets. A blue-and-white teapot teetered on the edge of the table and dropped from sight.

"Oh God," I choked, trying to convince myself what I'd seen hadn't happened. Her words as she unpacked it from the factory, only a few days before, echoed in my mind: "I think Royal Copenhagen is the most beautiful porcelain ever made."

Doc blew an imaginary puff of smoke from the end of the barrel. "Aw, I missed him."

"You idiot," I burst out, yanking the gun away and retreating into my bedroom. Emptying the cylinder, I kicked the stubby bullets under Jerr Casey's makeout sofa and sank onto it in a poof of dust mites. What could I do? Tell Doc to take a hike? Would he leave?

"After Pa finds out about this, you won't see what's left of my ass outside this room for the rest of the summer."

"Stop worrying. Tonto think Lone Ranger better gettum butt down 'dere and clean up mess before anyone see what happened."

"Your Indian talk isn't very funny," I said, sourly.

At the disaster scene, Doc turned over several pieces of deceased teapot in his hands. I slammed the lawn chair upright.

"What now, Einstein?"

"My fertile imagination will think of something. It's one of my sterling qualities."

"From what I've seen in the past few minutes, I'd say it isn't worth dog turds."

He turned on me, serious for the first time since he'd arrived.

"Hey, I'm your guest, remember? I drove over here to welcome you to Denmark, and what do I find? A new kid so bored, all he can do is hang around in his room and kill seagulls."

"So you do your best to ground me for the rest of the summer. Thanks a lot."

"Look, Andy. I've been here two years. Denmark is the niftiest place I've ever lived. I can show you how to take advantage of Copenhagen, and have the best summer of your life. Assuming you go to Frankfurt this fall, I know girls who will make your head spin. I'll fix you up with Copper Hopkinson. She's June Everett's best friend. June's my girl." He paused. "Well, sort of. We can double-date. How's that for starters?"

"I don't give a damn about the girls in Frankfurt. What about right now, huh? How am I going to get out of this mess you've gotten me into, hotshot?"

"Yes, Tonto think of something." He picked up the teapot spout.

"Yeah, you do that," I said, putting the surviving creamer, a half-empty cup and saucer, and a butter plate onto the solid silver tray. It was a gift to my parents when we left Chile, and had engraved signatures of attachés and diplomats all over it. Inside the French doors of the living room, I saw Elena watching us with a half-smile. She turned away, shaking her head.

"Heap good silver bullet miss silver tray," said Tonto.

"Maybe Mom won't notice the teapot is missing. I'll buy her another one, and …."

"Of course she'll notice. She's a mother."

Out on the street, the black Embassy Ford slowed and doom on four wheels came to a stop in our graveled driveway. Aage, the chauffeur, hurried to open the rear door.

# *Mom*

Clutching several shopping bags and her favorite alligator purse (which matched her shoes), she stepped out of the car. Fox pelts—the ones from Chile that were biting each other's tails—hung like sleeping weasels over her shoulders. From a childhood of poverty, she had grown into her role as a Navy wife—skilled at taking care of her children, organizing, packing, and decorating. An expert at quickly turning a few temporary rooms, an empty apartment, or house into a genuine home, she was talented artistically and musically, socially popular, and intuitively savvy about how to schmooze the right people to subtly enhance Pa's career. Sometime during the Korean War while Pa was gone she'd discovered religion, but was the only one in our family to do so. Once, when she was pushing Pa to read the Bible, I heard him grumble,

"Your only defect is that you read that damned book too much. I'm not ready to start cramming for the finals."

Doc waved. She smiled and headed for us. I was seconds away from becoming toast.

"Doc, what am I going to do?"

"What are we going to do, Andy—we."

It was a defining moment. Whatever happened next, I

knew I wouldn't face the music alone. This new kid, cool and relaxed, was going to stick with me. But was it too late? Was there anything he could do that might save my miserable ass? "Tonto got Lone Ranger into this fix, and Tonto get him out of it," Doc whispered, fitting together several larger pieces of broken teapot in his hands. "I've got an idea, but you have to do exactly as I say."

"Anything—just do it quick," I croaked.

"How nice of you boys to clean up the leftovers from my morning tea," Mom beamed, crossing the grass. "Who is your friend, Andy?"

"Hullo, Mom," I replied, trying to keep the dishes from rattling on the tray.

"Hello, Mrs. Barnes," Doc said as the distance between us closed. I realized that to Mom, it looked like he was holding a normal teapot. She was closing fast.

"Hold out the tray—now," he hissed, from the corner of a big smile glued across his face. His eyes sparkled with excitement.

Turning slightly, as if placing the real teapot onto my extended tray, he stumbled. The teapot slipped from his grasp, disintegrating against a sizable rock at his feet.

Dropping her bags, Mom rushed toward us.

"Are you all right?" Her attractive face a mixture of anxiety and concern. Then a gasp. "My teapot."

Wincing, Doc got up, rubbing his knee. "I'm Frederick Gordon, Mrs. Barnes, and I'm so sorry. It's all my fault. My mother will be furious when she finds out. This is not how I normally meet people."

Although I knew she was in shock, Mom smiled and held out her hand.

"I'm Isabel Barnes, Frederick. Don't worry, dear— accidents happen. Besides, it's a good reason to make another trip to the Royal Copenhagen factory, isn't it? I'm so grateful you weren't cut by those sharp fragments. Come, you must stay for some of Elena's butter cookies."

"Everybody calls me Doc," he replied, shooting me a glance of triumph.

As we crossed the lawn, Doc's lesson on how to hoodwink adults continued.

"Please," he said, reaching for her shopping bags as we approached them. "Let me." At the porch, he stepped ahead to open the French doors.

"I'm delighted Andy has found such a courteous new friend," Mom said, giving me a "why can't you have manners like his?" glance.

Inside, she excused herself to find Elena.

"You really like to cut things close, don't you, Gordon? What if you didn't figure it quite right? What if it hadn't worked?"

"But I knew it would," he answered. "More exciting that way."

Exciting? The way he said it was almost like he somehow found shooting the table and the whole teapot catastrophe stimulating. So cocksure of himself, wired for excitement. I envied Doc's self-confidence. But when Mom arrived and the chips were down, he'd stood with me —I was not going to face the consequences alone. Then he'd brilliantly gotten us out of the mess he'd created, almost like he felt it was his duty to save us. I'd never met someone who seemed to get so much satisfaction from escaping a tight spot like that. Man, was I confused. And yet, something deep down attracted me to him. Charisma? Sincerity? Desire to be my friend? I certainly needed one.

Mom returned, followed by Elena with a different tea set, glasses of milk, and cookies. Winking at Doc, she retraced her steps, making the skirt of her maid's outfit swish back and forth.

"Mouthwatering," he commented, as her shapely hips disappeared into the kitchen.

"Yes, Frederick," said Mom, passing the cookies. "They do look delicious, don't they?"

"So, Mrs. Barnes," he asked, taking several, "how do you like Copenhagen?"

"Of all the places we've lived," she began, warming to her favorite topic next to God, "Taarbaek is definitely the nicest, most lovely house—it's a castle."

She launched into the beautiful yard, lovely Dyrehaven, and the quaintness of Taarbaek village. I knew where this would end—Pa's career and all the places it had taken us— but Doc kept asking questions which, I had to admit, seemed offered out of genuine interest. I took a handful of cookies and settled back, looking out the window in time to see the seagull reappear on the dock railing with a piece of fish carcass. Damned bird.

"Our house got bombed during the Japanese attack," she was saying.

"I already told him," I interrupted.

"Andy's father spent the whole war flying in the Pacific," she continued. "While he was gone, Andy and I lived in Coronado, California."

"Was he in the Battle of Midway?" asked Doc, putting down his glass.

"No, thankfully," she replied. "He broke his collarbone crash-landing in one of those old fighter planes the week before."

"A Grumman F4F Wildcat," I said, for historical clarification.

She stood, turning toward the roses outside. "So many

of our close friends were killed out there," she said quietly, her thoughts far away in another time.

"What happened after Midway?" Doc asked, when she had returned to the present.

"At the Battle of Leyte Gulf, he was shot down and reported missing in action."

"The Solomon Islands, Mom," I interrupted, trying to speed things up. "He floated around for a week, Doc. The only thing he had to eat was a large bird that landed on his rubber raft. He was going to shoot it but decided not to, in case he put a hole in the raft. So he broke its neck, pulled out the feathers, and ate it raw. The eyeballs provided a bit of fresh water."

Looking queasy, Mom put down her teacup.

"But Frederick—I mean Doc—please tell us about your family. Andy's father and I met your parents at a party last week, and I remember your dad is an Air Force officer. Is he a pilot?"

Doc glanced in my direction, hesitated, and then repeated what he had told me earlier. Mom started to say something about God's will, but my new friend stopped her.

"It happened a long time ago, Mrs. Barnes. I learned that losing someone you love is part of life. Sooner or later, it happens to all of us. The important thing is how you deal with it. I'm fine now. I love my stepfather, and my four little sisters adore me. I couldn't ask for anything better."

While Mom glowed, Elena entered with a refill of cookies.

"I sure do like Elena's goodies," Doc commented, as

the two of us watched her rustle toward the kitchen.

"You seem a bit older than Andy," Mom said, following our stares.

"I'm almost 16, Mrs. Barnes. My birthday is at the end of June."

"Oh, you're almost exactly a year apart. Andy will be 15 in July. But I was wondering, Frederick—I mean Doc—how you liked Frankfurt High School this past year."

"That's the real reason she invited you for cookies, Doc." I was rewarded by Mom's momentary flash of irritation.

"It's a great place, Mrs. Barnes. Much better than that boring freshman year I spent at the Copenhagen American School doing correspondence courses. I got so little accomplished that my father took me to his office every day, where he could watch me work."

"Oh? Andy just finished his algebra doing one of those. We left Jacksonville two months ago, before his school year was finished. His father hired Knut, a Danish university student, to tutor him. He was such a nice young man."

We didn't care much for each other, Knut and I. He wasn't interested in fishing, and I disliked my tutor's favorite subject. But he got on famously with Elena. He would finish my algebra assignment in ten minutes, and spend the rest of the hour in Elena's room with the door closed. Pa mailed the work to the University of Whatever somewhere in Kansas, and I got A's, which pleased Pa and earned my tutor a bonus. I suspect Elena, however, gave Knut his real rewards.

"Remind me to tell you about Knut sometime," I said to Doc.

"Last year I lived in the Frankfurt dormitory," he

continued. "Kids there are from military and civilian families in Germany and all over Europe. I loved it, and I know Andy would, too—much, much better than staying here."

Mom nodded, but I'd had enough.

"Kee-rist, Doc. You're making Frankfurt sound like the Land of Oz. We just met. How the hell do you know what's good for me?"

Mom recoiled. "Andy! Your language is deplorable. Apologize right now."

"No need, Mrs. Barnes," Doc interrupted. "If he goes to Frankfurt, I plan to shape him up."

"My husband and I are a bit at odds about it," she replied, calming down. "He wants Andy to go on the training ship Danmark for a long cruise next year."

"I already told him, Mom."

"Well," said Doc, trying to keep things upbeat, "at this point, it seems Andy's school next year is a three-way toss-up. Anyway, I hope he ends up at Frankfurt."

The phone rang, and Mom excused herself. Doc snagged the last cookies and leaned back, munching contentedly. Mom returned, no longer the relaxed hostess interested in Frankfurt. Apologizing, she told us she had to get ready for a dinner engagement at the American ambassador's.

"Embassy business," she said.

"My folks are also going to dinner at the ambassador's tonight," said Doc, after she left. "Mother has to sit next to Captain Kossiakoff, the Russian naval attaché."

"Our parents are eating with Commies? What are you talking about?"

"All part of the job, Lone Ranger. My dad told me that the booze at those parties gets people talking, and sometimes they say things they shouldn't. My mother is very good at remembering that sort of stuff. I'll bet yours is, too."

"You mean our folks are secret agents fighting against communism? Mom, an American spy? Pa actually running a network of undercover agents from his office in the Embassy?"

"You've been reading too many comic books," Doc replied laughing, as we crunched across the driveway to his father's red Volkswagen Beetle. "By the way, do you know how to sail? I crew on my neighbors' junior boat, and there's a big race at Taarbaek Harbor this weekend. Want to come?"

I'd never sailed in my life—canoes and rowboats, yes, but not sailboats.

"Sure, Doc."

As I watched the little car turn out of the driveway one thing was certain, that off-the-wall June afternoon in 1956: I was already regretting the day we would have to say goodbye.

# *Sailing with Doc*

I did go sailing with Doc—once. The weather was lousy that Saturday afternoon, but he wouldn't hang up until I agreed.

"Grab your foul-weather gear and meet me at Taarbaek Harbor in half an hour."

"You mean my raincoat?"

"Look, Barnes: we need you for ballast, so be there, understand?"

"I'll bring my fishing gear, okay?"

"No, it's not okay." He hung up.

When I asked Elena if she'd fix me a peanut butter and jelly sandwich, she pinched her nose. "The boat will smell of peanuts. Everyone will be sick."

I stuffed her ham and Havarti cheese on dark bread into my pocket, and hurried outside.

Taarbaek Harbor was a forest of masts with sails crackling in a strong easterly wind. Beyond the breakwater, whitecaps laced the Øresund under an ominous sky. In Jacksonville, I would have scratched plans to go fishing on the wide St. John's River without a second thought. To the Danes, however, threatening weather apparently didn't matter.

I had no trouble finding the blue sailboat Doc had described, the one at the end of the quay with one mast and two triangular sails.

"At last," he said. "Where have you been? If we don't shove off, it'll take forever getting out of the harbor. Andy, meet my next-door neighbors, Inge and Kirsten Dahlström. They're Danish girls, in case you hadn't noticed."

Two similar freckled faces smiled up at me from the boat's cockpit. Tanned legs extended from yellow slickers like Doc's.

"Twins, aren't they?" I observed.

"Very good, Barnes. There might be hope for you yet."

"Thank you for inviting me," I said.

"You have sailed before?" Inge asked.

"Actually, no, but Doc said—"

"I see," said Kirsten, throwing a kapok life ring at his midsection.

He doubled over as if neutered.

"Get in boat," she laughed, disappearing under an armful of flapping sail. A barrage of orders followed.

"Up mainsail. Cast off. Trim jib." Around us, skippers hollered to scrambling crews. I had no idea what was happening, but our sails billowed, and we were underway. A gust of wind leaned the boat over, throwing me onto one of its varnished bench seats.

"Stay," Inge commanded.

Another boat crossed our bow, and I braced for a collision.

"Hard to lee," yelled Kirsten, shoving the tiller to one side.

Inge clapped her hand on my head and pushed it down, saving me from a cracked skull as the boom—a heavy piece of fir attached to the bottom of the big canvas mainsail—whipped by, missing my head by inches. Now we were headed straight for boulders that protected the harbor from the Øresund.

"The rocks," I screamed.

"Hard to lee," sang out Kirsten.

This time I ducked without being told as we came about.

"What rocks?" said Doc.

I looked up to see whitecaps and open water. The bow dipped into green waves, drenching me. Ahead of us, the starting line was coming up fast.

It's a good thing I've never been seasick, because the weather that afternoon got worse—much worse. By the time the race finished, the Øresund was a blizzard of froth, and boats with broken masts were being towed back to Taarbaek as angry clouds scudded above.

"I have a great idea," Doc announced. "Let's have some fun and ride the waves."

We stared at him. A shiver rippled down the back of my neck.

"Are you totally nuts? The race nearly got canceled. Time to quit."

"Worst day ever," Kirsten added. "Boat has limits. Crew, too. We go in."

"Good sailors know weather always stronger," Inge said. "We return."

"Aw, c'mon, ladies," Doc taunted. "This ship is built strong as a Viking longboat. It's the perfect opportunity to show us what good sailors Danish girls are."

I had grown up around the water, and I knew we didn't belong out here. Yet Doc was apparently willing to risk our lives for his idea of fun. What would Pa say, assuming we made it back alive? Until now, he trusted my judgment, but after this? Was that trust going to be ruined by someone I hardly knew?

"I'm with them, Doc," I shouted into the rising wind. "Whacking around in these seas is not my idea of fun."

"I'll forget I heard that, Barnes."

"This is a serious storm. The girls are right. Listen to them."

But he wouldn't give up, and the twins eventually wavered.

"Enough." said Kirsten. "We stay longer, but must wear safety coats."

As Inge reached for kapok life jackets, a monster wave hit the side of the boat. Three of us put ours on as fast as we could.

"I don't need a sissy coat," said Doc.

"Then I turn boat and trip over," snapped Kirsten. Her look left no doubt she meant it. "Put on—now."

He did as ordered.

I lost track of time as we surfed down dark rollers that catapulted us forward with exhilarating speed. Doc sat with a smile on his wet face, singing "Sailing, sailing, over the bounding main" in a cracked voice. The wind increased, and the rigging vibrated with an ominous hum. I wondered what we would do if something broke.

Kirsten finally turned the boat for home. For several hours, however, jarring seas kept us miles from Taarbaek. It seemed to me we were being pushed backward, and it was almost dark. Then, without warning, a powerful gust laid the boat on its side. Kirsten let go of the rope in her hands, and it sizzled through several pulleys. The boom swung free, a wave caught it, and half the Øresund poured into the cockpit. Our boat, which had a thousand pounds of lead in the keel and no flotation of any kind, began to wallow.

"Bail, Andy!" Doc screamed above the wind, as he threw a bucket at me.

While the two of us flung water to leeward like madmen, Kirsten struggled to bring the bow into the wind. Inge almost went overboard trying to free the sail from the sea's watery grasp, but Doc yanked her back in time. After an eternity, the boat righted itself, with the bow pointing into the wind. Gusts shrieked with an eerie sound I'd never heard before. Then, without warning, the boom and mainsail crashed down, trapping us under folds of wet canvas.

"*For helvede,*" cursed Inge, from somewhere under our impromptu tent.

"What happened, Doc?" I shouted.

"Halyard broke."

"The what?"

"The rope that holds up the sail."

"Is it serious?"

"Not if you know how to get us home without a sail."

"Can we fix it?"

For a few moments he studied the halyard block, thumping back and forth near the top of the mast, then grinned. "If I can put a spare line through that empty block …."

"You can't shimmy up there," I yelled, when I realized what he was thinking.

"Mast can have weak place," said Kirsten.

"No safety coat," added Inge.

"You won't be able to wear your life jacket up there," I pitched in, "and if the mast cracks you'll fall overboard or break your stupid neck." But he had already removed his shirt and was unbuckling his pants.

"The girls have been desperate to see me naked all summer," he laughed, tossing his Levis into the cabin slosh and starting on his jockey shorts.

"You better wear those if you don't want to leave important parts of your anatomy snagged on the mast," I shouted in his ear.

"Point taken, Lone Ranger. Keep bailing while the girls reef the main and jib. Kirsten, get the spare halyard."

With a worried look, she retrieved a fresh coil of line from a storage compartment in the stern and handed it to him. Silently, we watched his muscular body slither upward.

"Cheer up," Doc yelled down to worried faces looking up at him, as he swayed in figure eights each time the boat rolled in the waves. Then he extended both arms, using his legs to hold his body in place.

Inge gasped, hand against her mouth, as he started to slide. Somehow, he stopped himself, and began inching upward, eventually managing to replace the halyard and get down safely. Chest heaving, Doc struggled into his wet clothes while the twins threaded the new line through some pulleys.

"Nothing to it," he said, through chattering teeth.

"Weren't you scared?" I asked, shoving his life jacket at him.

"Well, after your comment, I was a bit concerned that Willy and the Boys might get left on a cleat when I slipped up there."

Darkness hid our visual reference points as Kirsten tacked us back and forth, insisting we were headed for Taarbaek. After another hour of smacking into unseen waves, I was stiff from bailing and half frozen. So were the others. No one spoke. An argument in Danish erupted between the sisters.

"C'mon, girls," Doc pleaded. "Let's not fight. What's happening?"

"Wind not right and boat is pushed back," replied Inge. "Never get to Taarbaek. "Rungsted closer. Must try Rungsted."

"Inge's right," said Doc. "We can't spend the night in these seas—we're so far into the shipping channel some freighter could run us down and no one would ever know."

Kirsten changed course, and the pounding against the hull immediately diminished.

"I can't see anything," I said. "Where's land?"

As the boat crested on a large swell, she pointed beyond the bow at winks of red and green in the distant night.

"Rungsted. There."

Two hours later, we were inside the harbor.

"We stay at friend's house," Inge said. "Need warm bath and eat something."

"Sounds good to me," said Doc. "But I'll need both of you to keep me warm. What do we do with Andy?"

"Only one bed," Kirsten teased.

After securing the boat, we went to a telephone booth where Inge called friends living nearby. After several tries she gave up.

"Gone, I think. Must stay in boat tonight."

I thought of the time in Florida, when a squall blew my buddy Ross and me three miles across the river. Mom was terrified. Eventually, we were picked up by a Navy patrol boat that Pa sent looking for us.

"I should call the folks," I volunteered. "Mom's going to be frantic."

"Think, Andy," Doc groaned. "Is she going to let us

spend the night in the boat with the girls? She'll call my parents and that will be the end of everything."

"You're not making sense, Gordon. We have no sleeping bags, no dry clothes, no towels, and we're freezing wet. I'm sopped clean through. The boat is wet. There isn't one single thing that isn't wet."

"Must be dry and warm," said Kirsten. She looked at Doc with a naughty expression. "Not possible in boat. Maybe another time."

"But Andy …."

His voice trailed off as I picked up the receiver and dialed. Mom answered right away. After asking again and again if we were safe and assuring herself we were, she promised to call Doc's folks and handed the phone to Pa, who said he was just about to call the Danish Navy.

While Aage drove to Rungstead to get us, we straggled into a nearby inn. The innkeeper placed us in front of the fireplace, passed out blankets, and ordered a waiter to bring bowls of hot soup with dark bread and butter. It was the best soup I'd ever tasted. He refused to let us pay for anything, but accepted Doc's promise to bring a case of Cokes as a thank-you gift when we returned to get the boat. In 1956 the iconic American soft drink—when available—was expensive and much appreciated in Denmark. Aage arrived, and the four of us scrunched under blankets in the rear seat of the Embassy Ford. I slipped my arm around Inge and made a mental note to never get in a boat with Doc again.

# *Rex*

"What's for lunch?" I called to Elena. I was sitting in the sun on the sheltered brick porch outside the kitchen.

She appeared in the doorway behind me, wiping her hands on her apron. "I will bring a shredded carrot and apple salad, with small open sandwiches of tiny shrimps and cucumbers on thin slices of dark bread."

"How about one of your delicious peanut butter and jelly sandwiches instead?"

"Peanuts in butter is disgusting American food. Even Danish pigs cannot eat it," she laughed, throwing her dish rag at me. A few minutes later she returned with my PB&J and a glass of milk.

"Your food smells," she said, wrinkling her nose as she set it down in front of me.

"You should try some," I replied, taking a big bite. A blob of Skippy's best, scooped from a large jar Mom had bought at the Embassy commissary, plopped onto the glass tabletop.

"Ants will come," Elena said, muttering something in Danish and putting both hands on her hips. Leaning across the table to wipe up the mess, she purposely brushed one of her ample bosoms against my shoulder. The sensation was magnificent. So was the view.

"You are not eating your sandwich, Little One," she smiled, brushing her other orb across my chest as she worked. "*Først må du se at blive voksen min dreng.*"

"English, Elena, English. What does that mean?"

"First, you must grow up," she replied, with a seductive smile.

Elena's loathing of bras, plus her habit of leaving the top buttons of Mom's required uniform shirt unbuttoned, made her an absolute joy to be near. Several times the two of them had exchanged words about this matter, and once, after a lecture on "appearances that tantalize young minds" (a veiled reference, I assumed, to me), Elena walked away in a huff. When I came into the kitchen later, she was still mad.

"This uniform is the same as wearing whatever you call it, a shell," she snorted, beheading several carrots in quick succession on her chopping board.

"You mean armor like knights used in the Middle Ages?"

"Yes. A suit of metal like Hamlet."

I couldn't remember if Hamlet wore "metal" around the house, but I was on Elena's side regarding this argument. Mom's prudish approach to our attractive housekeeper's relaxed Danish views of sexuality had been pushed over the edge one morning when she was standing on the dock, teacup in hand, watching the sunrise. Our neighbor, Hans Nilsson, appeared a few meters away on his dock to take his morning swim. After exchanging greetings, he stepped out of his slippers, dropped his bathrobe, and Mom spilled her tea at the sight of "pure Hans" diving into the icy water. After that, she drank her tea at the table in the backyard.

On the other side of the house, the Gordons' VW turned into the driveway. Doors slammed.

"Around front," I yelled.

"There you are," Doc said, coming into view with a slim kid a couple of inches taller than I. His handsome features were enhanced by dark, wavy hair cemented in place with an overdose of Brylcreem. An Ivy League shirt was tucked into summer khakis with turned-up cuffs, exposing well-shined penny loafers fresh from the States. He was as different from my red hair, glasses, freckles, and Keds tennis shoes as two people could get.

"Andy," Doc said, "this is Rex Holt. His father is my dad's new boss."

I extended my hand to this living advertisement for hair oil.

"Hi, Rex. Welcome to Copenhagen."

He took out a half-empty pack of Camels, extracted one, and stuck it on his lower lip. Returning the cigarettes to his shirt pocket, he fished around for his lighter. I lowered my unshaken hand and looked at Doc. He shrugged.

"Rex will be going to Frankfurt with us this fall," Doc said, stepping into the vacuum as the new kid lit up. "Oh, I forgot, Rex: Andy may be cruising on the Danmark instead. You know, the famous square-rigger? The Danish Navy's training ship?"

Rex looked around the yard. "Nice house," he answered, to no one in particular. "My father's the highest-ranking officer in Copenhagen."

Elena re-emerged from the kitchen to clear my lunch dishes.

"Hi, beautiful, I'm Rex," he grinned, immediately extending his Camels. "And who might you be? How about a date tonight?" His eyes were glued to the top of her blouse.

"That's Elena," I said, as she waved him off with a saucy shake of her head.

"Poor baby," she laughed. *"Først må du se at blive voksen min dreng."*

"What's she saying, Gordon?"

"Haven't a clue."

"It means 'First, you must grow up,'" I said.

"Good one," said Doc, with a chuckle.

"No, really. That's what it means."

Nodding, Elena laughed again and retreated into the kitchen, bolting the door in Rex's face. He continued to sweet-talk her through the mail slot.

I turned to Doc. "How long have you known this guy?"

He lowered his voice.

"I met him several weeks ago after his family arrived. My mother thought it would be wise if I showed him around. What I wanted to tell you was, my parents are having the Holts over for a cookout tonight, and I thought you might like to join us. You can meet my family, and stuff your face with my dad's grilled burgers, real baked beans, potato salad, and homemade ice cream. Afterward, the three of us can go to Bakken. You'll be doing Tonto a favor helping keep Rex company, Lone Ranger."

I wasn't crazy about this last part, but I hadn't had American hamburgers since we left the States. And going to Bakken was the clincher.

"Count me in. Thanks, Doc."

The red VW Beetle convertible swung into the driveway that evening, spinning gravel as it came to a stop.

"This'll be great, Andy. We'll eat, and slip away to Bakken while parents are yakking."

When we arrived, everybody was in the backyard, where a sweaty Colonel Gordon stood behind a glowing charcoal grill, doling out huge, juicy hamburgers. He brandished his spatula at us, and Doc's mother disengaged from the Holts to welcome me. His four younger sisters, faces decorated with rainbow smears of burger condiments, came running. The oldest, whom Doc called Chipmunk, looked about nine or ten.

"Time for Andy to meet our guests," Doc said to his little sisters, as he ushered me toward the Holts.

"Pleased to meet you," I said, in my friendliest tone, as I was introduced.

"Pleased to meet you, sir, young man," replied the general, without taking my outstretched hand. Although wearing a sport shirt and slacks, he might as well have been in dress uniform. "In the future, remember to address me properly."

"Yes, sir," I replied. "May I ask where Rex is, sir?"

He scowled, as if I had interrupted him in the middle of an important meeting. "Home on phone duty."

I started to ask what that meant, but Doc pulled me away.

"Generals don't like questions, Lone Ranger," he whispered, as we headed toward the food. "Any rank below a colonel, okay; but never a general. We'll find out what "phone duty" means when we pick up Rex."

As I was wolfing a second bowl of vanilla ice cream after a delicious all-American meal, Doc looked at his watch.

"Time to go."

I thanked his parents, said goodbye to Chipmunk, and followed him to the Beetle, where we put the car top down.

"Hope Bakken lives up to everything you've been telling

me," I said, sinking into the passenger seat.

It was a memorable evening drive. We chugged along a narrow, winding road at the edge of the Dyrehaven, under a shimmering umbrella of amethyst green beech tree leaves. I decided when I got a car it would be a convertible.

"What do you like most about me?" Doc asked, out of the blue.

I couldn't tell if he was serious. Half the time, he followed up a query like this with a totally different one—usually before I finished answering the first—so I decided to be vague.

"Dunno. What is there about you to like?"

"C'mon, Barnes. I'm trustworthy, loyal, friendly, courteous, considerate"—he paused—"and I always keep my promises."

"Okay, Mr. Boy Scout, promises this, promises that. You keep mentioning how you always keep them, but you haven't made any to me."

"Whad'ya mean? I promised to take you to Bakken. Isn't that what I'm doing right now? I promised to take you sailing. Didn't we do that?"

"Yeah, and we almost disappeared forever, somewhere between Denmark and Sweden."

"Now, now, Barnes, let's not be negative." His craggy face melted into a beatific smile. "I know: you like me because I bring sparkle into your otherwise dull existence." He was looking straight at me, oblivious to the curve ahead.

"Watch out, you conceited prick!"

The car swerved sharply, throwing me against the door.

"Jesus, Doc. One more move like that, and I walk home —assuming I'm still alive."

"How did you like the general?" he asked when we

stopped laughing.

"I don't see there's much to like. He was about to explode when I didn't say 'sir.' How's your father going to survive that guy?"

"My dad can handle people like that," Doc replied, adjusting the rearview mirror. "He's dealt with them for a long time."

"At least with Pa you can tell when he's about to blow up. It's like a volcano, and then it's over. After a while, he's himself again. Well, most of the time."

"Bet he blew his top when you got home after the storm," Doc grinned. "You probably told him it was all my fault, so now he blames me, right?"

"What do you think I am, a snitch? Yes, I was angry at you, but I would never make someone else a scapegoat."

"So, what did you tell him?" Doc persisted.

"Who?"

"Your father. We were talking about what you told him after the storm, remember?"

"Do you really want to know?"

"Yeah, I do."

"Nothing that night. I unfroze in the tub and went to bed. The next morning, he called me into his study to report—wind direction, wave size—technical stuff. I answered as best I could. I told him how scared we were, and how well the three of you handled the boat. I said that after the race the winds were too strong to get back to Taarbaek, and we got blown into the shipping channel. There wasn't any need to exaggerate. I even told him how you climbed up the mast to fix the halyard rope, and how the girls tied the sails smaller so we could get to Rungsted. I didn't say it was your stupid idea to stay out there in the first place, and therefore you were responsible, if that's what you want to know. Pa accepted what I told him, which was the truth."

Doc started to laugh.

"What's so funny? You wanted to know, so I told you. Stop laughing."

"I'm laughing because I told my dad exactly the same stuff, only when he asked me if it was my idea to stay out there after the race, I said it was yours."

"Thanks a whole, mole. If your father ever mentions that little tidbit of brilliance to Pa, I'll end up tied to a lawn chair and flogged."

"Oh stop worrying, Andy. Learn to appreciate the humor in life."

We slowed down alongside three attractive girls in tight sweaters riding bicycles, skirts trailing in the breeze. Doc tooted and hit the brakes. I felt a sharp bump as the little car jumped the curb onto the paved bike path directly behind them.

"What the hell are you doing?" I gasped.

The girls laughed and pedaled harder. Panties flashed as skirts flew above their waists. He tooted again.

"My, oh my, but the scenery is beautiful in this little country," Doc sighed. "Look at those drumsticks pumping up and down. You wouldn't get a view like this in the States."

"You crazy bastard. What if a police car comes along? I don't want to get arrested."

"You have a diplomatic passport, don't you? That means they can't put you in jail."

"Maybe not, but my father will see that I never ride in this car again. It won't make any difference because your driving days will be over, once your dad finds out."

The car bumped onto the road again.

"You sure can be a spoilsport when you want to, Barnes."

We turned into the driveway of an imposing house in an austere section of the neighborhood called Hellerup.

"Rex is in his father's study," said the Holts' housekeeper, pointing down a sterile hallway as she opened the mahogany door.

The cavernous dwelling was spotless. I was astonished to see one wall covered with General Holt's framed military citations.

"Pa has lots of fruit salad, too, but he doesn't show off his medals in the hallway."

"Yeah," said Doc. "My dad only wears his ribbons when he has to."

We found Rex pacing back and forth in a paneled room with modern Danish furniture.

"I take it you're still on phone duty—whatever that is," said Doc, glancing around.

"They're expecting a call from some war buddy and his wife who are supposed to visit," Rex answered. "They haven't arrived, so I'm stuck waiting."

"Why can't your maid do it?" I asked.

"My father wanted to stay here instead of going to the cookout, but my mother said that would be rude. So they ordered me to answer the phone if their friends call."

"Too bad," laughed Doc. "They should have sent you to the party instead."

I walked over for a closer look at a collection of trout fishing gear in the corner, which was more interesting than listening to Rex blow off steam. There were several fine American and British split-bamboo rods, a battered wicker creel, and boxes of old flies. My opinion of the general went up a notch.

"What a collection, Rex. Your father has great taste in fishing equipment. And get a load of these Hardy reels."

"I couldn't care less."

"This Orvis rod must be a hundred years old," I continued, reaching for it.

"Keep your hands off, Barnes."

"Okay, okay. No need to get in an uproar. Don't you ever go fishing with him?"

Rex pointed out the window at a sizable concrete pond in the backyard. Some large rocks had been arranged around its edges, and a log extended into the water to simulate a fallen tree.

"See that puddle? The first thing my father did when we moved in was to replace the goldfish with trout. Last Sunday, he put on his waders, took one of his stupid rods, walked out there to the Battenkill, or whatever he thinks it is, and caught two trout for breakfast."

"Only two?" asked Doc.

"That's all he can eat."

"What kind are they?" I asked.

"How the hell should I know? A truck dumped them in there."

"Doesn't anybody else in the family eat trout?"

"Fuck the goddam trout!" Rex screamed, whacking the telephone off the desk. Pieces of black plastic skittered across the floor.

"Sorry. I didn't mean to upset you," I said. "In Jacksonville, my father and I went fishing together a couple of times, and I thought—"

"Shut up, Barnes. Shut up. I don't want to hear about it, okay?"

The maid arrived, shaking her head as she picked up what was left of the phone.

"What will I tell your father?"

"Tell him whatever you want. Get me out of here, Doc."

"What about your phone duty?"

"Fuck it," Rex spit out.

"Since Bakken is closest to Andy's house," Doc said, pushing me toward the hallway, "we can leave the car there and hoof it the rest of the way."

"Just what I want to do—go for a walk in the park," Rex grumbled.

"It'll do you good. What exercise have you had lately? And by the time we leave Bakken, you'll be so drunk you won't know how far you walked, anyway."

For the first time, Rex smiled.

Leaving the car at my house, Doc led us across the street into Dyrehaven's woods. Once a hunting preserve for the royal family, it was a national treasure where the herds of deer paid no attention to people sharing their environs.

"Follow me, guys. I know a shortcut."

He waved to a soldier and his pretty companion emerging from some trees. She was folding a blanket.

"How many girls do you suppose get laid in these woods every night?" mused Rex.

"What did I tell you?" laughed Doc. "That's all he thinks about."

"Hey, I have to keep in practice for the Frankfurt skirts this fall."

As we approached the main gate, our path merged into a dirt road, crowded with horse-drawn carriages and rowdy working-class men kept on course by the pressing mass of humanity around them.

"Swedes," Doc said. "Probably got paid this afternoon,

and just arrived on the Bellevue ferry from Malmo."

"Are they drunk?" I asked.

"Of course they're drunk, you weenie," Rex sneered. "Don't you know anything?"

I bristled. The way he said it was demeaning. We hardly knew each other, but it was clear he didn't care for me.

"You'll see a lot of plastered people before tonight is over," Doc interrupted, before anything further could be said, "and I'll bet Rex will be one of them."

Inside the gate, Rex pulled out his Camels and headed for the nearest bar. A chesty girl with heavy lipstick and long legs smiled at him.

"I'm off to have a beer and begin my quest," Rex said, pulling out his Camels. "Maybe I can trade a few of these for a piece of ass."

"We'll rescue you later," Doc replied. "C'mon, Andy. I'll show you Bakken in all its glory, as only an expert can."

As we blended among revelers reeking of beer and cognac, Doc froze.

"Jimmy! Over here."

I turned to see a lanky, tough-looking kid with a chiseled, streetwise face walking toward us. He was wearing a leather jacket with turned-up collar, motorcycle boots, and a pair of shades anchored in swept-back hair combed into a ducktail. The cigarette tucked behind his ear cemented my image of him as a guy with an attitude. It was Jimmy's Danish girlfriend who captured my attention, however—long blond hair covering one shoulder, wasp-waisted,—I couldn't take my eyes off her.

"And who is your latest babe?" Doc laughed, planting exaggerated kisses on her extended hand and forearm as Jimmy introduced her. "For some reason, this guy attracts chicks like maple syrup draws bees."

Jimmy flashed a smile of perfect teeth, revealing humor and measured patience at Doc's demonstration.

"As you can see," Doc continued, "the prettiest Bakken chicks think he's real cool. Hey, Man, wanna come with us while I introduce Andy to this wonderful place?"

"Naw," Jimmy hedged. "Helga and me got a bit of private exploring to do."

"Nice meeting you, Helga," I said.

As the two of them melted into the crowd I turned to Doc.

"Who is he—a hood?"

"Jimmy's an Air Force brat like me, but he does seem older, doesn't he? Last name is Smith. He  arrived in Copenhagen a few months before you did, and will be going to Frankfurt with the rest of us this fall."

For the next few hours the air swirled with tobacco smoke and the sticky, warm stench of urine from open concrete-walled pissoirs. Louis Armstrong belted out "Mack the Knife" from every loudspeaker, while men with bloodshot eyes cursed as their kroner disappeared into slot machines. We turned into a narrow alley where a pair of crumpled pants at half mast gyrated between two bare legs next to a wall. Doc dragged me by.

"But, but did you see what they were …?"

"You'll see a lot of that if you don't break your neck first," he chuckled. "I come to watch people at the Fun House and talk to Ollie, who runs it, and some of the other guys who work the amusements. The roller coaster is my favorite. Still don't know the name of the wild man who operates it—he's never been sober enough to tell me."

I made a mental note to avoid Doc's favorite ride.

At length, we arrived at the Fun House.

"Hey, Ollie," Doc called to a rumpled man with a

mustached grin behind his ticket booth. "Long time no see."

"Doc," said a voice straight from Brooklyn. "Did'ja bring me another Yankee sucker?"

A blast of air shot up my pants, blowing out my shirttails. I jumped back and people laughed, including Doc and Ollie.

He held out his hand. "No offense—all part of the job. I'm Ollie."

I learned he'd gone AWOL from the 101st Airborne at the end of World War II, married a Danish girl, and never returned to the States. We watched as the master, using hidden jets of compressed air in the ground around us, blasted skirts above belly buttons. His most successful exposure was at the expense of a pretty university girl negotiating the Fun House exit, a long series of metal rollers. The crowd cheered as the maestro uncovered her lovely figure up to the armpits while she struggled over the rollers, holding onto handrails to keep from falling. She laughed, making no attempt to protect her privacy. We spent a long time at the Fun House.

Eventually, Doc pushed me toward screams coming from the roller coaster.

"Time for World War I Flying Ace Gordon and his intrepid observer, Andrew Barnes, to make a dangerous patrol over enemy lines in their Sopwith Camel."

"Doc, I have no intention of going on that thing with you."

"But you have to. It's like … like being initiated when you go over the equator."

He glanced at his watch.

"Is Bakken about to close?" I asked, grasping at any excuse to avoid riding in the rickety cars clattering overhead.

"I was wondering about Rex, that's all."

Rex had been on my mind. Were his Camels effective? Had those slick moves Elena brushed off—the ones he undoubtedly used on every girl he met—resulted in sharing a blanket with that pretty one at the first bar? I could never do something like that. Was I chicken? Jealous? Did Doc see something in Rex I missed?

"I'll go look for him while you visit your friend on the roller coaster," I said.

At that moment Rex, zipping up his fly, stepped out of a pissoir ahead of us. He stood, pondering a large, evil-smelling puddle at his feet.

"Over here," Doc yelled. "No, don't step in the … oh, well, never mind." His words trailed off as Rex splashed toward us. "Andy, remind me to throw away his shoes before he gets into the car tonight."

"I can't find Utta," Rex said, grabbing Doc's shoulder for support. "She said she'd wait while I peed in there."

"Who's Utta?" I asked. "What does she look like?"

"Grapefruits."

"What are you talking about?"

"Utta's knockers. How stupid can you be? She helped me finish my Camels. Then she introduced me to her friends. I bought them cognac and Tuborgs."

"Then what?"

"What the hell do you think, Barnes? We drank them."

"Do you have any money?" asked Doc.

"Three, no, five hundred kroner. Maybe seven. My wallet, somewhere …." He scratched at his rear end, unable to locate his pockets.

Doc withdrew the billfold and held it open.

"Looks like Utta got every kroner you had."

"She'll give it back when I see her."

"Look, Rex. Andy and I are going to ride the roller coaster. You come, too. Maybe you'll see Utta."

Female shrieks echoed from two cars thundering overhead as slivers from decayed rail ties showered down on us.

"Utta ... up there," said Rex, wiping wood dust from his face. "I will go to her."

"Good. That's all settled, Doc. Rex is going with you to find Utta."

Doc put his hand on Rex's shoulder and steered him toward the ticket booth. They climbed into one of the cars, and I watched the rails shake as it started up the cogged track to the top of the first steep descent. Reaching the edge, it plunged into the abyss with speed that defied gravity. The brakeman was totally insane. Ignoring the brake lever, he rode standing up, waving to the moon between long swigs from a bottle in his hand.

"Aquavit," Doc told me, later.

Flying Officer Gordon wasn't much better. As the broken safety bar flopped against his knees, he stood up and swiveled in place, machine-gunning enemy trenches as his Sopwith Camel careened through the skies. When they eventually landed, Doc saluted.

"Sah! Squadron Leader Gordon reports that after a fierce dogfight, the Red Baron has been vanquished, Sah!"

"I want Utta to come to me," mumbled Rex. He bent over and was sick.

"The concessions are starting to close," I said. "Shouldn't we be getting home?"

As we neared the house, Doc turned to me.

"Andy, his feet smell really bad. Can you find something to cover them, before I put him in the car?" He draped Rex over the trunk while I found a couple of burlap garden sacks, which we wrapped around his putrid shoes. He was asleep before Doc plopped him onto the front seat.

"Thanks to Lone Ranger, Tonto not need to fumigate stagecoach."

"What will you do with him?" I asked, as Doc closed the door.

"I'll think of something."

Early the next morning, the Holts' maid found Rex curled up in a car blanket, asleep by his father's fish pond. The sacks were still wrapped around his feet. It was Sunday, but she managed to get him into the house before the general, wearing his waders, creel and fly rod in hand, appeared to catch his two trout for breakfast.

# Part 2
## German Autumn

# My Seventh School

One afternoon, when summer was almost over, the dilemma over my education was finally solved. It happened when Pa returned from work.

"Andy, get down here, now!" You could hear him all over the house.

As I entered the living room, Mom hurried in, followed by Curt and Lissa—attracted by any commotion at big brother's expense.

"Calm down, dear," she said to Pa. The tone of her voice was soothing, but Pa knew this was a nonnegotiable order. "Now then," she continued, "whatever is the matter?"

He shook an official-looking letter bearing an embossed Danish Crown and gold anchor at me. "Only the most embarrassing thing that's happened in my entire career. By tomorrow, instead of congratulations, every attaché in town will be saying 'Too bad about Andy.'"

"Stop," Mom said, her voice sharp.

The house was her domain, a place where parents never "carried on" (as she referred to her husband's outbursts) in front of the children. He sank into his favorite chair, crumpled the letter, and threw it on the floor.

"I can't believe it—my own son."

"I still have no idea what this is about," she said, picking it up. "But this is from somebody in the Danish Navy. What does it have to do with Andy?"

"Make that Grand Admiral Torben Rasmussen," replied Pa, snatching the letter and shaking it at me again. His face was a mosaic of red and purple. "Do you have any idea who he is?"

I shook my head.

"The commander in chief of the Royal Danish Navy, that's who."

"I still don't know what you're talking about, dear," Mom soothed.

"I need a drink." he said, starting to rise from his chair.

"Not until you've calmed down. Is that clear? Now, let's start from the beginning."

"Andy didn't get accepted for the cruise on the Danmark. Why? Because he hasn't taken geometry and Admiral Rasmussen couldn't imagine how he would ever learn navigation.

I smiled to myself. I would not be spending the next year on my knees, freezing at dawn, scraping wooden decks.

"So you think it's funny, do you?" growled my father, rising from his chair. His eyes met Mom's, and he sank back again.

"But that's not his fault, dear. In Jacksonville, you insisted it was better for him to take Algebra II immediately after Algebra I, instead of geometry. And, for that matter," she replied, turning in my direction, "as long as we're on the subject, Andy wants to go to Frankfurt with Doc next week, don't you?"

Both parents looked at me.

"How about correspondence courses at home?" I managed. I'll work really hard …."

"You're going to Frankfurt, and that's that," Pa snapped.

Mom was in my bedroom packing clothes into a Navy cruise box. Constructed of heavy plywood with steel reinforced edges, it was the size of a large footlocker.

"I'm going to miss you so much," she sniffled, dabbing her eyes with a handkerchief. "You've never been away from home before."

"Yes I have," I replied, annoyed at her emotional display. "What about those two weeks of Boy Scout camp when we lived in Newport? And YMCA camp on Chesapeake Bay?"

"Those weren't the same, Andy. From now on, you'll be home only for vacations, and then college in a couple of years, and then …."

"Mom, if you don't stop crying, you'll have to put my shirt you're folding in the dryer."

On a cool morning in early September, I said goodbye to everybody except Pa, who was flying me and the other eleven Copenhagen kids and their fathers to Frankfurt in the Navy plane. Since his official title was Naval Attaché and Naval Attaché for Air to Denmark, the Navy saw fit to provide him with a flying machine. It was a twin-engine R4D, complete with a three-man flight crew.

"Mommy, why are you sending Andy away? Did he do something bad?" asked Lissa.

"No, no, dear. We're not sending him away," she said, sniffling into the depths of her handkerchief. "He's going to school in Germany. He'll be back soon, at … at Thanksgiving."

"Can I use your room while you're gone?" asked Curt.

"No," I answered, laughing.

After hugs all around, including one from Elena (the most memorable), I slipped into the Embassy Ford and Aage closed the door. As we sped through Copenhagen, images of Taarbaek and my now terminated summer—hands down the best of my life—raced through my mind: 3 a.m. sunlight shining through my bedroom skylight every morning; luscious Elena and her delicious meals; the hours spent standing at my window with binoculars, studying nude sunbathers at Bellevue Beach; diving off the dock into the ice-cold Øresund; mackerel fishing; nights at Bakken with Doc ….

Forty minutes later, Aage drove us through an unguarded gate at Kastrup Airport, stopping in front of a hangar at Pa's plane. In charge was a grizzled Navy chief whom Pa—and only Pa—called "Gunner." Later, when I asked why, he said Chief Fleming had been the turret gunner on his torpedo bomber in the Pacific. Now, their careers had crossed again; only this time, the chief's responsibility was to make certain this aircraft, a fancy Navy version of the classic twin-engine DC-3, was ready to fly at all times. It transported the ambassador to meetings in Denmark and Europe; family members to Germany for medical appointments; and us school kids to Frankfurt. Pa was furious when a group of congressmen and their obnoxious wives requisitioned it for a two-week partying jaunt to European capitals, which they justified as an inspection of NATO defenses. The Berlin crisis of 1948-49, the recent Korean War, and the specter of a Red Army invasion of Western Europe were enough for taxpayers back home to ignore such waste.

Climbing aboard, I dropped into a plush dark-blue seat

with plenty of leg room next to Doc for my first plane flight. While we waited for Rex to arrive, Doc kept us entertained with volleys of sick jokes, which, in 1956, were all the rage.

"But Mommy, that's not my baby sister." "Shut up, Billy. It's a better carriage."

Or, "How do you tell a Russian airplane? By the hair under its wings," etc.

Outside, General Holt's staff car screeched to a stop beside the plane. As Chief Fleming stowed Rex's trunk, portable record player, and golf clubs, the general argued with his son, stopping only as they boarded the aircraft. After taxiing to the end of the runway, the plane turned, its engines roared, and Kastrup's buildings slipped past. The tail lifted, a slight bump, and the earth fell away. Airborne, we banked as Pa set a course for Rhein-Main Air Force Base and a year that would become a turning point in my life.

For the next two hours, we throbbed along at 150 knots through skies that, a decade or so before, had been full of Luftwaffe Focke-Wulfs and Messerschmitts. I stared out the window as we approached Frankfurt. What if I hated living in a dormitory?

"You'll like it, Andy, I promise. It's a fun place," said Doc, reading my thoughts.

"I've been to plenty of new schools. But living in a dormitory makes everything different," I answered, staring out the window at green farmlands blotched with cloud shadows thousands of feet below.

"Tonto forgot. Lone Ranger never camp away from home before."

"If you don't stop this Lone Ranger crap, Doc, by the second day I'll be known as the Lone Ranger all over school."

"Sorry, I was trying to cheer you up. But dorm life is great. You'll have new friends and know everybody worth knowing in no time. I'll see that you meet June and Copper and all the cutest girls. The best part is that they're so close —right on the other side of our building. Every weekend the downstairs partitions, separating our side from theirs, are opened into one big room for dances and socializing."

White tendrils of cloud whipped over the wing, reminding me of foam passing over flat rocks in a stream. My ears popped. The plane bounced in pockets of unstable air. I gripped my armrest.

"Bumps are normal in cloud cover," said Doc, looking at gray nothingness outside. "I've decided you're going to room with me."

I stared past raindrops now squiggling across the window, at ghostly smudges of blinking red on the port wing tip.

"Guess so."

He looked at me. "That was pretty lukewarm."

"Why not Rex?" I asked.

He leaned closer. "Really, Barnes. How could Rex benefit from rooming with me? Would he require assistance getting a date? You, on the other hand, can profit greatly from my experience." His expression became serious. "You really want to know why I'd rather have you instead of Rex? You are totally honest. You say exactly what you feel and, most of the time, anyway, it makes sense. Furthermore, your innocence is so transparent it's unbelievable," he added with a grin. "I can read you like a book."

"Cut the bull, Gordon. I'll agree on the condition that you stop calling me Lone Ranger."

I stiffened at several jolts followed by a high-pitched

whine as we dropped below the cloud deck.

"That's the landing gear locking into place. It's what you want to hear."

Pointed evergreens zipped below our window. A chain-link fence, mown grass, a blue bus turning onto a narrow paved road, wide white stripes … I barely felt the wheels touch down on the rain-swept runway.

"Nice job," Doc commented. "Your dad greased us in beautifully. Welcome to Frankfurt am Main, Roomie."

Stepping onto a prairie of wet tarmac mirroring the dismal sky, we slogged through puddles to a waiting Air Force bus.

After stopping for lunch at Rhein-Main's large Dependents Hotel, our group climbed into taxicabs for a caravan ride into Frankfurt. Pa and I, along with the Gordons, got into a dinged Mercedes 180D. Its driver, yellowed cigarette dangling from his lower lip, smiled a mouthful of bad teeth as he loaded our luggage. Slamming the door, he flipped on the fare meter and crushed the gas pedal. Weaving in and out of traffic, we rocketed down the Autobahn as he laughed, cursed, and blasted a path through traffic with the horn. Only one windshield wiper worked, and it barely kept up with the rain. He tailgated so close I couldn't see the license plates of cars in front of us.

"This son of a bitch is certifiably insane," gasped Pa, after a near miss.

"Standard operating procedure, Barney," smiled Colonel Gordon. "Doc and I have done it many times, and we're still here."

Thirty minutes later, we climbed out of the taxi into the rain in front of Frankfurt American High School's main entrance, identified by a soggy Stars and Stripes clinging to its flagpole. The gloom was oppressive. With over six hundred students, Frankfurt High was then one of the largest American schools in Europe. Academics and personnel were the responsibility of the Department of Defense, but facilities and everything else fell under jurisdiction of the United States Army. One building housed administrative offices, classrooms, an auditorium, gymnasium, and cafeteria; the other, an H-shaped, two-story dormitory, was home to approximately 150 inmates, grades nine through twelve. The "five-day kids" (who lived in the Frankfurt vicinity but too far away to commute every day) were bused home on weekends; "seven-day kids," like Doc and me, whose families resided outside Germany, went home for Thanksgiving, Christmas, Easter, and summer vacations. Dependents from all branches of military service, as well as a smattering of those whose fathers were diplomats or businessmen, made up the student body. It was multiracial and desegregated—something unheard of at Robert E. Lee, my previous high school in Jacksonville—but few students were black. It wasn't a big deal: military bases had been integrated for nearly a decade.

Inside, a man dressed entirely in brown ordered us into a classroom, where he distributed fistfuls of forms.

"I am Silas Slimbaugh, the school psychologist and guidance counselor," he lisped. "Other than our principal, Mr. Pulaski, no one has been here longer than I have." He paused to wipe spittle from thin lips with a handkerchief, and continued. "I hold a Master of Arts in counseling from the University of Maryland. Only eleven percent of Department of Defense school employees worldwide possess this academic degree."

I had no idea what a Master of Arts was, but the adults

nodded approvingly. During the next hour, between pauses to clear away mouth drool, Slimbaugh asked appalling questions about delicate personal information. For me, it started when Pa, still stinging from the Admiral's letter, signed me up for geometry.

"Ah, Captain Barnes. I see that last year Andy's grades in algebra were terrible."

Rex snickered.

"Then," Slimbaugh went on, "he received an A for the last quarter. Might I inquire how that happened?"

"Andy had to finish his sophomore year taking a correspondence course with a Danish tutor," Pa replied.

Slimbaugh fixed his eyes on me. I made myself as small as possible.

"I know for a fact that the Danes are extremely good in mathematics. How much of the work did you actually do, Andy?"

"I tried my best, sir," I replied, evading his question. I was not about to tell this man what Doc already knew—that Knut, the university student Pa hired, did all the work. "I'm very good in history. Can I take that instead of geometry?"

The corner of Slimbaugh's lip curled.

"But Mr. Barnes, you got an A in algebra for the last quarter. I should think geometry would be a snap."

Pa gave me a curious look, and I knew the man in the brown suit had me. I resigned myself to taking geometry.

"It is done," said Slimbaugh. "Plane geometry with Miss Agnes Earl. She is one of our finest teachers and," his eyes bored into me, "the recipient of the Lobelia L. Muller Medal for Innovative Teaching."

Doc clasped his hands and closed his eyes as if in prayer. He was rewarded by smiles from kids present (including me), and frowns from parents. In addition to geometry, Pa and Mr. master's degree scheduled me for American history, government, English, and chemistry.

Setting my paperwork aside, the guidance counselor picked up Doc's. "I see no changes from last year, so you may proceed to register at the dormitory."

"We're out of here," he whispered, standing up. "While you're stuck listening to Slimebum, I'll find us a decent dorm room."

The remainder of the session was not pleasant. The school psychologist next turned his attention to Alfred Duncan, a timid ninth-grader sitting next to me. He was noticeably younger than the rest of us, with a round, pink face, thick glasses, and plump middle. Chubby fingers writhed back and forth on the handle of a large briefcase beside him. The green Tyrolean cap he was wearing, complete with some sort of turkey feather, marked him as, well, different.

"Has your son outgrown his history of bed-wetting, Major Duncan?" asked Slimbaugh, looking up from Alfred's opened file.

Rex laughed out loud, and the boy's face reddened. Pa scowled and started to say something, but Major Duncan beat him to it: "Personal information like that does not need to be discussed here."

"I'm sorry, Major, but health problems can affect other students so I must pay attention to them. What about Alfred's unlucky roommate sleeping on the lower bunk?"

More titters around the room. Major Duncan's eyes narrowed. "I'll talk with you about this in private. Do I make myself clear?"

The room fell silent, except for Alfred's sniveling, and our tormentor turned his attention to Jimmy, who was sitting apart from the rest of us in the back of the room. As their eyes met, Jimmy leaned back and yawned.

"Sergeant Smith," Slimbaugh said, "I see here that your son has a criminal record for shoplifting. Are there any recent episodes that should be noted?"

"Not that I know of, sir. If he was doing that again, he knows I'd whop him good."

Jimmy grinned.

"Ah, I've no doubt. Yes, er, thank you, Sergeant Smith."

After humiliating several more students, Slimbaugh gathered up his papers.

"Mr. Horace Pulaski will be with you in a moment."

Pausing to let the guidance counselor pass, our principal strutted into the room. His eyes drilled into us like those of an eagle about to dive on a bunch of prairie dogs for dinner. His accent was unmistakably Southern, and I got the impression he didn't smile much. An image of a redneck Southern sheriff from a movie I'd seen in Jacksonville flashed through my mind. After several minutes of telling us how wonderful Frankfurt High School was, he launched into his primary message.

"I want to make it very plain that at my school you will be expected to heed authority—mine, Mr. Slimbaugh's, your dorm supervisor's, and, of course, your teachers'. From this point on, you will be treated as adults, responsible for the choices you make, all of which have logical consequences. If you make bad choices, you will pay the price."

Adult nods were unanimous.

"I advise you to pay special attention to all dormitory regulations, particularly curfew hours, which are cast in stone. There is a total prohibition of alcohol, and no smoking anywhere, except in 'The Weed Pit.'"

Jimmy's hand shot up.

"Excuse me, sir, but where is this 'Pit'? I need a smoke."

Pulaski pushed his glasses to the end of his nose and gave Jimmy an icy once-over. "Next to the entrance of the cafeteria," he replied, adding, "I advise you to watch yourself in my school, Son." Jimmy grinned at him.

Glancing down at his watch, our principal removed his glasses. "You now reside in a foreign country, where you will be watched by the German people. You are their guests, and I expect you to exhibit impeccable conduct at all times. Never forget that whatever you do, wherever you go, you represent America."

Parts of Pulaski's presentation made sense—representing America, suffering the consequences of bad choices—but I felt that every step I took in this place would be watched. Slinging my raincoat over my shoulders, I followed our group to the dormitory.

# The Dorm

Inside, we lined up in front of a paunchy, balding man barricaded behind a wall of forms on a card table. Glancing at his watch, he gritted out a smile.

"I'm Stanley Kreebert, supervisor of the boys' dormitory. The sooner we start, the sooner we finish. Who's first, please?"

Pa and I stepped forward.

"Name?"

"Barnes, Andrew R.," replied Pa, before I could say anything.

Mr. Kreebert pushed pages of small print and a fountain pen at me. "Sign."

"What is this?"

His eyes became sesame seeds. "The forms say you agree to obey all dorm rules—mine, in other words. Your signature, please. You're holding up the line."

While this exchange was going on, Doc appeared. With a wave, he flipped my cruise box onto his shoulder and retraced his steps upstairs. Kreebert pushed a key and thick booklet of rules in my direction and motioned to the Smiths, who were behind Pa and me.

"What happens now?" I asked. "What room am I in?"

"The number is on your key. Since you asked, you will be with Mr. Gordon. It appears he has already taken up your things."

"But I wanted to room with Doc," Rex burst out.

The supervisor inhaled a gurgling snuffle, swallowed, and blew his nose. After apparently examining the handkerchief's contents, he stuffed it into his pocket. "Like everybody else," he said to Rex, "you will find out who your roommate is when your turn comes."

Doc reappeared and I started toward him, grabbing my guitar case.

"While you two are getting squared away," Pa said, "I'll check in at the Ambassador Arms Hotel across the street. Doc's dad and I will be back in an hour to take you for Dependent ID cards so you can use the PX. We fly back to Copenhagen at 0730 tomorrow," he added, "so I thought it would be nice if all of us had dinner at the Officers Club tonight."

"That Kreebert guy downstairs is pretty unpleasant," I said as we continued past rooms with people talking and unpacking. "And what's wrong with his schnozz?"

"You mean all that nose noise and gurgling? Last year my roommate asked his father—an Army doctor—about it. He said it was probably severe chronic postnasal drip. You'll find that The Kreebs is definitely a drip. At least he didn't use his paper cup."

"Huh?"

"Last year he honked into a crinkled Dixie cup he kept in his pocket. Maybe over the summer the Army passed a regulation against it."

Doc kicked open the door to #15, and I stepped inside.

"I like this room," he said. "It's far enough away from the toilets so we won't hear all the farting and flushing, and the window faces east, so we get the morning sun. Best of all, it looks out at the girls' dorm across the patio. We can wave to them as they're getting dressed."

I surveyed the austere cube that would be my home for the coming school year. There were two closets; a large metal double desk with two chairs, two dented metal bureaus and a filing cabinet. All were painted the color of Army jeeps. Under the window was an iron steam radiator. A layer of fresh paint (which Doc christened "vomit green") covered the walls and ceiling. The mattresses on our metal bunk bed frame weren't much thicker than doormats, and my stained pillow smelled suspiciously of chicken feathers. Folded at the foot of each bed were clean sheets, one pillowcase, one towel, and two Army-issue wool blankets. I stuck my fingers through several holes in one of mine.

"I'm going to freeze."

"Made by musket balls during the Spanish-American War," Doc laughed. He motioned toward the radiator. "It'll get so hot in here you'll be throwing those miserable rags on the floor every night. I suggest we make beds and then unpack. I'll take the top bunk."

In no time, he transformed it into a tight olive-green cocoon and stood back, watching me. "You haven't the foggiest idea how to make a bed using hospital corners, do you?"

"Of course I do. I'm just more familiar with those goose down Danish quilts at home."

"When you read The Kreebs's booklet of dormitory rules and regulations, you'll see that if you don't make your bed using hospital corners, you fail room inspections and we get restricted."

"What?"

"Jail. Imprisonment. The Kreebs writes us up in his little black book, and we don't leave our room for days."

"You didn't mention restrictions when you were chatting up my mother about Frankfurt last summer."

"An oversight on my part. Probably just forgot."

"I wonder how many other things you forgot."

"C'mon, Andy. It was important to impress her. I had to give Frankfurt my best shot."

"I'm beginning to realize that even your best is none too good, Gordon."

"Yeah, well, I'm telling you now. The Kreebs gets a hard-on whenever he finds something he can issue a restriction for, and I know from experience that a bed without hospital corners is one of them. Allow me."

Two minutes later, my bunk could've passed a Parris Island boot camp inspection.

Our fathers arrived. After commenting that my bed never looked that good at home, Pa took out his wallet and placed a pile of colored paper notes in my hand.

"Twenty dollars," Pa said. "From now on you will be expected to study for a living. Do whatever you want with it, but I suggest spending wisely and making it last. When it's gone, that's it—no more until payday, the first of each month, understood?"

"Monopoly money?" I asked, looking at Doc.

"Don't knock it. It's military scrip. Army money. I'll clue you in later."

It was still raining as our taxi drove through downtown Frankfurt, giving me my first glimpse at the legacy of World War II. After eleven years, the pounding the city and its people had endured was visible everywhere: ornate buildings pockmarked with bullet holes; blocks of rubble covered with weeds; Frankfurt's once-exquisite opera house, a gutted shell. Open to the rain, the roof of the central train station was a twisted piece of wartime art. In spite of the damage, however, a vibrant urban renaissance was underway. Shoppers stood in front of store windows full of merchandise. Streetcars sparked and rumbled along tracks set in repaved streets, while Volkswagens and streamlined minicars I had never seen before zipped in and out of traffic.

"Made by Messerschmitt from surplus fighter parts," said Colonel Gordon.

We crossed over the Main River Bridge and I swiped at my fogged window for a quick look. Plane trees, their wet leaves dull with the approach of fall, lined its grassy banks. A barge chugged upstream.

"We'll go kayaking there next spring," said Doc. "I promise."

"Dinner at 1830 hours sharp," said Colonel Gordon as we arrived back at the dorm.

Later, as we waited for our fathers downstairs, Rex appeared.

"What's up, Daddy-O?" asked Doc.

"I'm going to the Officers Club with my father for dinner."

"So are we," I said.

When Doc suggested we sit together, hope flickered in Rex's eyes, but he shook his head. "Don't think so. He wants me to meet a couple of his friends. I'll be stuck at a private table with several generals, listening to war stories while they get plowed."

"But wouldn't firsthand accounts from people who took part in battles that we read about in history books be interesting?" I asked.

"Yeah, right," Doc broke in. "About as interesting as

that night last summer when we didn't make it to Bakken because you forced me to look at your father's World War II pictures of Navy fighter planes and aircraft carriers."

"I think history is important. It's why we're here in Europe," I replied.

"Skip the lecture, Barnes." He turned back to Rex. "What room are you in?"

"The one next to the bathrooms."

I started to ask if he could hear farting and flushing, but a horn honked outside. Rex leaned against the door. "That's for me."

"Don't forget to sign out," Doc reminded him.

"Fuck it." He took his time crossing the patio in the rain to his father's waiting staff car.

After a pleasant dinner at the Officers Club in the nearby I.G. Farben Building, we returned to the dorm, where Pa surprised me with a hug.

"Well, Andy, you're on your own now. I know you'll learn the ropes quickly. Have fun, but remember the reason you're here is to do well, so try to develop good study habits."

"I will, Pa."

"Your mother and I will miss you. Don't forget to write."

Blinking back tears, I watched his taxi pull away, severing me from my family.

"Quit blubbering, Barnes. Only ten minutes to the warning bell. We have to sign in and get to our room. Move it."

"I'm not blubbering, and I don't give a damn about your stupid bell."

"You better. It means we have ten minutes after that one before the lights out bell. Ten and ten are twenty, right? That's how long we have until bed check."

"What's that?"

"The Kreebs's nocturnal visitation. He opens the door, shines his flashlight in your face, and if you're not in bed you get restricted."

We were climbing into our bunks when the last bell sounded. In a futile effort to get comfortable, I banged my head against Doc's sagging mattress springs above me.

"Oww. My hair is caught."

"Quiet. Do you want to get us restricted on our first night?"

"Of course not. Stop moving around. Every time you move, it pinches more."

"What are you talking about?" His flashlight beam fixed on my hair. Then he buried his head in his pillow.

"Stop laughing and help me, Gordon."

He froze. "Shhhh. The Kreebs is coming."

Out in the hallway a door opened, then clicked shut again. Footsteps stopped at the next room, and we heard our dorm supervisor conversing with its occupants.

"You better unsnag yourself, fast, Roomie."

"I can't. Do something."

Jumping down, Doc snatched up a pair of scissors and I felt his hand on my head. A quick snip and I was free. Shoving the scissors under his pillow, he vaulted into bed.

"Pretend you're asleep."

Our door handle turned, and a beam of light swept my face.

"Uhhh," Doc groaned, rolling over.

The light shifted to him, paused, and the door shut. Slippered footsteps padded to the next room, and the next, while our bed quivered from my roommate's silent laughter.

"Thanks," I said to his mattress. "If Mr. Kreebert had seen me, it's too embarrassing to think about."

"We would have been restricted, that's all. Don't worry about it, Lone Ranger. G'night."

Shortly, he was asleep.

I lay in the dark, wide awake. So much had happened. Last night I was home in my own bed, listening to waves lapping against the seawall outside my balcony. Now I was stuck in this crummy room, serenaded by car horns, ambulance sirens, and the clang of Frankfurt's streetcars. My tin of Elena's cookies was empty—Doc had eaten some and given the rest to his friends. How could I avoid Kreebert, Slimbaugh and Mr. Pulaski? What was tomorrow going to be like?

# *June*

The next morning I awoke before six to Harry Belafonte singing "Sylvie" on Doc's clock radio. Without television, we relied on nearby AFN, the Armed Forces Network station, for our news, sports scores, and stateside pop music hits. In addition to its steady diet of Elvis, Fats Domino, Patsy Cline and all the others, from 6 to 7 a.m. on weekdays an Army DJ played songs that kids dedicated to secret (or not-so-secret) loves, sparking rumors at breakfast about who had the hots for whom. For me, AFN's morning mishmash meant reveille.

Reaching for my glasses, I blinked at sunlight casting its warmth through the window. Doc, a towel around his waist, was opening our door. There was no fat on him at all.

"Morning," he said, pausing, like some Greek statue come to life. "Belafonte's fantastic, don't you think? I like his calypso stuff, too, but 'Sylvie' is my favorite."

I continued listening to the unique voice and lilting melody, committing it to memory.

"Get a move on, Andy. If you wait, there won't be any hot water in the showers."

I grabbed my towel and hurried after him.

We were the first ones in the upstairs bathroom. Showers were in a large open room with a long wooden bench and hooks for towels. As we were drying off, the mob arrived. Doc smiled at cries of "This water's fuckin' freezing" from latecomers. Kids crowded sinks to brush teeth, shave, pop pimples, and drown themselves in after-shave lotion. A great deal of time was spent sculpting hair into swept-back ducktails and waterfalls, cemented in place with gobs of Brylcreem.

"If I had hair that long I'd never make it to the mess hall in time for breakfast," Doc commented, giving his flattop a couple of quick licks with his comb.

We were dressing in our room when, after a quick knock, the door swung open. Doc was pulling up his Levis. Kreebert's head appeared, said "Good morning," and disappeared.

"What was that about?" I asked.

"The Kreebs was taking his morning peek to see if we were playing with ourselves."

"There's a regulation against that, too?"

Outside, wisps of rising steam from patio puddles swirled into a fresh blue sky. I stopped to tie my shoe.

"Hurry up, Barnes. Breakfast is the best time to check out the new quail from the other side of the dorm, and I don't like to rush it."

He was right: we were in a sea of girls. Most were in sweaters and straight skirts, but some wore poodle skirts— wide affairs decorated with hand-sewn felt poodle dogs— floating on several layers of crinolines that flared out 360 degrees. Nobody wore slacks.

"Hello, Frederick," said a pleasant voice with a slight New England accent behind us.

"June. Love of my life." Doc dipped her backward,

helping himself to exaggerated neck and ear nibbles—a repeat of that first day in Copenhagen with Elena. The exhibition drew giggles from her passing dorm mates.

"Control yourself," she fussed, making a show of pushing him away and straightening the thin aqua scarf that covered small blue and green fish swimming together on her round-collared blouse. "Let me go. Behave yourself."

But I could tell she was enjoying his attentions.

"Aren't you going to introduce me to your friend?" she asked, extending her hand.

I stood, giddy from the warmth of her touch, mesmerized by the most gorgeous face I'd ever set eyes on. The energy in her green eyes melted me. A delicate shade of light rose lipstick accented enticing lips, and her friendly smile, complete with dimples, swept me away. If she was wearing makeup it was hardly visible—and certainly not necessary—as her cheeks glowed with health. The wholesome, sensual aura surrounding her thrilled me. Intelligence? Integrity? Self-assurance? She had all these and more, wrapped into the most perfect package of female perfection I had ever encountered. Shivers went through my entire body.

"I'm Andy," I croaked, staring without brain waves at her short, dark hair.

"It's naturally curly," she laughed. "I never go to a hairdresser."

"I … I like your fish blouse," I managed, dropping my eyes. "Blue and green are my favorite colors."

"Then we have something in common, don't we?" she replied, raising her lovely eyebrows at Doc.

"You can let go now," he said, a bit surprised. "Her hand doesn't belong to you. June, allow me to present my roommate, Andrew Barnes, Esquire. He can't decide which he likes better—fish or girls—so let me apologize for him in advance. His father is the naval attaché in Denmark. Andy, June Everett. Her father is the naval attaché in Turkey."

She studied my face with mischievous eyes. "Andrew Barnes, Esquire. Hmm. I seem to remember from history class that 'Esquire' was a title for candidates to knighthood in the Middle Ages. I've never met someone that old before. I'm honored, sir."

My face could have lit one of Rex's Camels.

Doc gave her a squeeze. "Personality plus. Now you know why she's my favorite girl. Last year I persuaded her to go steady, but she wasn't keen on the idea. This year I'm confident she will come to her senses and realize what a wonderful catch I would be."

"A slim possibility," she replied, with a look of coy indifference.

"But I live in everlasting hope," he said, dropping on one knee. "May I carry your books to the mess hall?"

"I guess I'd better take advantage of his gallantry while it lasts," she said, winking at me as she transferred her stack of spiral notebooks, piled neatly on top of a blue, hard-backed three-ring binder, into his arms.

I was kicking myself. Why didn't I think of that? Now they were walking together, three steps ahead of me, and I was out of the conversation. All I could do was listen as she told Doc about some Turkish army barracks in her neighborhood getting blown up, followed by soldiers shooting and arresting people called Kurds.

"That must have been really exciting," I said, trying to create a three-way conversation. "I've never been in the middle of a revolution."

She gave me a curious look.

"How long did it last?" I asked.

"Most of the summer, unfortunately." She shifted her gaze back to Doc.

"You should have been in Copenhagen," he said. "We sailed, fought off hordes of beautiful Danish girls at Bakken …."

Before Doc finished his exaggerations of our summer, we arrived at the mess hall. Stepping inside, I stared at my future dining surroundings. Off to one side was the serving line, which provided a barrier between us and the rest of the kitchen, where the walls, the eight-foot formica tables, and chairs all matched the paint in our dorm room.

"Vomit green," Doc mouthed silently as June waved to a table of girls and turned toward them. Their presence was the only thing that made coming through the door seem worthwhile.

"Nice meeting you, Andy," she said with a smile, as she left us.

"Behold the princesses of Frankfurt High, Roomie," Doc said, nodding toward June's table as we sat down some distance away. "The redhead is Copper—Ginger Hopkinson—the one I told you about last summer. She's perfect for you: swims like a fish, and is a beautiful high diver. I watched her give a demonstration last year when we went to the indoor pool in Wiesbaden. She's on the tennis and golf teams, and chairman of the social committee."

"I'd like to know June better," I said.

"I'll introduce you to Copper at lunch," he replied, somewhat surprised.

"Who are the babes?" asked Rex, scanning the table Doc and I had been discussing as he sat down. "Boy, I can't wait to hop into bed with the one in blue—warm, soft … I'll bet she's a real tiger between the sheets. What a piece of ass. Who is she?"

"Her name is June Everett, and she's from Turkey," I replied.

Rex stared from me to Doc.

"How the hell does he know her? We just got here last night. Is he for real?"

"Pretty much," replied Doc.

"We met on the way here this morning," I said. "Too bad you didn't get up earlier."

Rex's eyes narrowed.

A chair scraped beside me as Jimmy sat down. During the school year, I would learn that underneath his perpetual cigarette fog, Jimmy was a really nice guy. Gradually, as he let slip some details of his life—the tragic death of his mother and little sister in a fiery car accident; street gangs in Detroit while his father was in Korea and he lived with his grandparents—I came to admire him as a resilient survivor, observant of others' feelings, interested in foreign cultures, and possessing a gifted ear for languages.

"Who's the troll?" he asked, dipping his chin toward a table where Stanley Kreebert was sitting with two women. There was no mistaking the one Jimmy meant—flabby, hooked nose, excessive amount of fuchsia lipstick, unpleasant mouth, and bloodhound jowls. Sparse strands of coarse hair above plucked eyebrows were partially obscured by a multicolored bandanna.

"Why don't you crawl into bed with that one, Rex?" I asked.

He flipped me his middle finger.

"Aw, c'mon, guys," said Doc. "Let's not fight. The fat

one paralyzing your eyeballs is Lola Franklin, head supervisor of the girls' dorm. She's a real battle-ax. We call her 'the Frankfurt Pirate.' The other lady is Maybelle Marbury, her assistant. Miss Maybelle is really nice. Whenever you need help regarding the girls or anything connected with their dorm, always see her." I'd already decided to avoid Miss Franklin at all costs.

"I'm starved," said Jimmy. "How's about we eat?"

# *The First Day*

In their white aprons and paper hats, the kitchen staff behind the cafeteria-style serving line reminded me of a row of grandparents. They all knew Doc. When he leaned across the counter and gave one grandma a hug, she said something in German and wiped damp eyes with her sleeve.

"Amazin'," said Jimmy, extending his tray for a spoonful of rubbery scrambled eggs. "A few years ago we were killin' these folks, and they were killin' us. Now we're all kissin' at breakfast."

"Save my place," said Rex, nudging Doc. "I'm going over to invite the girls to eat with us. I want to meet the one in blue."

"Not a prayer of sitting with them this morning," I said. "They're too busy catching up with each other to want to sit with us. Maybe at lunch, though."

"What have you done to him, Doc? One night here and this weenie is giving me advice about girls."

"Andy's right," Doc replied. "There may be hope for him yet."

I passed by a ladle of bubbling, gray lumps and exchanged glances with Jimmy.

"Oatmeal?"

"Oliver Twist wouldn't have eaten this stuff," he replied.

"Two slices of bacon. Only two per person," said a pudgy, red-faced man standing behind the servers. A starched white apron obscured the front of his Army greens, and a puffy chef's hat enhanced his short stature. He clapped his hands. "Keep moving, moving, moving."

"Who's the mushroom head?" asked Rex, back at our table.

"That's Sergeant Marc Normand," answered Doc, crunching through a piece of bacon. "He's in charge of the kitchen. Besides his native French, he speaks English and German. Thinks of himself as a French chef, though his heritage has no influence on his cooking. Rumor has it he was in charge of food at a POW camp in Korea."

Jimmy submerged a piece of pancake into a syrup puddle on his tray and forked it into his mouth, washing it down with a swallow of coffee.

"This is the worst breakfast I ever tasted. Remind me never to join the Army."

"Quit beefing." said Doc. "By next week you'll be used to it."

"I miss Elena's cooking," I said. "I wish I was home."

"Then you wouldn't have met June, would you?" Doc had a point; if I was going to survive this place, I'd have to look on the bright side.

The homeroom bell clanged. Chairs scraped, and students hurried to return trays.

"The chicks are leaving," said Rex. "Damn, I wanted to go over and talk to them."

"I'm glad you know where we're going," I said as Doc navigated me through crowded halls. We turned into a bright classroom with a "Welcome" banner over the door.

American history maps decorated the walls. As I sat down, Doc twisted my head.

"Look. Over there."

June was sitting behind Ginger Hopkinton, next to the window. Her reddish-auburn hair, burnished by the morning sun, made it easy to see why she was called "Copper." They whispered something, laughed, and waved at us. I had a sudden fear that June might be relating what a simpleton I'd been when we met on the way to breakfast.

"Welcome, everyone."

Our teacher's pleasant voice, which reminded me a little of Mom's, caught everyone's attention and the room became quiet.

"I'm Mrs. Flood, and I hope you had a wonderful summer. I teach American history, and I'm looking forward to getting acquainted with each of you. First, let us stand for the Pledge of Allegiance and the Lord's Prayer."

We stood to face the flag, right hands over our chests. For the next few minutes the room was a jumble of the memorized words. Through the window, I watched a couple of crows on the football bleachers fighting over a piece of sandwich. Both Doc and I had American history first period, so when the bell rang we stayed where we were. So did June and Copper.

Mrs. Flood brought the class to order and started passing out note cards. "I know it's tedious, but I like to start the year by getting some particulars about each of you. Please write your name as you wish to be called in class, where you live, and your favorite subject in school."

She smiled as Doc extended his card when she got to us.

"Hello, Doc. It's nice to see you. How was your summer?"

"Hi, Mrs. Flood. It was great. Are you going to be good to us this semester?"

"I'm always good to my students," she laughed. "And who is your friend?"

"This is my roommate, Andy Barnes. He's also from Copenhagen."

"I'm pleased to meet you, Andy," she said, giving my card a quick glance. "I see that you are interested in American history."

"It's my favorite subject," I answered, instantly regretting this reply.

"Apple polisher," said Rex, from across the room. His comment focused the attention of every kid on me, as Mrs. Flood asked me what aspects of American history I liked most.

I cringed, but there was no way out.

"It's all interesting, but I guess I like the military stuff best—the Revolution, Civil War, World War II, that sort of thing."

"You must have a good memory for dates," she continued, refusing to let me off the hook. "Do you remember what happened from July 1 to July 3, 1863?"

"Gettysburg, ma'am. The single most costly battle of the Civil War."

"Very good. And June 6, 1944?"

"D-Day, the Normandy Invasion."

"How about December 7, 1941?"

"The Japanese attacked Pearl Harbor. Our house got bombed." It just slipped out.

Laughter erupted. My teacher frowned. "Andy, history is too important to joke about."

I looked at Doc, desperation in my eyes.

"It's true, Mrs. Flood. His mother told me about it last

summer in Copenhagen. He was five months old in his crib when a Japanese bomb exploded outside his window and blew the house all to hell. He remembers it like it was yesterday," he grinned.

Laughter rippled around the room, but it was at my roommate's comment, not me.

"That must have been a terrifying experience, Andy," Mrs. Flood said, after restoring order. "I'll look forward to having the two of you in class this year, and to hearing about your experience at the proper time, Andy."

"Thank you, ma'am," I murmured.

After history, Doc steered me through the hallway mayhem to geometry. "Have fun with Miss Earl," he said, grinning as he disappeared into the scramble of bodies and books.

I sat down in a back corner, where I hoped she wouldn't notice me. Every blackboard was covered with chalk dust. The only personal touch was a framed picture of some Greek in a toga and sandals. I was counting his toes when Jimmy, jacket collar turned up, entered. He slid into a vacant seat next to me, pulled a pack of Lucky Strikes from his shirt pocket, and tapped one into stained fingertips.

"Jesus, I need a smoke."

"Put it away, Jimmy. If the teacher sees you with a cigarette, you'll end up in the office and Mr. Pulaski will crucify you."

"Yeah, I guess you're right." He placed the Lucky behind his ear.

"No. Put it back in your pocket where she can't see it."

He gave me a penetrating stare. "Okay, Daddy-O. I'll vanish the cigs. What is this class? It gives me the creeps."

"Geometry," I answered. "I'm no good at it. Are you?"

"Some kinda algebra with maps, ain't it?"

"I guess that answers my question."

A formless dress above bright green shoes that clicked against the floor tiles with quick, commanding steps floated across the room. An inverted triangular head at the end of a spindly neck extended from a chest as flat as a fillet of dried salt cod. The entire class gaped.

"A praying mantis with fluorescent feet," Jimmy exclaimed. "Didn't Slimbaugh say she got some kind of prize?"

The boy sitting in front of him turned, his magnified eyes staring at us through Coke-bottle glasses. "Miss Earl won the Lobelia L. Muller Medal for Innovative Teaching."

I recognized the bed-wetter from the day before—the one Slimbaugh had humiliated.

"Who asked you?" said Jimmy.

The youngster turned away, embarrassed.

"Hey, amigo, just kiddin'. What's your name again?"

"Alfred Duncan. My friends call me Alfie," he said, glancing down.

Jimmy patted Alfie's shoulder.

"I'm Jimmy. Sorry, Alfie. No hard feelings, okay? Us problem chillun got to stick together in this nasty place."

The kindness in his voice surprised me. He nodded toward the portrait of the toga-clad Greek.

"Who's the cat on the wall—the one wrapped in sheets with leaves in his hair?"

"That's Euclid, the mathematician. He's the father of plane geometry," said Alfie. The tone of his voice left no doubt that his command of geometry was probably equal to, possibly better than, that of our teacher.

"If you're nice," I whispered to Jimmy, loud enough so our new friend could hear, "maybe Alfie will help us with our geometry."

"Cool," Jimmy replied.

The green mantis picked up a brass hand bell and rang it three times.

"Give me your attention. I'm not in the habit of asking twice." She was looking straight at Jimmy and me.

"Kee-rist. She's on our case already," Jimmy said, out of the corner of his mouth.

"Young man, language like that will not be tolerated. Do I make myself clear?" As she was taking roll, he scribbled something on a piece of scrap paper and tipped it toward me. It read: "She's got ears like a fuckin' elephant."

"Bring me that note, young man. Immediately."

"Shit," said Jimmy to himself.

"What did you say?" Her lips pursed under flared nostrils. "I said, give me that note."

He stood up and started forward, stopping about halfway down the aisle.

"What is your name?" she demanded, her voice beginning to quaver.

"Jimmy Smith, ma'am. I apologize if I offended you. I didn't mean to."

"You should have thought of that beforehand." She snatched up a pink slip and scrawled several quick sentences. "Go apologize to Mr. Pulaski. I'm sure he'll be delighted to see you on the first day of school. And for the last time, give me that note."

Without taking his eyes off her, Jimmy stuffed it deep inside the front of his pants. Agnes Earl's eyes transformed into quail eggs.

"Get out of here! Get out, get out, get out!" she half gasped, half screamed.

I knew geometry was going to be bad news, but I never

expected anything like this. Nor, I suspect, did anybody else. Saying nothing, Jimmy took the pink slip and walked toward the door, closing it quietly behind him. With a grim smile, The Mantis snapped her pencil into pieces and dropped them, one at a time, into her empty wastebasket.

"You are here to learn something. Now that the distractions are over, we shall get down to business," said the winner of the Lobelia L. Muller Medal for Innovative Teaching.

Doc yanked me into the lunch line where he and the girls waited for the cafeteria to open.

"How was your first morning, Andy?" June asked, her voice warm and sincere behind that beautiful smile.

Brain cells misfired. My tongue refused to make sounds. Smiling stupidly, I looked into her eyes, which held mine with a mixture of humor and relaxed curiosity.

"Hi," I managed, desperate to make a good impression. "Um, okay, I guess—I mean, um, it wasn't what I expected. You saw what happened in history class, and—"

"Yes, that was a bit awkward for a few minutes, wasn't it?" she smiled. "But I thought your Pearl Harbor connection was interesting. So did Mrs. Flood and others. I was born in the Philippines, but we were sent home to Coronado a few months before the war began."

"How was geometry with Miss Earl?" inquired Doc.

"Don't ask."

"That bad?" It was Copper. She had been listening to our conversation, silently observing me with amber eyes that missed nothing. I felt like a fruit fly under a microscope. She was almost as exquisite as June, but more athletic looking, and her voice lacked June's softness. It crossed my mind that she and Doc would make a good pair.

He nudged me toward her. "Sorry, Copper. This is my

roommate, Andy Barnes. I forgot to introduce you."

"Never mind, Gordon. Hello, Andy. I'm Ginger. You were starting to tell us about geometry. June and I had that woman last year."

June nodded. I gave an abridged rendition of what happened, omitting the part about Jimmy stuffing the note inside his pants.

"How many pencils did she break this time?" Copper asked.

"I wasn't counting. Is that normal?"

"I'm afraid the abnormal is normal in her class," replied June. "Miss Earl doesn't inspire any love of subject in her students. The only thing is to grit your teeth, get your A, and get out."

"Hopefully, with your pencil still intact," laughed Doc. "What you just heard is about the worst you'll ever hear June say about anyone—unless she's really mad at you."

She gave his arm a knock and pushed him away.

"Hold my place," he said. "I have to see a man about a horse."

I turned back to the girls. "I don't see how I'll ever get an A in that class ...."

That's when Rex appeared, butting into the lunch line in front of me.

"Hi, beautiful ones. I'm Rex. Pleased to meet you." He made a show of hastily pulling out his Camels and then stuffing them back into his shirt pocket. "I was going to offer you one, but I just remembered Doc said neither of you smoke." He flashed them an Errol Flynn smile and launched into his repertoire.

My heart sank. How did Rex get away with the same crap he used on every girl he met? Clearly, he was after June. His advances did not impress Copper, however. She rolled her eyes, and turned back to me.

"Doc said it's true that you really were bombed at Pearl Harbor."

"Yeah, but I was too young to remember any of it," I replied, still focused on June and Rex. "I was only nine months old when Mom and I got evacuated to California, Copper. What about you?"

"I was born in the Philippines. My father was an Army pilot flying for General MacArthur. My mother and I were shipped back before the war started. In fact, we were on the same boat with June's family. We didn't know each other, then, of course," she smiled.

I glanced quickly at June, but Rex stepped in to block any possibility of my conversing with her.

"What happened to your father?" I asked, looking back at Copper.

"He spent three and a half years in Japanese prison camps, but survived to return to us."

"My father spent the war bombing the hell out of the Krauts and getting medals," interrupted Rex, turning away from June in midsentence. "He was a full-bird colonel when he was twenty-four."

Doc reappeared with Jimmy in tow.

"Are you going to introduce me, Gordon, or do I have to do it myself?" Jimmy asked, giving his hair a couple of swipes with his comb.

"Jimmy Smith," said Doc. "One of the Copenhagen crew."

"He specializes in shoplifting," said Rex.

I was delighted to see June give him a look that would have frozen a polar bear.

"All in my past," grinned Jimmy. "I'm a big boy, now, so I only rob banks."

"Are we going to have a school mixer?" Doc asked Copper. "I told Andy what a great time everybody had at that square dance you organized last year. He's an old hand, you know."

She looked at me with new interest. "You are?"

"Well, not really. Doc's just saying that. But it sounds like fun."

"It is," Doc cut in, grabbing June and twirling her around several times.

During lunch Rex continued to monopolize June, leaving me no chance to talk with her.

My last class of the day was chemistry. I entered to find Rex still trying to impress June. Jimmy sat nearby, talking to Alfie. A massive demonstration bench with rusty sink, hoses, and spigots occupied the front of the classroom. Dr. Wilson, his stained lab coat flapping like dirty white schooner sails on his tall frame, stood rummaging through debris on his desk.

During class I got lost taking notes. Fortunately, Alfie explained each test tube and beaker. Although he was a freshman among juniors and seniors, by the end of the hour it was plain that he knew more about chemistry than any kid in the room. When the bell rang, Dr. Will (as students called him behind his back) told us to study our handouts, read the first chapter in the textbook on the scientific method, and begin memorizing the periodic table. My first day of classes at Frankfurt High was over.

The next day was the same: get to the shower before the hot water ran out, then breakfast, if you could call it that. My enjoyment of first-period history was eclipsed by the gruesome Mantis, whose class was the low point of each day. Then government; an uninspiring lunch; and a stimulating English class with Miss McCafferty, followed by chemistry. After 3:30 p.m. sign-in to the dorm and mail call, it was sign-out for the PX or whatever, and then hustle back for dinner before 6. Missing a meal meant restriction. Sunday through Thursday at 7 p.m. the dorms closed for required study hours, which lasted until 9 (Friday and Saturday nights we could stay out until 11). The last hour of our day, prior to lights out at 10, when Kreebert did his nightly bed check, was free time. He hid in his room, ignoring all the horseplay, shouting, and loud record players that blasted our eardrums up and down the halls. Doc loved commotion, and was usually in the middle of it. I couldn't understand how my roomie thrived on this stuff. It didn't bother him at all, and somehow, he managed to keep one step ahead of Kreebert. Initially, I tried closing the door and practicing my guitar, but gave up.

By the end of the first week I knew two things for sure: one, I would never, ever, join the Army; and second, meeting June was the only good thing that had happened to me. Being near her in history, English, and chemistry every day, even though I could barely manage to speak straight, made my life at Frankfurt High bearable.

And so it went—the next week, the next—my calendar blurred.

# *The Washing Machine*

Thanks to Doc, my second weekend of the school year was my first on restriction. We had gone to see Gregory Peck in Twelve O'Clock High at the nearby Army theater and, afterward, were several minutes late returning to the dorm because he insisted we go for hamburgers. The PX snack bar was half a mile away at WAC Circle.

"It's already 10:30, Doc. We'll never get down there, order, eat, and get back by 11 to sign in."

"No problem, Lone Ranger. I know a shortcut. I'll get us back in time."

The Kreebs was at the door, waiting.

It was Saturday afternoon, and we were in our room. I was playing my guitar, wondering what June and Rex were doing. He never missed a chance to let everyone know when he had a date with her. Pacing round the room, Doc stopped in front of my laundry bag, took a deep sniff and fell on the floor, gasping for air.

"A bit ripe," he gagged, "wouldn't you say?"

I stopped playing chord progressions and looked down as he rolled, clawing at his throat. "Not any worse than yours. What's the big deal?"

He pinched his nose. "Let me put it this way, Roomie. If

you wash your clothes, the girls might sit with us at meals. Now, grab that bag of compost and come with me."

I followed him down rough-planked stairs to the basement, past a room with photo developing equipment, which Doc peeked into as we passed, to a dimly lit room smelling of dried soap and mold. My eyes fixed on a frayed electric cord coiled in a puddle of water on the uneven concrete floor and connected to an ancient washing machine with two wooden rollers on top. A wooden bench, rusted sink, bucket, and a broken baseball bat completed the equipment list for the dorm laundry.

"Impressive, Doc."

"Looks like nothing's changed since last year," he said, plopping his clothes on the bench. "At least the photo lab seems okay. Now, Roomie, pay attention, because you will be doing this once a week from now on. First, we put in water."

"I didn't know that," I yawned, as he connected a short length of brittle garden hose to the sink faucet. A twist of its handle produced a lukewarm trickle that quickly went cold. As the scummy washtub slowly filled, he tossed in everything—whites, darks, blue Levis, wool sweaters—the works. Half a large box of Ivory Flakes followed.

"This next part is dangerous as hell," he said, reaching for the electric cord. "Be sure your hands are dry and you aren't standing in any water when you plug it in, or our German 220 current will fry Willy and the Boys before you can let go." Lining up the tines with the plug receptacle, he shoved it in, leaping back as a blue spark shot out of the socket. The washer's engine emitted a puff of smoke as its wooden paddles shuddered against the oversized load.

"Just like we knew what we were doing," Doc said, beaming.

"Does it always spark and smoke like that?" I asked. "Wouldn't it be safer to take the clothes to the Army laundry? I'm not keen on getting fried."

"I hope the wringer works," he said, as if I hadn't spoken. A flip of the switch beside two wooden rollers on top of the tub produced another flash of blue, accompanied by a ferocious electrical snap. Doc jerked his hand away.

"Oww! The damned thing shocked me."

He was rubbing his fingers when the machine growled to a stop.

"Hotter than a firecracker," I said, touching the motor housing. "Now what?"

"Not good. Never did this last year," he replied, yanking the plug. "Your sleeves. Roll them up."

"You mean stir all that stuff by hand? Rinse and squeeze them ourselves?"

"Now you're getting smarter," he grinned. "I'm impressed at what a quick learner you are, Roomie. Good exercise for those puny wrists and forearms. Afterward, we dry everything on the radiator in our room."

"Why not take the clothes to the laundry?" I repeated. "They'll come back clean, the girls will be able to breathe, and we won't end up turned into carbon."

"Here," he said, shoving the busted baseball bat at me. "Stir."

By the time he let me stop, the water was sewage brown with no evidence that soap had ever been part of the equation. Doc pointed to the dinged-up pail.

"Don't tell me: I get to empty the tub, right?"

"The drain pump never worked. While you're bailing, I'll start wringing out the clothes."

"I'm going to take my stuff to the Army cleaners. That's

what normal people do."

He threw a wadded-up shirt at me. "Let Tonto put things in perspective, Lone Ranger. Which would you prefer—paying three dollars a week for starched underpants? Or taking Copper to several movies with hamburgers and shakes afterward? Living on a budget means cutting corners."

"Make that June instead of Copper, Gordon, and doing this might be worth it. I seem to recall last summer you promised to fix me up with her, and you 'always keep your promises,' remember? I'm still waiting."

"As usual, you have things confused. Tonto offered to fix you up with Copper, so the four of us could double-date. You said, 'I don't give a damn about the girls in Frankfurt.'"

"You had just shot up Mom's new Royal Copenhagen teapot, and I was about to get restricted for the rest of my life. Did you expect me to be pleased?"

A wadded-up sweater hit my face. I heaved my pail of dirty water at him, drenching the clothes he was wringing out. Wet socks splatted on the wall behind me. A pair of Levis followed. When it was over, the laundry room was filthier than when we'd started. So were we.

"Look what you've done, you jerk," I laughed. "Now we're both soaked."

Forty minutes later, two naked guys ignored catcalls and wolf whistles as they ran down the hall with armloads of clothes to dry on the radiator in their room.

*Alfie*

I slapped my geometry text closed and looked across our desk at Doc. As usual, he was waiting for any excuse not to study.

"It's been half an hour, and I'm still on the first problem," I groaned. "There are nine left. What am I going to do?"

"At this rate, you might finish by the weekend, Barnes. Not good."

I scrunched up my geometry paper and tossed it.

"You know," he pushed his chemistry book aside, "we should make a deal with Alfie. The kid's probably finished all his homework, and is sitting in his room listening to Mozart while he does a crossword puzzle. He might be the answer to our prayers."

Alfie Duncan loved Mozart. He arrived at school lugging a collection of old 78 records of the eighteenth-century genius's music. As soon as he touched his phonograph needle to the first one, he was forever branded a "square." The combination of Mozart, however, Alfie's thickly magnified glasses (which quickly earned him the nickname "Guppy"), his bed-wetting problem, and his feathered Tyrolean hat guaranteed him the life of a social outcast.

"Might not be a bad idea to take him under our wing," Doc continued, squirming around in his seat as he tried to scratch an itch between his shoulder blades. "The lad could use a couple of friends. As I see it, everybody has something to offer."

"I'm listening."

"Alfie is a treasure, with abilities just waiting to be tapped. Why don't we waylay the boy, buy him a sandwich at the snack bar, and make some arrangement that'll help us do better in chemistry and save you in geometry?"

Monday though Thursday nights after study hours we could buy candy bars, Cokes, and sandwiches from the dorm snack bar. The kids running it smeared peanut butter and jelly, or oily tuna fish mixed with mayo, between slices of white balloon bread—the same stuff that helped "build strong bodies twelve ways" (or whatever it was that Wonder Bread wrappers claimed). Because Alfie was so good at math, his peers let him do all the accounting. We found him making change at the counter.

"The tunas are fifty cents," he said to a hulking kid twice his size. "You only paid twenty-five cents."

I recognized Mike, a not-too-swift guard on the football team, who was always after Doc to bring him Danish porn magazines.

"I gave you fifty cents, Guppy Face."

Alfie recoiled, but held his ground.

"I'm very good at calculations," he replied, "and you did not pay the full amount."

Mike grabbed him by the collar. "You calling me a liar?"

"Mike, Mike," said Doc, draping a powerful arm around the sandwich thief's shoulder. "I'm sure Alfie meant no such thing."

Mike released the freshman. "Uh, hi, Doc. This pop-eyed fish face called me a liar."

Alfie took a step back, rubbing his throat.

"I didn't hear him say anything like that. Did you, Andy?"

"Absolutely not."

"Really, Mike, another twenty-five cents is no big deal. You know it all goes for dorm parties, so why not pay up and enjoy your sandwich?"

Mike whispered something in my roommate's ear.

"Is that all?" Doc put a paper quarter on the counter. "My treat."

"I'll pay you back tomorrow," said Mike, looking sheepish.

"By then you'll have forgotten all about it," Doc replied, laughing.

"Thanks," said Alfie, when Mike had gone. "I thought he was going to hit me."

"Certain people require a little finesse, that's all," replied Doc.

"But I was right. He only paid half what he was supposed to." Alfie started tallying up the nightly proceeds.

"Alfie, Andy and I could use some help, and we thought you might be a good person to ask," said Doc.

The freshman's pencil stopped moving. "What sort of help?"

"Well, as you probably know, neither of us is doing well in chemistry, and we were wondering if you could—"

"Help us with homework," I cut in. "And I'm totally lost in The Mantis's—I mean, Miss Earl's class."

"How much help do you need?"

"Lots," Doc answered.

"So you both need my assistance with chemistry, and

you," he turned his magnified eyes toward me, "need it in geometry. Chemistry and geometry—my two favorite subjects." He finished his additions and recorded the total. "What's in it for me?"

"You need friends," I said.

"Andy's right. Especially someone like me who knows this place, and can stand up for you in situations like you just had."

"We take you under our wing," I said, glancing at Doc.

"Can I sit at the same table with you in the mess hall?"

"Of course. You'll be one of us, Alfie," my roommate smiled.

"Deal," said the science whiz.

Doc and I barely beat the late bell back to our room.

"For half the price of Mike's sandwich," he said, "we've gained a friend who can make us respectable students in Dr. Will's class, and just might pry you from the jaws of The Mantis."

# *The June Dilemma*

Doc's relationship with June puzzled me. At first I thought they were steadies; on weekends, however, she was blitzed with dates, and the person who got most of them was Rex. If she was my girl running around with half the school, it would have really bugged me, but it didn't bother Doc. In fact, the thought crossed my mind more than once that he almost seemed to prefer being in a group when he was with her. Several times whenever he referred to something they had done together last year, I saw shadows of sadness creep over her lovely eyes.

Then one Friday evening several weeks into the semester, Doc announced he had a date with her, and Copper and I were going as "chaperones." For some reason, he was still convinced Copper was the girl for me.

After seeing Friendly Persuasion with Gary Cooper and Dorothy McGuire at the base theater, we hit the PX snack bar for ice cream sodas. Copper was witty, easy to talk to— and I didn't get tongue-tied every time I opened my mouth. That night, however, June occupied most of my thoughts, and this did not escape my date.

When we said goodnight on the dorm patio, Copper took my hands. "I hope you enjoyed your evening with me,

Andy. I wasn't sure at times."

A wave of guilt swept over me. "Of course I did, Copper. I had a wonderful time, really. You were a great date. Thank you so much for going out with me. It's just that—"

"Your mind was somewhere else? You're not much of an actor—or liar—you know."

"It showed, didn't it?"

"'Fraid so," she smiled.

I looked away. Why hadn't I paid attention to her? She deserved better.

"Copper, I'm so sorry for being a jerk to such a nice girl as yourself. You're a wonderful, fun person. Hurting your feelings is the last thing I would ever want to do, and that's the truth."

"You didn't hurt my feelings, Andy—well, maybe a tiny bit." She paused. "If I read this correctly, it's June, isn't it?"

I nodded. "But we can still be friends, can't we?"

"I wouldn't have it any other way," she replied, a warm smile on her lips as she gave my hands a squeeze and turned to leave.

Sudden fear gripped me: by breakfast, would everyone know that Andy Barnes had the hots for June Everett? What if Copper told her?

"Copper … you won't …."

She surprised me with a light kiss on my cheek. "Of course not. This is strictly between us. I don't discuss my private life with others, so nobody—even June—will ever know. And Andy, I hope it works out for you two. G'night."

When I got back to our room, Doc was radiant.

"Looks like things are going well between you and Copper. She doesn't kiss everybody on the first date.

Congrats. The two of you are almost going steady."

"You sneak. You were watching through the window."

He pantomimed having Copper in his arms, bending her backward onto my bunk and falling on top of her.

"Doc, can I ask you something personal?"

"Let me guess: you got up enough nerve to ask her for another date, and she accepted. You need advice on what to do next."

"Quit clowning. It's not what you think, okay? For your information, Copper knew immediately that I'm interested in June, not her. I don't know how, but she could tell. She even wished me well."

Doc sat up, serious at last. "Are you trying to tell me you want to ask June for a date?"

"That's all I've been thinking about for weeks. Where have you been?"

"So, what's the problem? Ask her."

"It would help if I knew what's going on between you two. You're the one she really likes, but I honestly can't tell if you care about her or not. If you do, fine, I won't interfere. If you don't, or you're stringing her along for some reason, that bothers me."

"Let's get this straight, Roomie. June and I are close friends—not steadies. That's all you need to know. If you have the hots for her, that doesn't bother me. If you asked her, I'm sure she'd accept—assuming she hasn't already been asked by Rex." He grabbed his toothbrush and headed for the door.

I knew this was the end of it for now, but the fact that he seemed upset convinced me I had touched a nerve. I wanted to know about the two of them—I had to know if I was ever to get close to her—and his "close friends—not steadies" comment was a good place to start.

In the weeks that followed, I hungered for a date with the nicest girl in school. There were two major problems: June's impossible social schedule, and me—more specifically, my tongue's inability to work properly whenever I tried to ask her out. Well-rehearsed words turned into strangled croaks. My back got clammy. My face burned fire extinguisher red. If I could stand in front of history class and give a report, why couldn't I face June and ask if she'd like to go to a movie with me? Eventually, however, the day came when I approached her without making a total mess of things. She was on the path beside the gym when I caught up with her.

"June, could I speak with you a minute?"

"Of course, Andy. What is it?"

Fighting an attack of mental pablum, I began. "June, um, would you please, no ... like to me, uh, to the—"

She touched my arm. "Stop. Take a couple of deep breaths. That's better. Now, what is it you want to ask?"

"I wanted to know ... if you would go with me to the —"

"She's going to the Teen Club dance this Saturday with me, Barnes, if that's what you're getting at." Rex sauntered past, smirking. "I already asked her."

"Andy and I are talking, Rex, and it doesn't concern you," she said to him, icily. She waited until he was out of earshot before continuing. "I'm afraid he's right, though. I did say I would go with him. I'm so sorry; I would have loved to accept your offer, so please ask me again. But next time," she touched my arm, "do it before anyone else does, okay?" She smiled over her shoulder and resumed walking toward the dorm.

I leaned against the building. June would have accepted. She said she'd like to go out with me. I couldn't believe it.

That night a few minutes before study hours, I recounted the whole episode to Doc. When I got to June's blunt words to Rex, he chuckled.

"Excellent, Lone Ranger. She meant what she said. She regards her private affairs as sacred, and doesn't go for people butting in."

"That's all fine, Doc, but a lot of good it does me with Rex slobbering after her."

"Don't blame him. You know every pair of antlers in Frankfurt—including yours—is pointed in her direction. He isn't a bad catch, either. Is she going to refuse him while she waits for you to get around to asking her out?"

I sank onto my bunk. "What am I going to do? She must think I'm a total idiot."

The study hour bell clanged, and we sat down across from each other at our desk, opening books we had no intention of reading.

"I don't think so," he replied, looking around for a pencil with an eraser that wasn't chewed. "But you do need to be more daring—more persistent. Remember, when it comes to getting a date with June, the early bird gets the worm."

He thought for a minute. "Tell you what, in the meantime, maybe I can show you Rex isn't doing as well with her as he lets on."

A couple of days later, Doc, Rex, and I were walking back from the PX when Rex started crowing about another date with June.

"This Friday I'm going out with my sex goddess," he said, glancing in my direction. "Man, is June ever hot for me. Can't keep her hands off my bod. Hey, Barnes. Stick around and I'll tell you what this is for." He waved a package of silver foil from his billfold in my face.

"Go screw, Holt."

"How did you know?"

I felt a tug on my sleeve as Doc stepped in. "So, Romeo, what's happening with you and June these days? Things cooling off a bit?"

Rex gave a terse laugh. "Come off it, Gordon. She practically throws herself at me when we're out together. Whatever gave you that idea?"

"Well, it seems to me that talk and action are opposites, and lately, you've been doing a lot of talking."

The swagger faded, and Rex looked uneasy. "You're not making any sense, Gordon."

"I'm saying that when guys aren't getting any action, they cover it up with talk."

Rex's face flushed. "What the hell are you getting at?"

"No biggie. I take it that despite all the recent attention you've given her, things aren't quite working out as you'd hoped, and I'm wondering what's happening, that's all."

I remained silent, fascinated by this exchange. Until now, I had never seen the slightest crack in my adversary's armor.

"Let's say," Rex replied, cautiously, "that she's too old-fashioned for my tastes."

"Old-fashioned?" I broke in, unable to stop myself. "C'mon, Don Juan. What you're really saying is that you— the great lover—have struck out. Your Camels don't work and you can't get anywhere with her, so now it's her fault? Your problem is that you can't handle a quality girl."

Rex tightened his fist and Doc stepped between us, mouthing a silent "Shut up" at me. But the conversation was over.

"Brilliant," he said, as Rex stormed off. "If you'd kept quiet, you might have learned something helpful about

June and her relationships with other guys—particularly Rex. He won't forget this, and you'll never hear a useful word about her from him now."

"Sorry," I said, realizing Doc had orchestrated the whole conversation to help me see that June was capable of taking care of herself.

# *Jimmy*

Living in the dorm was difficult for Jimmy: smoking inside or on school grounds was forbidden, except in the Weed Pit—a concrete stairwell outside the entrance to the mess hall. He had an endless supply of  cigs, but the problem was finding a place to smoke them when he needed to, which was often. The Kreebs was hyper about enforcing the ban. Along with being drunk, or trying to sneak a girl into your room, getting caught smoking meant immediate expulsion. Jimmy smoked in his dorm room whenever The Kreebs wasn't around. He would prop a chair against the door, open the window, light up, and flip the glowing butt into the night whenever Kreebert showed up. Warnings had no effect, and surprise inspections failed to catch him red-handed. This cat-and-mouse game between them went on for weeks.

"Mr. Kreebert was outside my window last night," said Alfie through a mouthful of gluey oatmeal at breakfast.

"Were you undressing, Guppy?" asked Rex.

Doc, who had stuck two pancakes on opposite ends of a pencil which he was rolling back and forth on the table, paused and turned his full attention to Alfie.

"Could you see what was he doing out there, Alfie?"

"He seemed to be looking up at the second floor. Then a couple of red sparks dropped on the grass, and he wrote something in his little book and went away."

"He's on to you, Jimmy," said Doc.

Jimmy stopped stirring uncounted spoonfuls of sugar into his coffee.

"I guess The Kreebs is on to me, then."

"But he's building a bulletproof case against you—that's his way. At some point he's going to go to Pulaski, and you know how sympathetic he'll be."

"You'll get kicked out of school," said Rex.

Jimmy put down his coffee and looked at Rex. "Get this straight, Holt: whatever happens, I can handle it, okay? I was puffin' long before Kreebert was sniffin'." He looked down at his breakfast and shrugged. "Besides, if I get kicked out, what am I missing?"

"Can't you stop smoking?" asked Alfie, trying to be helpful.

"No," Jimmy snapped back. People at surrounding tables, including June, looked up.

"Stay cool," said Doc. "Keep your voice down. Maybe there's time to think of something."

Time, however, had run out. That evening, Jimmy told us he had had a meeting in Pulaski's office with The Kreebs and Slimebum. We crowded around.

"What did they say?" I asked.

"What do you think? I'm being expelled for smoking in the dorm, and they're notifying my father. Man, is he going to be pissed."

We were crushed. "Damn," was all Doc could say.

The next day, Master Sergeant Harry Smith arrived for a meeting with school administrators about his son. I was surprised to see Pa with him.

"When Smith phoned to say he needed to fly down regarding Jimmy, I took the opportunity to make an appointment with Mr. Pulaski to talk about your progress in geometry—or lack thereof. At 1600 hours I want you sitting outside his office door in case questions come up. We have to fly back to Copenhagen tonight, so be there on time, got it?"

All this had been precipitated by an unfortunate incident during my first-quarter geometry exam. As I struggled to explain the Pythagorean theorem, The Mantis leaned over my shoulder to see what I was writing and a blob of her makeup fell off her face onto my paper. It smeared, making my answer unreadable. She took so long bringing me a clean page that time ran out before I could finish. I got another D, which really bugged me—especially since Alfie felt that after a month of tutoring I was showing signs of progress.

As Pa and I sat outside the principal's office waiting for Jimmy's hearing to finish, we could hear Pulaski presiding over my friend's fate.

"The evidence is clear, Sergeant Smith: your son repeatedly smoked in his room. He ignored warnings and broke a strict dormitory rule—not once, but many times. It is recorded right here in Mr. Kreebert's notes. I see no option except expulsion."

Jimmy's dad held his ground.

"The school allows students to smoke, and has a specific place for it called the Pit, I believe, but it isn't available after hours. Why is there no place in the dormitory where he and others can have a smoke when they can't go to the Pit? Yes, my son broke a dormitory rule, and should be punished for that. But he did not break a schoolwide regulation that allows smoking. Therefore, he should not be prevented from continuing his education here."

"The Sarge should have been a lawyer," commented Pa.

After Jimmy and his father left, we had an abbreviated meeting with Mr. Pulaski—abbreviated because The Mantis never showed up. Pa was not pleased. Neither was Pulaski. Later, I heard that the winner of the Lobelia L. Muller Medal for Innovative Teaching had been chewed out, which made her venomous toward me in class. When first-quarter grades came out, Alfie took my D- as a personal insult, insisting I was now doing at least C- work. I took him to the PX snack bar, where we drowned our sorrows in root beer floats.

That evening at dinner we crowded around Jimmy.

"So what's the deal?" Doc asked.

"I'm out of the dorm, but still in school. Andy's father suggested contacting the USO or Red Cross to see if they could find me a room in a boarding house, or maybe with a nearby German family. I've picked up enough German now, so I should get along pretty well with either."

"You'll be in a place all by yourself?" There was envy in Rex's voice.

"Why not, Holt? Us big guys can handle it. Hey, man, this has possibilities. Imagine, there I am, living unsupervised in my own pad, my dad hundreds of miles away. No Kreebert around, just me, alone in my garret room. Wisps of smoke rise from a glowing Lucky in my ashtray, curling upward toward ancient ceiling beams that survived the war." He paused for effect. "I look out the window at rain falling on tiled rooftops, pour a shot of cognac into my empty beer stein, and take a sip or two.

Then I get stumped studying my Kraut lessons, but the landlord's daughter, a lovely Fraulein of unsurpassed talents, knocks on the door to assist me. Cool, huh?"

"If it didn't stink so much, I think I'd take up smoking," said Doc.

# Cold War Jitters

"Did you hear about the combined dorm meeting this evening?" June asked as we walked back to the dorm after dinner. It was the third week of October 1956.

"What about it?" replied Doc.

"Apparently, it's pretty important. The announcement on the front door says seven o'clock sharp in the lounge. Required attendance. No sign-outs for any reason."

I took a long look at the street on the other side of the football field. Shrouds of black exhaust smoke seeped through what remained of fall's foliage on the trees and bushes lining our school fence. The growl of heavy transmissions shifting gears, chains clanking against trailer hitches; the ominous rumble of motorized weaponry and troop carriers, as they stopped and started—all heading toward the Autobahn. I could feel the ground shaking, even though we were standing at least fifty meters away. All this had been going on for several hours, but until now I assumed it was just another 3rd Armored Division exercise.

"Maneuvers?" I asked.

"More than that," Doc replied. "They're sending out the kitchen sink. I'll bet the meeting is about all those big

Army toys out there."

When Doc and I arrived a few minutes before seven, the big room, normally full of chatter and kidding around in mixed company, was sober. Every seat was taken. We stood behind Alfie, settled on one of the sofas up front. He looked worried.

"Do you know what this is about, Doc?"

"Not a clue," my roommate replied, squeezing our tutor's shoulder. "But we're about to find out, aren't we?"

In front of us, Mr. Pulaski and several Army officers stood looking at a map of Europe on an easel. A major with a boxer's nose, rows of ribbons, and a cigar stub clenched between his teeth listened to a captain briefing him from notes on a yellow tablet. The major snapped his fingers, and a lieutenant immediately produced a wooden pointer. Off to one side, Miss Maybelle and Miss Franklin whispered with The Kreebs. He moved to the lectern and the room fell silent.

"Your attention, please. Mr. Pulaski will now speak to you, followed by Major Broderick Westfield, an intelligence officer from the 3rd Armored Division. Mr. Pulaski."

"This meeting," our principal began, "has been called in response to events in Hungary which, although at the moment do not pose problems for us here in Frankfurt, have the possibility of doing so in the days ahead. If this occurs, we must be ready to react at once."

"What is happening there?" a shaky voice interrupted.

"I know everyone is concerned," replied Pulaski, "but kindly hold your questions until after the presentation. Since you asked, Miss Farrer, a revolution against the communist authorities has broken out in that country. If the Russians get involved and war occurs—"

Westfield whacked the side of his immaculately creased

trousers with his pointer. Alphie flinched. A fly buzzed in a spider web on a nearby window.

"At present, chances are low this will occur," Pulaski continued, "but if so, we do not intend to let anything happen to you while you are in our care at Frankfurt High. Should evacuation be required, you must cooperate immediately and follow directions. Now, please listen to Major Westfield, who will tell you all you need to know."

Placing his cigar in an ashtray extended by the lieutenant, Westfield struck the green and brown surface of his topographical map with his pointer.

"Hungary is behind the Iron Curtain, which is here," he boomed, as if we were troops on a parade ground. His stick swished from the Baltic to the Balkans and back again, stopping at a spot close to Frankfurt. Westfield's eyes gleamed. "This is the Fulda Gap, a natural corridor on the East German border leading straight into the heart of West Germany. If Russki T-34s—um, medium tanks— start pouring through on our doorstep here at Fulda—" his pointer stopped at a town very close to Frankfurt "they're sonsabitches to stop. These babies have 85 mm cannons that can destroy anything in front of them. We'd have a helluva fight on our hands."

In a few sentences, this man, spoiling for battle, had us face to face with communist tanks. My imagination flipped into overdrive: the distant rumble of heavy artillery fire; sirens wailing as trucks packed with soldiers grind by on the Miquelallee; Rhein-Main's fighter jets screaming overhead; explosions getting louder; machine guns— desperate small arms fire; Russian tanks flattening the school ….

Noticing teary faces around the room, Westfield looked uneasy. "Um, put another way, they have more tanks than we do. But—" students jumped as his map took another brutal hit "—we have an ace in the hole: Davy Crockett shoulder-mounted tactical nukes. One GI can take out a whole division of their tanks."

"Sweet Jesus," said Jimmy's voice from the back of the room. "World War III?"

The Kreebs snuffled into his handkerchief, returning it to his pocket without examining its contents as he usually did. Apparently, this maniac with medals considered battlefield nuclear explosions reassuring, but every kid present wondered if we would soon become another Hiroshima. An aide whispered something into Westfield's leathery ear and he nodded, perhaps realizing his comments were overkill.

"The point is, not to worry, because we have things under control. If the bastards break through, we'll nuke 'em while you're being evacuated on Army buses to Rhein-Main, where you will be airlifted out as fast as the planes can take off."

Mr. Pulaski coughed and Westfield stopped again. "Any questions?"

"What if it's foggy?" asked Doc.

Westfield looked past my roommate as if he didn't exist.

"What about our parents?" June asked. "How do we reconnect with our families?"

It was an important question on everybody's mind, but no reply was forthcoming.

"In conclusion," Westfield said, "you must be ready to evacuate on a moment's notice." He turned to the captain. "Did I cover everything?"

"Yes, sir."

"Thank you, Major Westfield," said Mr. Pulaski, "for that clear and reassuring briefing. And now, Mr. Kreebert will give you important instructions."

"Yes?" Our dorm supervisor looked directly at Alfie, huddled into the sofa.

"Sir, if an atomic bomb goes off, are we supposed to 'duck and cover'?"

Nobody laughed, although I couldn't help smiling at a phrase I hadn't heard since fifth grade. It was during the Korean War: Pa was gone, this time flying from a carrier somewhere in the Yellow Sea. Mom said he was near a place called Inch'on. Every afternoon, my class listened to a movie about Bert the Turtle. "If you duck and cover you will be much safer," Bert told us, as the school buses arrived. He quickly became "Bert the Turd," his slogan a joke.

"I don't think it will come to that, Mr. Duncan," replied Kreebert, evading Alfie's question. "But we must be ready for any eventuality. The most likely scenario is evacuation to Rhein-Main on short notice." For the remainder of the hour, he told us how to pack a suitcase.

"Westfield ignored your question about the fog," I said to Doc, back in our room.

"Yeah," he replied. "But it was a good one. Last Christmas, we had to stay overnight at Rhein-Main because the fog was so thick the Copenhagen plane couldn't take off."

For several days the Hungarian crisis cast its shadow over the school as we waited for a possible rendezvous with a nuclear nightmare. Between classes, at meals, and out on the grounds, little knots of kids talked, and steadies stayed close together. Rumors abounded: the semester was about to be canceled; we would be sent home; we were to be relocated at a similar American school in Bushy Park, England.

Rex was his cynical self. "Listen, the school evacuation plan is so fucked up we'll all be french fries half an hour after the shit hits the fan, so what's the use of worrying?"

Doc was more optimistic. "My father called to say he doesn't think anything is going to happen, because the risks are too great for us to go in and help Hungary. It would mean direct contact between Russian and American armies, and war would result, which nobody wants."

In my case, I didn't worry so much about becoming a french fry as about whether I would see my family again. I wrote several letters home, including, for the first time ever, one to Curt and even one to Lissa. Pa wrote back saying not to worry, things weren't as bad as they seemed; and Mom commented that she hoped she would not have to wait for another international crisis to get more than one letter from me. A huge tin of Elena's butter cookies arrived.

Several days later, I saw June heading back to the dorm. She was alone—unusual for her. As I hurried to catch up, I rehearsed what I wanted to say: "June, next to my family and Doc, you are the most important person in my life." No! "June, I really care about you, and I want to be with you when Russian tanks arrive." No, No, No! "June, if trouble comes in the days ahead, let's run for it together" … I stopped beside her.

"What is it, Andy?" she asked, turning to face me.

I reached for her hands. "Whatever happens," I began, "I want you to know that you are the most wonderful girl I ever met. Next to my family, you are—next to my family, I … can I sit with you on the plane from Rhein-Main if we get evacuated?"

Why did I say that? Why? The spell was broken. I looked down, "Sorry, June. I can't seem to get this right. I feel like a total idiot." I released her hands, their softness slipping from my fingertips like drops of liquid silk. She was silent as moist green eyes softly searched my burning face. I felt her hand under my chin, gently pressing upward.

"That was a really nice thing to say, Andy," she smiled, as our eyes met. "Thank you. And yes, you can sit with me on the plane if it comes to that."

Within a week, it was obvious we weren't destined to become nuclear french fries. Doc's father was right: President Eisenhower realized that, short of melting down a good portion of Europe, there was nothing the United States could do to help Hungary break free from the Soviet Union's grip. So, while the 3rd Armored and its sister units stood by across the border, Hungarians died throwing rocks at Russian tanks. Frankfurt High returned to normal, and we transitioned back into the humdrum bubble of our daily lives, safely surrounded by American military might. Major Westfield must have been the most disappointed Army officer in Germany.

# The BFV Shave-Off

"What's that?" Doc asked, looking at the Sunbeam electric razor I was turning over in my hand. I was standing in front of the small mirror hanging next to his closet.

"A hand-me-down from my Dad. Probably too dull to cut his whiskers anymore. Now I'm stuck with it."

"Does it work?"

"He got it before the Korean War, for God's sake. I have no intention of using it."

"Then I will." Plugging it in, Doc made a pass along the side of his neck.

"Yeoww. This thing sucks the whiskers out roots and all."

He handed it back, and I started to drop it in the wastebasket.

"Hold on, Andy. I have a better idea."

On the way to the PX, Jimmy asked about the "Barnes Face Vac." I was mystified. By the time I entered the mess hall for dinner, several others had inquired about the "shaving contest."

"Count me in," said one kid, handing me a dollar as I sat down with my tray.

"I'll take that, thank you," said Doc, grabbing it. "Can't

trust Andy with the purse, you know." He jotted the entrant's name on a list from his pocket.

"Okay, Gordon, what's going on?"

"Thanks to me, your razor is famous. Seven contestants have already signed up at one dollar each."

"Signed up for what? Do you mind telling me what you've done—without my consent?"

"I put a notice about our shaving contest in the upstairs bathroom," Doc replied, with self-satisfaction. "Behind the wall next to the sinks, where The Kreebs won't see it, because he never goes in there to pee."

"What contest? All I know for sure is that it's something against the rules."

"See for yourself after dinner, Lone Ranger."

Later, I went into the bathroom to examine Doc's handiwork.

> *Hear Ye, Hear Ye!*
>
> *Contest to see who (if anyone) can get a full shave using the Barnes Face Vacuum (BFV). Think you're tough? Try this device brought back from Korea, where it was used by the Commies to torture American POWs. Experience the pain. How long can you take it? Two-day growth of whiskers required; winner gets the pot, minus judge's fees—one half the pot. Entry fee $1.00. Time and date to be announced. See Doc Gordon to register.*

Back in our room, I found him on my bed counting a fistful of colorful military scrip. In those days, it was used at all U.S. bases. The idea was that scrip would prevent the Germans from buying American products at our PX facilities, forcing them instead to buy locally made goods with marks—the official German currency—which would strengthen West Germany's economy.

"So, how much have you collected from guys looking for an excuse to grow a beard?" I asked.

"Almost twenty dollars," he replied, without looking up.

"Doc, let's take a minute to think about this crackpot scheme, okay? The announcement says minus judge fees."

"So?"

"Who's the judge? You?"

"Now you're getting really smart, Roomie."

"Did it ever occur to you, Einstein, that this could get out of hand? I assume your 'contest' will have to be done while The Kreebs is asleep. How long is it going to take to give twenty people time to shave their two-day beards? All night? And the longer it goes on, the greater the chances he'll wake up, right? Stop the enrollment now and give back the money."

After considerable debate, in which he refused to stop the contest, he agreed to give refunds to the five-day kids (who went home every weekend, thus reducing the contestants to a manageable number), and have it in the upstairs bathroom the coming Friday at midnight.

"And what about The Kreebs?" I asked.

"It's his weekend off. His substitute is an old man with hearing aids. No problem."

Friday midnight, as sleet drummed against the dorm windows, five sleepy shavers, plus Doc, Rex, and me, padded down the hall to the upstairs bathroom, where contestants drew cards from Rex's deck to see who would go first.

"What's the towel for?" somebody asked.

"Use your head," Doc replied, wrapping the BFV in it. "You don't want to wake up some snitch who hears a B-52 flying around and tells the substitute, do you?" He plugged in the razor and handed it to the first challenger. With a gasp of pain, he quit with one side of his neck full of skin divots. I handed him a styptic pencil and hot washcloth, and he sat down on one of the toilets to recuperate.

"Next," said Doc, jamming the plug of the BFV into the socket again. In short order, the second contestant's upper lip was reduced to uncooked flank steak. As he passed the shaver to the third hopeful, it slipped out of the towel and clunked against the wall. Number Three reached down.

"Oww. This thing's hot."

"Supposed to be," replied Doc, wrapping the towel around it again. "Melts the whiskers and they get sucked out by the roots. Of course, if you can't take it …."

Number Three grabbed the Sunbeam and attacked his stubble. He was working on the front of his face when Rex said, "I smell something burning."

"There's smoke coming from inside the towel," said Alfie, who had appeared from downstairs. Doc yanked the plug and threw the BFV—towel and all—into the nearest toilet.

"Phew," he said, as steam hissed upward. "That was close. Thanks, Alfie. You showed up just in time."

"I came to warn you that Mr. Kreebert is here in the dorm."

"But I saw him leaving with his suitcase," said Rex.

"He had his galoshes on," said Doc. "This is his weekend off."

A switch clicked, paralyzing us with light.

"Things don't always go as planned, Gordon. Word gets around, you know." Stanley Kreebert stepped into the lavatory, pencil and little black notebook ready. "Now, boys, what is going on? Oh," he said, spotting Doc's small pile of entrance fees on a sink. "I see that money is involved. Gambling means expulsion, you know."

"Yes, Mr. Kreebert, money is involved, but we weren't gambling," I said.

"Let me guess, Barnes. You were raising money to buy Girl Scout cookies." He laughed at his cleverness. "No, I think you were betting on some sort of contest, and that constitutes gambling. Ringleaders," he looked at Doc and me, "will face the music."

"Actually, Mr. Kreebert, we were trying to make some extra money for the dorm fund," said Doc, "so we can pay for the, ah …."

"Square dance we want to have," I broke in.

Rex's jaw dropped and he started to say something, but Doc kicked his shin, hard.

Kreebert laughed again, enjoying himself. "You want me to believe that red-blooded he-men like yourselves do square-dancing? Do-si-do, boys. C'mon, you can do better than that."

"But it's true," Doc said. "We've been talking about it for weeks. Last year we had a great square-dance mixer …."

Kreebert cut him short. "So? That has nothing to do with your gambling tonight, eh?"

"We weren't gambling," I repeated.

"I say you were, Barnes, and around here what I say is law."

"But Andy's right, Mr. Kreebert," Doc insisted. "Look: the problem is paying for the band. We need live music to do it—a fiddle player, guitar, a couple of banjos, and a special square-dance caller. It's expensive, so, we came up with this great idea to raise money, using Andy's razor."

The Kreebs glanced around. "I don't see any razor."

"It's in the toilet," Rex said, pointing to the towel hanging out of the bowl.

"What the hell are you talking about?" Kreebert exclaimed.

"We were using an old electric razor my dad gave me," I replied. "It started to burn up, so Doc threw it into the toilet."

"The toilet? An electric razor?" The Kreebs gasped, stepping back from the commode. "You could have been electrocuted."

"It was starting to smoke, but we unplugged it first, sir," Doc said.

"My God. That's what I smelled. You stupid kids might have burned down the dorm. Everybody asleep—we could have had a disaster."

"We even put up an announcement about the contest," said Rex.

"What are you talking about, Holt?" For the first time, Kreebert was hesitant.

"That's right," said Doc.

I started to say something but stopped. Doc's announcement didn't mention anything about a square dance.

"Prove it, Gordon. Show me the notice that says the purpose of this illegal gathering was to raise money for a square dance. I want to see it right now."

While this exchange was going on, Alfie had the

presence of mind to remove Doc's announcement from the wall behind the furious Kreebs, and tuck it into his Bugs Bunny pajamas.

"It's in my book locker at school," Doc went on. "I can't get it until tomorrow."

"I've had enough of this. You are all restricted. Gordon, I want to see that announcement at breakfast, do you hear? Now, hand over the money you collected. I'm keeping it for evidence. And the razor."

"But sir," said Alfie, "it's still in the toilet. Shall I fish it out for you?"

The Kreebs was unable to answer. "Wrap it in a dry towel that doesn't smell and deliver it to my office. Now, get back to your rooms—immediately."

The BFV Shave-Off was over.

"I can imagine Pa's reaction when he gets the telegram from Pulaski saying I've been kicked out for gambling," I said to Doc's sagging mattress above me.

"Cheer up, Andy. Just because we lost the battle doesn't mean we've lost the war. If we play our cards right, something positive will come of this. We need to get the girls involved."

"I have no idea what you're talking about."

"It's too bad the razor got fried," he mused. "If it still worked, we could tie Kreebert to his bed, gag him, and vacuum his balls."

I was too depressed to laugh.

At breakfast, Doc gave The Kreebs a revised shaving contest notice stating that its purpose was to raise money for a dorm square dance. With a snort, he passed it to Battle-ax Franklin, who scowled and passed it to Miss Maybelle. Miss Maybelle smiled.

"I think a square-dance is a wonderful idea," we heard

her say. "It would be fun."

"I think we're off the hook on this one," said Doc. "Good thing The Kreebs didn't see the original notice on the bathroom wall last night," he continued, looking at Alfie. "What did you do with it?"

Alfie stopped sawing at his breakfast waffle. "I don't remember," he said, apprehensively. "I either threw it in my wastebasket or left it with some papers on my desk."

"Brilliant move, Guppy," said Rex, at his sarcastic best. "You realize what will happen if The Kreebs pulls one of his surprise inspections? You'll be pissing in your pants all the way back to Copenhagen with the rest of us."

"Stay cool, guys," said Doc, his eyes glittering with excitement from this unexpected crisis. I don't think anyone else noticed, but I did.

"Something needs to be done—fast."

"But how can I get into the dorm during school hours?" Alfie removed his glasses and rubbed his eyes.

"That's up to you, Alfie," Doc told him. "Everything depends on destroying that piece of evidence."

For the first time all year, Alfie was late for second-period geometry. Eventually, he entered and handed The Mantis a hall pass, which she signed and put into her desk. He gave Jimmy and me a big smile as he sat down. After class, we cornered him in the hall.

"Rex was right. The Kreebs was just starting inspections on my floor as I arrived. But we're safe."

"Amazing," said Doc. "How did you pull it off?"

"After first period, I stopped at the drinking fountain in the hall and splashed water on the front of my pants. Mr. Pulaski was checking hall passes, so I said I wet my pants and could I please go back to my room to change. He gave me a pass, which got me past Mr. Slimbaugh, Mr.

Kreebert, and back into Miss Earl's class without a hitch."

"Where was the notice?" I asked.

"My trash can. I tore it into little pieces and flushed it down the toilet."

"'You done good,'" said Doc, tousling Alfie's hair. "Allow me to buy you a soda at the snack bar after school this afternoon."

Alfie grinned.

# *The Square Dance*

That night before study hours The Kreebs told us that, against his better judgment, Miss Maybelle had prevailed on the issue of a square dance, and he was putting our restrictions on hold so we could "get it over with as quickly as possible." After arguing about all the preparations that needed doing—especially getting the band—he agreed to a week from the coming Saturday.

"How can we put a square dance together in that short a time?" I asked Doc afterward.

"Easy. I'll tell June about our predicament. She'll be glad to help. She'll tell Copper, who will create a dance committee and invite other girls to be on it. That will guarantee success, because girls do all the work once they get involved in that sort of thing."

"What?" June's eyes glowed like green auroras. "You got caught lying about gambling, and now you want Copper and me to save you? You must be out of your mind."

"Aw, June, don't be mean," Doc wheedled, in his most vulnerable tone. "You wouldn't want to never see our smiling faces again, would you?"

"How anybody could be so stupid. It serves you right." She turned back to her Wheaties and looked around for milk.

"Allow me," I said, passing her my glass.

She hesitated.

"It's okay—I didn't sneeze in it."

"You better not have," she replied, trying to look severe. But her eyes flickered with amusement as she poured it into her bowl. I saw it, and so did Doc. He pressed ahead.

"A square dance would be fun for everybody. It's tragic that the social committee decided not to have one this year. Aww, c'mon, June. We need your help. Please?"

She took a long sip of tasteless orange juice, picked up her spoon, and crunched through a dainty mouthful of cereal.

"So, you'll help us?" he said, giving her his most defenseless grin.

"I'll talk to Copper," she answered, without looking at him.

He winked at me.

After school, Copper surprised me on the PX steps.

"Andy, are you coming to the square dance?"

"Sure, if there is one," I replied. "But isn't there a problem getting live music?"

"Not anymore. I just ran into Whitey Trapp, that great caller we had last year. He told me he still has his band, and when I asked if he would be interested in another dance, he said, 'Sure.' We could use your help."

"Me?"

"You. What about being on the social committee? Pretty please?"

"But Copper, I've never been on a committee."

"Then it's time you were. You can sit next to June at our meetings," she added, batting her eyelashes.

I attended every session. When Copper announced that Whitey had acquired a draftee banjo picker who had played professionally in Nashville, I nodded like everybody else—even though I had never heard of the Grand Ole Opry. The girls were all business. We set a date, reserved the gym, and narrowed refreshments to Cokes and cookies. The biggest concern was how to make guys want to come.

"No cowboy outfits," Doc insisted. "Remember last year?"

I looked at Copper.

"They thought it was sissy stuff," she said.

"What about a wet T-shirt contest during intermission?" Doc suggested. "That would bring 'em in droves."

"Other suggestions?" asked June.

"Why not make it one of those Sadie Hawkins things?" I said. "Isn't that where the guys have to come if the girls ask them?"

Female faces sparkled in agreement.

"Congratulations, Andy," said Copper. "You are now chairman of publicity."

I made a mental note to be more careful making suggestions in committee meetings.

"Has June asked anybody to the dance yet?" I queried my advisor on matters of love as Saturday approached. "She hasn't said a thing to me. How about you?"

Doc stepped to the window and stretched.

"No, and I don't think she wants to stir up old memories by going with me again."

"Feel like talking about it?" I asked. "I'm a good listener."

He smiled at my latest attempt to worm information out of him regarding what had happened between them. "Not now, Andy. Maybe later. Anyway, Copper asked me. I'm also the official yearbook photographer, so I'll be busy taking pictures."

"I was hoping June would have said something, but not a single word. I must be at the bottom of her list."

"Who knows, Lone Ranger? Your hat's in the ring; maybe you've got a better chance than you think."

Then, the next morning, she pulled me aside in the hall.

"Andy, I feel I owe you an explanation about why I haven't asked you to the dance tomorrow night."

At least she considered it, I thought, as my heart sank. The only good thing was that she hadn't asked Rex, either—he hadn't been bragging about it.

"You are going, aren't you?"

"Don't look at me like that," she said, touching my arm. "Yes, but it wouldn't be fair—to you, or anybody, for that matter. I wouldn't be much of a date, honest."

"You're not making any sense. Of course I'd go if you asked me."

"I'm taking admissions and counting the money. And I volunteered to be in charge of the cleanup and closing the gym. We would end up spending all our time working. Not exactly my idea of fun, if you know what I mean."

The bell rang, and we started for homeroom.

"I'm able to decide what I think is fun, thank you, Miss Everett. As long as we can do stuff together—I don't care what it is—that would be a great evening, in my book."

"In that case, Mr. Barnes, I know you have better things to do, but would you like to go to the square dance with me?"

I floated through Mrs. Flood's history class. In geometry, Alfie cringed when The Mantis sent me to the board and I used the formula for a triangle to find the area of a square.

"What's wrong with you? Last night I spent an hour explaining squares and triangles, and you haven't remembered anything."

"What's with the stupid grin on Barnes's face?" asked Rex at lunch.

"Someone destroyed his powers of concentration when she asked him to go to the dance," replied Doc. "That's all he can think about. His antlers are tingling with excitement."

He wasn't far off.

Saturday evening, I went downstairs to meet June in the dorm lobby. She was wearing a green knit sweater with Scottish tartan skirt and knee socks. Her face was radiant.

"I'm not very experienced at this sort of thing," I said, "but you look fantastic."

"That's a good start, sir. How about helping me with my coat?"

Besides the janitor, we were the first ones in the gym. She put me to work fetching a table and two chairs while she got the money box and tickets. Whitey Trapp arrived with his musicians, who began hooking up microphones and tuning their instruments. Food wasn't allowed in the gym, so we set up another table in the hall with Alfie in charge. Despite the raw weather, hordes of people came. At one point Jimmy sauntered in, arm around a willowy brunette in skin-tight pants and a soft leather jacket. He winked at us: "Elke, my German tutor."

The noise level in the gym dropped several decibels as Jimmy and the stunning Elke entered. June nudged me under the table.

"You're my date tonight, remember?"

At 7:30 Copper welcomed everybody, and introduced the 3rd Armored Division Hoe Downers. The evening was underway.

Whitey explained that this would not be "grade school

stuff," but the new Western square-dancing, with the dancers performing moves that the caller told them to do, in the order he said to do them.

"Now," he said, "take a partner and get into squares of four couples, with everybody facing the center of the square. When each tip is over, you will end up back in the same spot where you are now—that is, if all eight people did everything correctly."

June and I stood in the doorway, trying to listen. "One more couple," the caller was saying, "we need one more, so everyone can dance. Is there another couple in the hall?"

"I can tell you two are dying to dance," said a voice behind us. "Go. I'll watch the table."

It was Miss Maybelle. Thanking her, we hurried across the floor to take our places in the last square. The other three couples were all teachers and their husbands, including Mr. and Mrs. Flood. A flashbulb popped.

"That's a great picture for the yearbook," Doc beamed, inserting another bulb in his prewar 35 mm Leica III, a family heirloom.

"Holding hands with your partner is very important," said Whitey. "It keeps the square small, and helps you maintain proper position."

I took June's hand and lost track of what he was talking about, recovering in time to hear him say something about giving your partner a "Yellow Rock."

"For those of you just starting, that's a big hug," Whitey clarified.

I locked us together in a magnificently long embrace, and decided I was definitely going to take up square-dancing.

"Andy," she gasped, trying to catch her breath, "I think you …."

"You're supposed to release your partner after a Yellow Rock," said Mrs. Flood, smiling.

It was a wonderful evening. I hadn't realized how often I would be holding June close, savoring wisps of her peppermint breath and the citrus fragrance of her hair when it brushed my face, feeling her arms around my neck, breasts pressing firmly against my chest when I swung her. And so it went—great exercise, marvelous fun, laughter, and physical contact with the girl I adored—over and over. I had no time to think of my latest D from The Mantis, or dorm restrictions, or the coming test in Dr. Will's chemistry class. If the school had been on fire, I wouldn't have cared. I never wanted this night to end.

Later, after we cleaned up the gym, it was almost dorm curfew time.

"Look," she said, tossing her head back as we stepped outside. "It's snowing."

In the streetlight's glow, we watched large, wobbly flakes meandering the last few yards of their long journey to earth.

"First snow I've seen in Europe," I said, putting my arm around her waist.

"Thanks for your help, Andy. I apologize for everything you had to do."

"We make a good team, don't we—you tell me what to do, and I do it."

"It wasn't that bad, was it?" June asked, laughing.

"Thank you so, so much for inviting me, June."

She put her arms around my neck.

"I'd say you had a pretty good time, in spite of the extra work. I did."

I brushed some snowflakes from her hair. Her eyes closed, and for the first time I felt the softness of her lips on mine—lightly at first, then firmly. I slipped into reverie, overwhelmed by tenderness. She stepped back and, arm in arm, we walked to the dorm in silence. At the door, she gave me another kiss.

Back in our room, Doc was waiting. "Okay, Lone Ranger, let's have it. Every sordid detail laid bare for my expert analysis—no stone unturned."

"Sorry, Tonto. What's under those stones is strictly between June and me. Ask Rex about his exploits. On second thought, save your breath: he'll tell everybody everything anyway, whether they're interested or not."

"But, but Andy," Doc sputtered, looking like a dog whose dinner dish had been removed for no reason at all. "How can your advisor on matters of love properly counsel you if you won't cooperate? I'm crushed."

"Doc," I answered, climbing into bed, "I'll need your advice—probably many times—and I feel really good knowing that it's there. But let me be the one to ask for it, okay?"

After a long minute or so, I heard sounds of pillow-smothered fake blubbering coming from the upper bunk. Pulling my threadbare blanket around me, I relived the entire evening—our first genuine date: getting into that last square; laughing over dancing mistakes; sharing ourselves. I could feel June's body twirling in my arms. I dozed off, dreaming of us going steady.

# Part 3
## The Long Winter

# *Doc's Femme Fatale*

Thanksgiving vacation was short, from noon Wednesday to Sunday evening. When I asked June what she was doing, she said she and Copper had been invited to stay with one of their friends at Rhein-Main.

"Aside from whatever I can do to help, I'll probably spend the time relaxing and reading ahead for chemistry."

"With all those guys who live out there? You won't have a moment's peace."

"I suppose that's a possibility," she replied, a hint of mischief in her smile. "And you?"

I told her about my family and Taarbaek; hanging around the house, possibly taking a bike ride through Dyrehaven, enjoying Elena's cooking.

"Sounds wonderful, Andy. I wish my dad worked in Copenhagen, instead of Ankara."

"I wish so, too."

Driving home from Kastrup Airport, Pa asked if I would like to go hunting with him the day after Thanksgiving.

"I'd love to, Pa."

"It won't be what you're used to, Son. Eigil Hansen, one of the wealthiest men in Denmark, has invited several

guests to his estate for a Danish hunt. When I mentioned
you are a good shot and I haven't seen much of you this
fall, he said, 'By all means. Bring your son.'"

"Am I going to be the only kid there?" I asked. "Is Doc
going?"

"Colonel Gordon has been invited, so it's possible Doc
will be there. Do you want to go hunting or not?"

The slight edge to his voice told me decision time was
now.

"Sure, Pa. Thanks. I haven't used my shotgun since we
left Jacksonville."

"I've missed you so much," Mom said, hugging me hard
enough to dislodge my glasses. "This is the longest you've
ever been gone."

Even my siblings seemed glad to see me, although Curt
cringed when Lissa said he had taken over my room while
I was away.

"And yesterday it was still full of his comic books," she
added.

"It better not be," I growled, grabbing her in my arms
and pretending to take a chomp out of her neck. She
screamed with laughter as I dropped her on the sofa.

I spent Thanksgiving morning in the kitchen helping
Elena, who was preparing her first American turkey dinner.

"I have read about this holiday in a schoolbook. It was
when the Indians saved the Pilgrims from starving, so the
Pilgrims took away their land, correct?"

"Something like that, yeah, Elena."

She pushed a bowl of potatoes and a paring knife
across the counter top. "Peel, yes?"

I told her about living in the dorm, Doc, the school,
Sergeant Normand's awful food, and how much we
enjoyed her cookies. She asked if I had found a girlfriend,

so I told her about June.

"I think your June would like Denmark, Little One," she commented.

On Thanksgiving Day, Elena's turkey dinner—minus American cranberry sauce—was fantastic. I savored the closeness of my family as they told me all the news while I'd been gone. Outside, leafless beech tree branches shivered in the oncoming Danish winter. I was surprised to see the dock stacked in the back yard next to the sea wall, a precaution, my brother told me, so it wouldn't be destroyed by ice. But nothing had changed inside—my room, all the touchstones of home, were still there. And yet, something was different. I kept thinking how glad I was that Pa had made me go to Frankfurt, instead of letting me stay home doing correspondence courses. I would never have met June.

The next day, without Doc to pull me out of bed for 6 a.m. showers, I slept late. After lunch, I grabbed my shotgun case and started to the car with Pa.

"Leave it here, Andy."

"What? How can I go hunting without my shotgun?"

"Mr. Hansen will let you use one of his Brownings." Pa replied.

Aage got behind the wheel, and we turned onto the Strandvej for a pleasant hour-and-a-half drive to Eigil Hansen's estate. My father was relaxed as I gave him a detailed description of the dorm, Mr. Kreebert, life under Army regulations, the food, and my teachers, to which he paid close attention. At one point he astonished me by asking if I had met any nice girls. "Your mother will undoubtedly ask," he said, quickly. "I'm surprised she didn't last night at dinner."

I mentioned there were several, including one named

June Everett. He sat back, thinking.

"Is her father currently our naval attaché in Turkey?"

"How did you know that?"

"My office. I've seen documents from Ankara signed by him." Pa was quiet, lost in thought. "Actually, Andy, there's more to it than that. Butch Everett was skipper of the submarine that rescued me when I was shot down in the Pacific. And, as I recall, he had a daughter about your age. Your mothers were friends in Coronado while we were at sea."

"You and Mom knew the Everetts? Why haven't I met June before this? Lots of your Navy friends have shown up at places we've lived."

"Aviators and submariners have different career paths," he answered with a smile, "so they aren't often stationed near each other. But ask your mother; she can probably tell you about the Everetts better than I. And when you see June, tell her to say hello to her folks for us."

"I certainly will," I replied, excited about these tidbits. At last I had something significant to say to her. I couldn't wait to get back to Frankfurt.

We turned into a tree-lined driveway, stopping in front of a palatial dwelling.

"Welcome to my hunting camp," said a jovial, well-fed Mr. Hansen, standing on marble steps surrounded by a phalanx of eye-catching uniformed parlor maids. After initial formalities, one of them ushered me upstairs to an immaculate room with antique furniture and two single beds, one already claimed by a partially unpacked familiar suitcase with its contents scattered about. Wisps of steam curled from the bathroom, where singing escaped from a shower going full blast. There was no mistaking Doc's cracked voice.

Stripping to my skivvies I opened my suitcase, wondering what to wear for dinner. A soft knock, and the bedroom door opened a crack.

"Frederick Gordon?" said an alluring voice in accented English. "I may come in?"

"Just a minute. I'm not …." I lunged for the white bathrobe folded on the foot of the bed as a beautiful brunette stepped into the room. She wore a low-cut midnight-blue velvet evening dress that exposed more than the expensive string of pearls around her enticing neck. Her hair was pulled back and upward in a styled bouffant, with a soft curl over her forehead. Sensual lips curved into a smile as she glided across the floor. For a second or two I imagined Audrey Hepburn about to pounce on me. She seized my hands and kissed both cheeks.

"I'm Marissa Hansen, Frederick. I wish you to have a nice weekend."

"Doc is in the shower," I blushed. "I'm Andy Barnes. Pleased to meet you."

"But you are surprised, Andy. Is it that a stranger kisses you? It is the way with friends in Geneva, at my school."

"Switzerland?" I felt almost as awkward as the day I met June. At least then I had clothes on. "Do, do you like it there?"

"I hate it. The nuns allow no men, and it is very dull. This is my final year."

She shifted her gaze from me to the bathroom door, as a gargled version of Fats Domino's "Blueberry Hill" momentarily overpowered the shower.

"Your friend—the one you call Doc—perhaps he is not a singer," she smiled. "His name is Frederick Gordon?"

"Yes, but everybody calls him Doc. I was unpacking while he finishes in there."

Marissa glanced at the antique clock on the bureau. "Dinner is soon and it is impolite to be late. You must dress. I will help."

She retrieved a pair of tan slacks from my suitcase, a blue jacket, long-sleeved white shirt, and the blue necktie mother had included.

"These. Put them on."

"But, I can't dress with you in here …."

With one lightning movement, she seized the collar of my bathrobe and whipped it away. Naughty eyes studied my body, but I didn't have time to be embarrassed.

"Put shirt on," she ordered. "Tie also."

"But I have trouble tying these," I said—which was true.

In an instant, she was behind me, chin resting on the back of my neck, breasts caressing my shoulder blades as her fingers whipped the tie into a spiffy knot in front of the full-length mirror. Seizing the slacks from the bed, Marissa held them open for me to step into.

"When you finish school will you go to college?" I asked, as Marissa tucked my shirttails deep inside the front of my pants. I hoped she wouldn't notice that things were getting embarrassing down there.

"College?" she puzzled. "Oh. What you say is college we call university, yes?"

"If you say so."

"I will go to the university to become a doctor. I will study male anatomy."

"Do you, I mean, you, you know, men's, um—?"

"Penises, testicles, prostates—everything," she replied.

No girl had ever said these taboo words in my presence. This was 1956, and I had never heard of a woman doctor, much less seen one. Nurses, yes, but they were supposed to be females. A vision floated through my mind of me lying nude on an examining table as Marissa—white lab coat, magnifying glass in hand—examined my penis.

"But now you must finish dressing. Hurry."

The shower stopped, and she started toward the bathroom door.

"Marissa, don't open—"

"That you, Andy? Oh, excuse me," Doc said, adjusting the towel in his hand across his middle with a big smile.

"I'm Marissa Hansen," she said, kissing him on both cheeks, "My father wishes me to make your weekend pleasurable."

"It is already so, I assure you, Miss Hansen. Doc Gordon at your service."

Later, conversation ceased in the reception room as Marissa stepped forward and took her father's arm.

"My daughter Marissa, everyone. She is home from school in Geneva, and I have assigned her the pleasant task of accompanying our two youngest guests."

Then Colonel Gordon and Pa introduced Doc and me, and we completed a round of handshakes and names, none of which I could pronounce.

"Please," said Marissa, ushering us to the hors d'oeuvres. She spent a long time leaning over the punch bowl filling three cups and handing them across the table to us. At the tinkling of a bell, everyone headed for the dining room and its elegant table, set with Full Lace Royal Copenhagen china. I sat down, dazed by the place settings, bowls, multiple pieces of silverware, and crystal goblets with dangerously tapered stems arrayed before me. Church spires of thin blue and white candles rose from a narrow carpet of wildflowers traversing the middle of the long mahogany table. It was a far cry from the campfire setting

I envisioned when Pa first asked me about going hunting.

After dinner, a jolly band of hunters adjourned to Mr. Hansen's den for aquavit, schnapps, and cigars. Reflections from the stone fireplace shimmered across imperfect glass panes of very old windows separating the cozy room from November's darkness. In one corner I noticed a beautiful harp, but before I could ask about it, I felt Pa's hand on my shoulder.

"Time for bed, Andy."

Doc started to follow his father inside, but Colonel Gordon shook his head.

"I think it's time you turned in, like Andy."

Marissa motioned us aside.

"Please. I may show you the house? First we will stop at my bedroom where I may change into clothes more comfortable, yes?"

Like hypnotized lemmings, we followed her up the staircase to her bedroom, where she stepped into a walk-in closet bigger than our dorm room.

"It will take a minute to get undressed," Marissa said, kicking off her shoes as she partially disappeared into racks of clothes.

We exchanged glances.

"My wildest dreams have come true," Doc whispered, falling backward on Marissa's canopy bed. Soft pillows rested against its rosewood headboard. Carved naked bodies on the bedposts left no doubt that beds weren't only for sleeping.

"You like?" she asked from inside the closet. A pink bra landed at Doc's feet.

"Yes," I replied. "I mean, I've never seen the inside of … of a girl's bedroom, uh, like this one." I stopped short of saying this was the first time I'd been inside any girl's bedroom, let alone one complete with a girl starting to undress in it.

"Doc," said Marissa, fumbling with her zipper, "this appears to be, what do you say—to be tight. You will help, please?" She turned her back to him.

"Absolutely. Let me see what the matter is." He began to fiddle with the zipper, which, from what I could see, had nothing wrong with it. Marissa's giggling was interrupted by a knock on the door. A maid entered, and a heated exchange in Danish followed.

"What was that about?" asked Doc.

"Father thinks it is nice for me to perform music on the harp while they play billiards," she replied, twisting away from him and yanking up her zipper.

"Do you have to leave now? Can't you show us the house first?"

"No. Leena says Father insists, so I must go."

"Okay," said Doc. "Play them a tune and we'll wait for you here."

She smiled, tilting her head in front of the mirror as she fluffed her hair.

"I am so sorry, but no. This happens often when he has guests. I play one, and another, and I have to play very many works by Chopin and others before he lets me finish. It will take hours. I will see you tomorrow. *Je suis désolée.*"

After giving me a peck on both cheeks, she planted a smudge of lipstick on Doc's lower lip and was gone.

Back in our room he flopped onto his bed, stuffing his fist into a cup of Marissa's pink bra. "I had a feeling this weekend was going to be fantastic."

"New souvenir?"

"She is simply the most gorgeous thing I've ever seen— a bod like the Venus de Milo, filthy rich—now there's a woman worth going for."

"Jeez, Doc. You sound like Rex."

"C'mon, Andy. Admit it: isn't she beautiful?"

"The most beautiful girl I've ever seen wouldn't undress in front of any guy, period—let alone two she'd just met."

Neither of us got much sleep that night. While Doc raved about Marissa, I stared at shadows on the ceiling, wondering how his fascination with this new girl might affect June and me. As I saw it, the problem was that in the aftermath of whatever their relationship had been the year before, he considered it finished and she didn't. Something still bothered her. Until this was resolved, I would never be able to get close to her. I wanted June all to myself so badly! If Doc just asked what was bothering her and they talked about it, wouldn't that help? And when would he tell her he had a Danish girlfriend? I'd feel terrible if I was about to begin a scorching affair without being honest to the girl I was leaving. How much did June mean to him, anyway? It was all so confusing.

At breakfast, Doc cheerfully polished off everything in sight. Marissa did not appear.

"She is not a huntress," Mr. Hansen said by way of apology, when Doc asked about her.

The hunt didn't last long. Shooters in tweed coats climbed into several lorries, which deposited one hunter and a Danish gun bearer about twenty-five meters apart along a dirt road that went through an open field. It faced dense woods, where unseen men whistled and whacked trees with sticks. Without warning, critters of all kinds burst into the open to face a broadside of flame and smoke. I fired both barrels and it was over. As groundskeepers put crumpled corpses of fur and feathers into burlap bags, I saw my roommate picking himself off the ground. His gun bearer was doubled over in hysterics.

"Wow," said Doc, dusting his pants. "That shotgun really knocked me on my butt."

"Let's walk back to the manor house," I said. "I don't feel like sitting in a truck listening to men bragging about what they shot."

"On a happier note, Lone Ranger, do you think Big Chief's beautiful daughter is waiting for Tonto in teepee?"

"You're acting totally nuts, Doc. You've known Marissa less than twelve hours, and you talk like she's about to marry you. Tomorrow we'll be back in Frankfurt, and you'll never see her again."

"It is written in the stars. Marissa is the girl for me."

We stepped aside as a lorry filled with hunters and burlap bags rattled by.

"What about June?" I asked as the dust settled.

He wrinkled his brow. "What about her?"

"When are you going to tell her about Marissa?"

"Why do I have to say anything? It might hurt her."

"I suppose it will, Doc. But isn't honesty important with someone you care about?"

He grabbed my arm.

"Let's get a few things straight, Andy: I've told you before—we're not going together, and I don't owe June anything."

"Hey, no need to get violent—we're only talking." I pulled away and resumed walking. For a minute or two, neither of us said anything.

"If I had to guess, Doc, I'd say June's feelings for you go deeper than you think. That's why you owe her the truth."

"I can't do that, Andy. I don't know why, but I can't. It's the way I am, I guess." He kicked at a dried cow pie, scattering pungent dust. "What do you want me to say? 'Hi, June. I'm wild about this Danish beauty I met over Thanksgiving. Do I have your blessing?' I sure don't know what you're getting at, Barnes."

"I'm not sure, either, Doc. Maybe what I'm trying to say is that if you don't talk about Marissa, I'll never have a chance with her—even if I get my act together. So I need to know: is she, or is she not, your girl? Please tell me."

"June goes out with all sorts of guys. You know that, okay?"

I looked at my friend—covered with dust, confusion on his normally confident face.

"I guess it doesn't matter, Doc. But you're the one she really cares for, not me."

"Where did you get that crazy idea, anyway?"

"By the way she looks at you, sometimes, when you're not watching. Her eyes are sad, and there's pain in them, too."

"Dammit, Andy. You know exactly how to rub it in, don't you?" He grabbed me in a headlock with one arm, twisting his knuckles into my hair, releasing me immediately. "So, Lone Ranger, I'll rephrase my original question: do you suppose Marissa is up yet?"

I sighed. It was useless to go on—for now. But getting to the bottom of Doc's relationship with June was not something I intended to drop.

Wearing loden-green slacks and a rust-colored turtleneck with matching headband, Marissa greeted us in front of the house. I got a peck on both cheeks, while Doc received a smear job. She tugged on his sleeve.

"I would give a private tour of the stables, yes?"

"Love to. Absolutely," he grinned.

As groundskeepers artistically arranged deceased fauna

on the front steps, the two of them disappeared behind the house.

"Have you seen Doc?" Colonel Gordon asked, a few minutes later. "It's time for group pictures, and he should be present."

"I'll find him, sir."

I ducked around the corner toward the stables. "Doc, where are you? Answer me."

"It's Andy," I heard him say, somewhere above the stalls.

"Make him to go away," Marissa giggled.

Doc's head appeared in one of the openings in the hayloft.

"Go away. We're getting down to business up here."

More laughter. I saw Marissa's fingers pluck some straw off his neck.

"Doc, listen to me. Your father wants you to be in the group pictures. He says it would be an insult to our host if you aren't."

"*Lort!*" she exclaimed, angrily. "You must go."

After what seemed longer than necessary, Doc appeared. "Where is it?"

"Out front. If it makes any difference, there's straw in your hair."

Doc and Marissa didn't make it to lunch; he told me she was helping him pack. When Pa was ready we thanked our host, and I asked Mr. Hansen to tell his daughter goodbye for me. Aage loaded our bags into the car, and I sank into the back seat.

"Well, how did you like it?" Pa asked, as I watched the house recede.

"It wasn't hunting, was it? Just a way of keeping the animals on Mr. Hansen's estate under control. Why did you bring me?"

"So you could see there are other ways of doing things, besides ours."

But the wisdom of Pa's words was lost, as thoughts about June, me, Doc—and now, Marissa, his femme fatale —churned through my mind. I stared at the sinking winter sun through the window of the Embassy Ford.

# Blood Brothers

Back at school, my roommate couldn't wait to hear from Marissa. Correspondence in those days was simple—fountain pen, paper, and stamps. Letters were our primary link to distant friends, or news from home. The ones I got were usually from Mom, wanting to know if I was alive, and, if so, why I hadn't written. Sometimes, she sent a picture or two of the house, Lissa in the rose garden, or Curt holding one of his cats. An occasional check providing a bit of extra spending money, or word that a care package from Elena was on the way, were more appreciated. Dorm kids who got a letter from home slouched into a lounge chair to read it right away. When the recipient went off by himself, you knew it was from someone special, and he wanted to be alone to savor its contents.

Several days after Thanksgiving, Doc and I watched The Kreebs massage the final envelope of mail call with his chubby fingers. Taking longer than usual to honk in his handkerchief and examine its contents, he passed the pale-blue envelope under his dribbly nose.

"Ooooh. From Switzerland. Mmmmm. Lavender. Unless I miss my guess, a young lady wrote this."

"Please don't get snot on my letter, Mr. Kreebert," said Doc.

"What lovely handwriting. And look at those graceful curves."

"It's against the law to withhold mail. I know it's for me, and if you don't fork it over, I'll complain to the Provost's office. You know the Army—somebody's sure to make a note of it in your personnel file. Now, are you going to give it to me or not?"

Kreebert extended the letter, squinting at it.

"Yeeees. It is addressed to Gordon, isn't it?"

Doc snatched it out of his hand and turned toward the front door.

"Aren't you forgetting something, Mr. Gordon?"

Bending over, Doc signed out in the log book and headed for the door again.

"Your signature is positively illegible, Mr. Gordon. Kindly redo it for me. You should ask your lady friend how to improve your handwriting."

Doc signed out in large block letters, pressing down so hard I could see them on the pages underneath for days.

Later, I found my roommate in a secluded corner of the library, scribbling with unusual concentration.

"Hey, stud. Writing to Marissa?"

"Mind your own business, Barnes. Open your history book and memorize the chapter on the French and Indian War."

"Already have. It's to Marissa, right?"

He got up and moved to another table. Eventually, he pushed his chair back and left.

"Did you get to the post office in time?" I asked, at dinner.

"Yes, if you must know."

"Don't want to pry, but I was sort of wondering what Marissa's up to."

He lowered his voice. "She says her school is a prison—can't stand the curfews, restrictions, or food."

I looked down at my boiled potatoes with schnitzelized meat swimming in creamed corn from olive-green cans originally intended for marines on Guadalcanal. "So, what's new?"

"She got caught telling a dirty joke about nuns," he said, laughing, "and they tried to wash her mouth out with soap. Imagine. Washing out a seventeen-year-old girl's mouth with soap. When she fought them off, they locked her in her room—tea and porridge, no mail, nothing."

"Sounds almost as bad as here."

He glanced around our empty table. "Get this: after making a ladder of bras and bed sheets, she climbed out her window. Now that's really impressive."

"Sounds like sooner or later she's going to get kicked out, if she doesn't break her lovely neck first. How did she get back into her room without waking up the nuns?"

He pulled out her letter. "Listen: 'I found a workingman's ladder from a nearby house and put it on the wall. Günther helped me to climb into my window.'"

"Günther?"

"Some student prince she met in a bar," Doc replied, uneasily. "She says the ladder worked so well they've met several times."

"Inside or outside her bedroom?"

"That's not funny. Promise you won't tell another soul about Marissa and me—not Rex, not June—no one. Do I have your word?" I agreed, but he insisted we shake on it.

And so it went. Doc salivated over every word she wrote. From portions he was willing to share, it seemed that here was a girl who enjoyed taking chances, and understood his craving for the wild side of life which, apart from her seductive body, was probably why she so mesmerized him. Marissa would ride on the Bakken roller coaster, or join in any dangerous, exciting escapade he might dream up. At one point, she wrote that he was the only American she had ever liked. Personally, I couldn't imagine any pair of testicles Marissa didn't like, but then, I was prejudiced. It struck me that my advisor on matters of love was in as much misery over her as I was with June.

As Doc's infatuation with his Danish pastry deepened, I worried about my own girl troubles. It was obvious June had no idea about Marissa, but she was bound to find out eventually. Doc showed no sign of telling her. I knew the longer this continued, the more she would suffer when he finally did.

Then one night everything changed. He had been unusually quiet during study hours, and I was about to ask if he was all right when he pushed his papers aside. "Andy, I think you should make a move for June. I know she likes you."

I sat upright. "Quit fooling around. You know that's a sensitive issue."

"I'm dead serious. What you said about not being honest with her has bothered me ever since we returned from Thanksgiving. I've been trying to figure out a way to break the news, but I can't. I want to, but I can't. You know why."

"You mean about hurting her?"

He gave the hallway outside our door a quick Kreebs check.

"Right. Now that Marissa's in the picture, things are definitely over between us, but I can't talk to her about it.

For that matter, as you know by now, I've never been able to talk to June about serious stuff. It's the way I am, I guess. I'm not a very good boyfriend, am I?"

I'd never heard him sound so miserable. "Of course you are, Doc. If Rex was in your shoes, do you think he'd care how June felt when he ditched her? The fact that you're so concerned proves you're a wonderful friend."

The hint of a smile crossed his face. "Thanks for the support, Roomie, but June needs someone worthy of her, and I don't think I am, anymore."

"You're lucky to have someone as classy as June like you so much," I said. "I'm jealous. As far as I'm concerned, she's in a totally different league from Marissa. How could you possibly want anyone else?"

"I don't know, I don't know, I don't know," he groaned, "but I do. And I feel really bad about it. I just want June and me to stay good friends. She needs someone who doesn't play around, who will be there when she needs a real companion. I'm not that person—if I ever was. Are you?"

He looked at me as if I were his last hope. Maybe so, I thought to myself. But I had been with Doc long enough to be cautious.

"What are you trying to say, Roomie?"

"Well," he replied, looking straight at me, "I thought if someone worthy of her took my place, I'd feel better knowing she was in good hands. Last year we tried going steady, but now we are … well, she's more like a sister to me, that's all. Once I thought it was more than that, but since I met Marissa …."

"You're saying June is great to be around, but Marissa's bod is more accessible, right?"

He started to say "yes," but turned and shook his head,

letting out an anguished moan. "I wish I didn't still like her so much, but I do. That's my problem."

"Your problem, Doc, is that you have a guilty conscience. You can't tell her the truth, so you want me to try for her to make you feel better."

His reply was a long time coming. I could feel his sadness.

"Something like that. Yes. Other than being friends, it's definitely over with June."

The Kreebs's footsteps stopped outside our door, and he jumped back into his seat as the knob turned. The piggy face looked in, said nothing, and the door closed.

"So, Lone Ranger," he said, after Kreebert had moved on, "am I looking at June's next boyfriend?"

"Okay, Tonto. I'm in."

"I knew I could count on you." He was grinning like the old Doc. "Now, we must seal our bargain in blood."

"Blood? What the fuck—?"

Flipping open his jackknife, he jabbed his opened palm. "Give me your hand."

"The hell I will!" "Oww!" I felt a stab of pain followed by a gush of blood.

"Lone Ranger and Tonto now blood brothers in noble cause," he said, pressing his opened palm against mine.

"Leggo of my hand, you crazy bastard. There's blood all over the place. What do you think this is, you jerk? Some cornball cowboys-and-Indians movie?"

I hustled to the bathroom to wash the cut with soap, leaving a trail of blood behind me.

"You can clean up the hallway, you butcher."

A vision of Doc waving my favorite bass rod around my room that first day we met—when he baptized me (or whatever it was) as his new friend—came to mind. I thought he was nuts; but by now, I knew that sometimes there was meaning behind his nuttiness, and he really did take his promises seriously. The trouble was, he should have promised to be honest with June.

# *Getting to Know You*

Becoming Doc's blood brother did little to advance me on June's social calendar. Friday and Saturday were the only nights available for dating, but someone always got to her first. Days passed, and I still hadn't found the right circumstances to tell her about what I learned from my parents at Thanksgiving.

"You don't seem very concerned," I complained to Doc during study hours one night when the subject of my dating her came up. He threw up his hands.

"Look, Andy. We both know you're a hopeless procrastinator. You take forever making up your mind; getting to the shower in the morning; you put off your homework until there's no time left to do it—I could go on and on."

"I don't procrastinate when Alfie's tutoring me," I replied. "We get together in the library for an hour almost every afternoon."

"We're talking about girls, Barnes, girls. Remember? Maybe it's because you're just too young for such things."

"Oh, stop it, Doc." He was right, though: I was younger than just about everybody else in my class, including June. This was because British teachers in Chile advanced me from first to third grade. Apparently, I was smarter then.

"All I can tell you," he continued, "is that when it comes to asking June out, you have to be decisive. It's a matter of getting to her before someone else does. Take Rex, for example."

"Yeah," I said. "That jerk's been after her since the first day of school."

"Do I detect bitterness? Envy? Both, maybe?"

"Whose side are you on, Gordon? We're supposed to be blood brothers. Every time he comes back from a date, he goes around boasting that she spent the whole time panting for him. It drives me nuts."

"That's just Rex. You and I both know June better than that."

"Easy for you to say. He's especially graphic whenever he's near me."

"He's doing it to get your goat. Or, could it be Rex is covering up for something?"

I leaned closer across the table. "What do you mean?"

Doc sighed. "Do you actually think she's swooning over a pack of Camels? June likes Rex. He's smart, good-looking, sophisticated, and witty. He showers her with compliments, has buckets of scrip to spend when they're on dates, and knows how to turn on the charm. Face it: that stuff is pretty nice if you're a girl. Whatever he's doing when they're out together, he's being himself—he'll never change. The good part, as far as you're concerned, is that he's not the type she's looking for."

"He's not? I don't understand."

"There's a whole lot you don't understand, Lone Ranger."

"Well," I said, "I know one advantage I have over Rex regarding June that Rex doesn't. But I'm not sure how to mention it to her."

Doc stopped examining shadows behind pulled window shades across the patio on the girls' side of the dorm. He turned, his face alive with sudden interest.

"So, what's the big secret, Lone Ranger? Tonto promised to help with June, remember?"

I sat down on my bunk, rubbed my eyes, and told him what I had learned at Thanksgiving—how our parents were old friends; how the skipper of the submarine that rescued Pa turned out to be June's dad; that we lived nearby in Coronado during the war—everything I could remember.

"And, get this, Doc: our mothers used to take us swimming at Coronado Beach without bathing suits. Imagine. So, what do you think?"

"Well, aside from the fact that your nude swims together happened fourteen years too early, I'm not sure what to say. Telling June all that would definitely get her attention. And it does set you apart from the competition, so that could make a difference. On the other hand, sometimes sharing past experiences has the opposite effect." He proceeded to tell me about an old girlfriend on some Air Force base in Minnesota, and losing contact when her family got transferred. Then, last year in Wiesbaden, he ran into her at a basketball game.

"I was so happy to see her, Andy. She was such a sweetheart. I asked for a date and we spent most of the time reminiscing, but nothing clicked. By the end of the evening, we both realized the old spark wasn't there anymore. It was over between us."

My spirits sank. "Jeez, Gordon. At times you can be downright depressing."

"The thing to do is grab any opportunity to connect

with her. And be yourself. Quality girls like June and Copper know right away when a guy's being a phony. That goes for making out or going steady—never push her into anything she doesn't want to do, or you'll ruin everything. I speak from experience," he concluded, after a pause. "Tell you what: I'll be on the lookout, and maybe we can get you fixed up with some time together."

My big opportunity occurred the following Friday night, returning from an away basketball game against Heidelberg. As we got on our waiting Army bus for the ride back to Frankfurt, I saw June sit down three rows ahead. Doc nudged me.

"She's all by herself. Quick."

Rex lunged, but Doc blocked him, shoving me into the seat beside her.

"Hey. What'd ya do that for? I wanted to sit next to her."

"Looks like Andy beat you to it," Doc said, pushing Rex down the aisle as he took the seat behind us, next to Copper.

"Hello, June," I said. "Mind if I sit with you?"

"Of course not," she replied, grabbing my coat sleeve and pulling me next to her.

As the bus left Heidelberg's cobblestone streets and accelerated onto the Autobahn, I began telling her about our Coronado connection.

"I remember Copper saying that both of you were evacuated on the same ship from the Philippines, and you were born there," I said. "Was your father a submariner?"

She looked at me with interest.

"Why, yes. He was on the submarine that took General MacArthur to Australia."

I knew MacArthur had escaped from Corregidor on a

PT boat, and then flew to Australia in a B-17, but I wasn't about to correct her. "Is his name Butch?"

She gave me a strange look. "That's his Navy nickname," she said, slowly. "How did you know that?"

"You're not going to believe this, but when I was home for Thanksgiving, I mentioned that I had met you, and my dad asked if your father was a submariner. Pa said the name of the skipper who saved his life during the war was Butch Everett on the Tarpon."

She shook her head as if doing a double take. "That was the sub he commanded during most of the war. But how did your dad end up on the Tarpon?"

I told her about Pa floating around in his raft (the bit about eating raw bird eyeballs didn't bother her at all), and finally, being rescued by her father.

"I can't believe it. What an incredible coincidence."

"And that's not all," I continued. "When Pa told Mom I was probably in the same class with Butch Everett's daughter June, that really set her off. She launched into all this stuff during the war, about when we were living down the street from Cora Everett in Coronado, and …."

June's hand flew to her mouth and she sat bolt upright. "That's my mother. So we met when we were little. Did your mom say for how long?" Her eyes sparkled like emeralds. And those dimples—I wanted to kiss each one. Suddenly, we were talking like we'd known each other our whole lives.

"I don't remember, exactly," I replied. "Two years? Three? It was while our fathers were in the Pacific. But there's more. Our moms …."

"Hi, Beautiful." Rex leaned over me, pulling out his pack of Camels. "I just thought of a cozy little place downtown where I haven't taken you yet. Since you're probably tired of talking to him, you could come sit with me, and we can make plans."

"Leave," she ordered. "I'm enjoying a private conversation."

"Sorry, My Queen. I didn't know Barnes could talk when he was around you."

"Go!" The tone of her voice left no doubt his interference was not welcome.

"As I started to tell you," I said, after making sure Rex was out of earshot, "Mom told me we used to play together on the beach without anything on. She can be nasty with her baby stories."

"Too young to remember anything, unfortunately," June giggled. "I'm going to write my folks tonight, and ask Mother about all this."

"You will tell me what she says, won't you?"

Her eye lashes flickered playfully as interest radiated across her face.

"Only if it isn't too embarrassing … of course, silly."

I took a deep breath. "June, maybe we could … um, go out somewhere and catch up on things since Coronado? My treat?"

"I'd like that very much," she answered immediately, taking my hand.

In that instant, all my insecurities about asking her for a date vanished, replaced by a new phase of our relationship.

"Can I put my arm around you?"

"That might be nice."

We scrunched together, and I rested my arm across her shoulder. I'd waited all semester for this—dreamed about it. It didn't matter that we were wearing winter coats.

The bus chewed up kilometers on the Autobahn, hurtling us closer to the dorm—a ride I wished would never end. Pinpricks of light from scattered farms twinkled like distant stars in the darkened countryside.

I broke the silence. "Rex aside, do guys offer you cigarettes often?"

"All the time." She leaned closer. "He knows I don't like being pressured. I'm glad neither of us smokes. Have you ever tried?"

I told her about my first and only time in Chile. I was eight years old and it made me sick.

She looked toward the window. "Smoking can't be good for anybody. I wish my mother would quit. She coughs a lot, and it's getting worse. But let's change the subject."

"I don't like beer or wine either," I said. "Give me vanilla ice cream any day."

"That's a drug, too," she laughed. "Tell me what Copenhagen is like, Andy. Doc says it's the best place he's ever lived."

"It is," he interrupted, from the row behind us.

"Gordon," Copper exclaimed from the seat next to him. "Are you paying attention to me, or is your goofball mind in the next seat with June and Andy?"

"It is here with you, my gorgeous, redheaded wood-pecker."

Sounds of struggle and giggling followed. In the muted light, I studied the pensive look on June's face, followed by a barely noticeable smile.

"What are you thinking?" I asked. "Two nude toddlers splashing on a California beach? Doc? Maybe even me, if I'm lucky?"

"All of those are on my mind," she replied. "In fact, a lot about you. Why, after so many years, have we been brought together again? And in Germany, of all places. Are the fates playing tricks on us or is there some reason?"

"Can't say," I replied, giving her shoulder a squeeze. "All I know is that from the day we met, you haven't been out of my thoughts, even during The Mantis's—I mean Miss Earl's—geometry tests."

"Maybe if I were, your grades in her class would be better, Mr. Barnes," she said, trying to frown.

"Aw, be nice, June."

She snuggled closer. "Now that the interruptions behind us seem to have stopped, I'd like to hear about Copenhagen."

The bus slowed as we turned into the school parking lot.

"Guess it will have to wait," I said, removing my arm from her shoulder.

"Thank you, June. This was the nicest non-date I ever had."

"I enjoyed it, too," she replied. "We share some unusual connections, don't we?"

Stepping down from the bus into the crisp night air, I took her arm as we headed toward the dorm.

"I wish we had more time tonight," I said.

"We'll have lots of time to talk during our evening out, Andy. Goodnight."

As I walked across the patio and pulled open the door to the boys' side of the dormitory, I was on cloud nine.

Inside our room, Doc was sitting at our desk, notebook and pencil ready. He motioned toward my chair on the opposite side facing him. My pair of spare glasses wobbled on the end of his nose. I couldn't help grinning at his homespun entertainment. How many other friends had I ever known who would have created such cornball drama in order to find out the details of my love life?

"Have a seat, m'boy. The doctor is in."

"What is this, a séance? You some kind of shrink?"

"As your advisor on matters of love, it is my duty to record all details of a romantic nature that might be helpful in guiding you toward happiness."

"Well," I began, "I can't say it was a real date, but it was the first chance I've had to talk to her privately—in spite of your interruptions. I think it went well. And I'm sure glad you pushed me in next to her before Rex beat me to it. I owe you."

"Yes, you do. Rex wasn't pleased."

"Later, when he tried to butt in and June told him to get lost, I almost laughed."

"Good thing you didn't," Doc replied. "I'm surprised he didn't try to annoy you more. Now, get on with it."

"With what? Look, Doc. I appreciate all your efforts and advice, but I'm not giving you a blow-by-blow account of everything we talked about—that's between her and me. She let me put my arm around her and I told her about Coronado, that's all you need to know."

"You took a chance there, you realize," he replied, a bit annoyed I wasn't making him privy to more details.

"She wanted to know all about how our parents knew each other. I suggested we get together and catch up on happenings since California, and she said she'd like that very much."

"Excellent." He was rubbing his hands together, lost in his role of matchmaker.

"You could take her downtown to a good movie," he began, stopping to think. "I know: Around the World in Eighty Days with David Niven. It's perfect. She'll love it. Afterward, that little Italian restaurant near WAC Circle— The Grotto, or maybe Santa Lucia's … yeah, that's the one. Secluded, great pizza, booths with candlelight, two glasses of Chianti ...."

"I don't drink wine, and neither does she. You know that."

"Perfect atmosphere for love. Fabulous cannolis for dessert. Then the two of you can ...."

"Doc!" I had to admit, though, what he envisioned sounded pretty nice.

I did manage to take June to the Italian restaurant Doc raved about. She had been there before with Rex, but she said this was the first time she looked forward to it. We discovered we both had lived in Newport, Rhode Island, and Washington, D.C., but at different times. She told me about The Sidwell Friends School in D.C., where she was a ninth-grader before coming to Frankfurt; and everything her mother had written about living in Coronado. Afterward, on the steps of the dorm, she said she had more in common with me than any other guy in the school. Our evening was punctuated by a warm, lingering goodnight kiss.

# *Holiday Spirit*

The holiday season arrived, casting its spell over the dorm. It snowed once, depositing more than enough to have snowball fights and make creative pieces of winter art. The Kreebs never found out who was responsible for the five-foot phallus melting outside his window, but I'm sure he had a good guess. Christmas vacation was on everyone's mind. Miss Maybelle outdid herself playing Christmas records by Fred Waring's Chorus, and putting up tacky Santa decorations. Doc and I were so mired in schoolwork we hardly had time to scratch the days off our calendar, but Alfie wrote Christmas cards to all his teachers—even the administrators. I told him Miss Maybelle would be delighted, but sending cards to the rest of them was a waste of time. He did it anyway. All I could think about was going steady with June. But how to ask her? I rejected Doc's recommendation, involving a romantic dinner, wine, and a bouquet of roses, after which I would present her with my beautifully wrapped Christmas present (I hadn't a clue what to get her) as I got down on my knees to ask if she would go steady with me.

On the last Saturday before vacation, we were sitting by ourselves at breakfast. I lowered my voice.

"Doc, can you keep a secret?"

He rubbed his hands and leaned across the table.

"On matters of love, Lone Ranger always has Tonto's utmost discretion. What is it?"

"Be serious, will you? I want to give June something nice for Christmas, but I don't know what to get."

He drained his glass of powdered milk. "You've got it bad, Roomie. There's no hope."

I pushed my chair back.

"Thanks. All I said was I wanted to find her a Christmas present. Are you going to help or not? For that matter, what do you have for Marissa?"

"Good point. And I don't have anything for my sisters, either. They'll kill me."

"Same here. We've got some shopping to do today."

Half an hour later, pressed like pickled herring inside a jar, we were in one of Frankfurt's vintage streetcars that had somehow survived the war. Every seat and hand strap was taken. Its steamy windows were coated with grime and hair grease that had probably been there since before the Führer was born, and the smell of wet wool overcoats, cigarette smoke, and the occasional fart was stifling.

We missed our stop, but it felt good to walk back a few blocks in the frosty December air to a toy store Doc had in mind.

"Look at this Mercedes replica," he exclaimed, picking up a small metal car. "Really solid. Now that's quality. The doors open, the front wheels turn—you'd never find anything like this in the States. I ought to start a collection. My philosophy is, 'If you like it, buy it, and figure out who gets it later.' "

"What about Marissa and your sisters?"

"We have to go to another store for them."

On the way, I completed my shopping. Using the "Doc Doctrine," I purchased a fake plastic dog turd for Curt from a joke store; several French comic books about a dog for Lissa; a box of candles for Mother; and an ornate beer stein I found in a pawn shop for Pa—but nothing for June. Then I spotted a music box. It was a miniature Swiss chalet, handmade of dark wood, with a tiny goat on the roof. When I opened the top, it played the German Christmas carol "O Tannenbaum."

"I'm going to get her this."

"She'll love it. The goat has horns, so she'll know it's from you. Now for Marissa."

We stopped in front of a shop window, where a pale man with a thin mustache was stretching a pair of nylons onto a naked mannequin. Female customers stared as Doc dragged me inside. I tried to twist away, but his grip tightened on my coat sleeve.

"Kee-rist, Doc. Let's get out of here," I pleaded, feeling my face redden.

"Not before I find something worthy of my Contessa."

"In here? You haven't seen Marissa since Thanksgiving, and then for barely a day. How do you know what she likes? Do you even know her size?"

"Trust me, Roomie. For someone like myself with significant experience concerning the fair sex, this task is a piece of cake. Besides, I've studied her letters."

Eyebrows went up as he peered underneath a silk slip covering the lower half of an anatomically correct plastic female figure. Moving on, he pawed through a tray of panties, raising a particularly skimpy pair. "What do you think, Lone Ranger? Something like this, perhaps?" He bulged out the crotch with his fist.

"May I assist you?" asked the unsmiling man from the

window in perfect English. "What, exactly, are you looking for?"

"Enough, Doc. It's late, and we have to get back for supper. Look: after we eat, you can show me how to use your camera, and I'll take a bunch of pictures of you. Then you can develop them in the dorm photo room, and pick the best one for Marissa. For that matter, your sisters and parents would be delighted if you gave each of them one, too."

Looking thoughtful, he tossed the panties into the bin. "Once in a while, Andy, you come up with a really good idea. Let's eat."

The first morning of Christmas vacation, kids scurried back and forth loading suitcases on Army buses parked in front of the patio. I couldn't wait to give June her music box. She emerged from the girls' side of the dorm dressed in a striking blue suit, carrying her suitcase and a blue-striped cloth bag with brightly wrapped packages poking from the top.

"Let me help," I said, taking the suitcase. "I've never seen you wearing that outfit before—I like you in greens, but blues are definitely your best."

"Thank you," she smiled.

"Can we talk? It's important."

She glanced at her watch. "Okay, but let's go inside where it's warmer."

We sat down on one of the lounge sofas.

"Perfect. I'll be able to see when my taxi comes."

"You're not flying home to Ankara?"

She shook her head.

"Phooey. I was hoping I could sit next to you on the bus to Rhein-Main."

"Not this time. How about Easter vacation instead—

assuming you can wait that long?"

"And maybe by then I'll have a bombshell Danish girl like …." Thank God I stopped in time—that was close.

Her eyes, on full alert, drilled into mine. "Oh? You have someone else up there in the frozen North? Interesting. I've needed to trim some dead wood from my social list for a while. I'll start with you."

"June, no. Don't say that. I would never cross you off my list."

"Is that because I'm the only one on it, Mr. Barnes?" She collapsed in laughter.

"Go ahead and enjoy yourself. See if I care. So," I said, when she had recovered, "where are you spending Christmas?"

"Paris. Dad arranged everything and sent an overnight train ticket. Imagine. Our family in Paris. I've never been there. Have you?"

"Not yet. But the naval attaché and his wife are old friends, and Mom talks about visiting them. Probably her excuse to see all the stuff in the Louvre."

"'Stuff in the Louvre'?" June repeated, slowly. "Stuff?" I searched her face. She giggled. "I'm so excited, Andy. I'll tell you about everything when we get back."

"Can you write me? A postcard, care of the U.S. Embassy, Copenhagen, Denmark?

"I'll try … . By the way, I made something for you," she said. Reaching into her Christmas bag, she handed me a soft package. "I thought you might be able to use these, but don't open them until Christmas morning."

"Feels like mittens. Hope they fit."

"Andy. That's not what you are supposed to say." She stood up.

"No, please don't go. I didn't mean …."

"I'm not leaving, silly. It's getting a bit hot at this end of the sofa, so I thought we might switch places."

"I have something for you to open in Paris. I didn't make it, but I picked it out and wrapped it all by my lonesome—well, Miss Maybelle gave me the paper, and she said you'd like it." I handed her my wrinkled green-and-blue package.

"That's so sweet of you." Her fingers pressed sides and corners, tracing the contents. She shook it gently next to her ear.

"Music box. Wood, with rocks on the roof. Probably one of those little Swiss chalets like the one Doc gave me last …." She gasped. An expression of heartbreak crossed her face. She looked miserable.

"I'm … I'm terribly sorry, Andy. It just slipped out. I love music boxes. I do. And I will especially love this one because it's from you. I really, really appreciate the thoughtfulness behind your gift. Please believe me."

"I wish Doc had said something," I answered. "I wouldn't have picked it out if you already had one."

"I'm so ashamed. I never meant to hurt you."

I gave her shoulder a gentle squeeze. "Do you still have Doc's music box?"

"It's not important," she answered.

"I think it is—at least to me, anyway."

She looked away. "No. In fact, I never really did."

"Come again?"

"There's not much to say. Last year, he gave me one for Christmas. Before I finished unwrapping it, he grabbed it out of my hand. 'Let me show you how it works.' Then he broke the spring winding it. He thought it was funny—which it was, sort of—but I was crushed."

"What happened then?"

"He promised to fix it, but I never saw it again."

I touched her hand. "It's okay. I know you didn't intend to hurt my feelings. Don't worry about it. I really appreciate that you went to all that effort to make mittens for me. I never got a Christmas present from a girl before except from Lissa, my kid sister. Thank you."

She fixed me with a look of tenderness. "I always feel comfortable when I'm around you, Andy. You say what you feel, and don't kid around all the time—like Doc," she added softly, as if to herself. She glanced away, trying to conceal a slight blush creeping over her cheeks.

"I know it's not my business," I said, pressing into uncharted territory, "but in a way it is—I'm having a hard time when it comes to you and Doc."

Her expression changed from warmth to uncertainty. "I'd rather not go into it."

"Please, June. I'm confused. Last summer he referred to you as 'my girl,' yet you aren't going steady—at least it seems that way on the surface. I feel guilty that I want to steal you away from my best friend. What I'm trying to say is that I need to know if I have a chance with you. If you are still Doc's girl, tell me."

Her half-smile was painful to see.

"Not in 'going steady' terms, if that's what you mean. Not anymore. However, there are still things to settle between us. I'm not sure if it's more my problem or his, so I need to work it out. That's all I can say, right now. Please understand, and don't give up on me in the meantime."

"Not a chance."

Outside, several sharp beeps announced the arrival of a Mercedes 190D taxi.

"That's my ride," she said, standing up.

I helped her on with her coat, managing a soft hug in

the process. "Have a wonderful Christmas with your family. I'll be thinking of you."

"You, too, Andy." Her eyes were shining. "And I'm going to be very careful winding your present—I can't wait to find out what song it plays."

I carried her suitcase to the driver, who tossed it in the back and slammed the trunk. She put the blue-striped bag on the back seat and turned, wrapping her arms around my neck.

"Thanks for caring," she whispered, touching my ear with her lips.

As the small car pulled away, she blew me a long kiss through the rear window. From that moment, not even Christmas was as important to me as June—the love of my life.

# Home for Christmas

When I arrived, a twelve-foot floor-to-ceiling fir tree dominated the living room. Along with old ornaments I recognized, there were new ones of straw with traces of red ribbon; but the real white candles that identified a true Danish Christmas tree amazed me. Each fit into a tiny cup at the end of a rod that screwed directly into the tree trunk. The bottom rods were longer than those at the top, so the result was a pyramid of white spires on the outer edges of its branches.

"Are we going to light them?" I asked.

"Of course we are," said Lissa.

"Not unless you want to burn the house down," Pa said, taking a sip of fortified eggnog from his sacred Lexington mug.

"Melvin jumped into the tree and it fell over" said Curt, laughing.

"Where is that crazy cat, anyway?" I asked.

"For safety, we're keeping him outside so he won't do it again," replied Mom. "Your father was furious."

He started to say something, but took another swallow of his drink instead.

"Daddy was going to take Melvin outside and shoot

him," my sister blurted out.

"Melissa, really," said Mom. "You know your father would never do anything like that."

I wondered if she had forgotten that night long ago in Chile when, after it savaged our garbage cans once too often, Pa sent a marauding pig squealing down the street with a .38 slug in its rear end.

After everyone had gone to bed, I sat on the sofa softly picking out the German carol "O Tannenbaum" on my guitar, pretending June was snuggled next to me. I dozed off, dreaming she was sharing the reflections of the tree decorations and the fire's flickering embers on the window panes. I was awakened by Pa's wardroom clock chiming 11 p.m. My guitar had slipped to the floor and the fire was out. I stretched, gazing through frost-encrusted glass at a full winter moon above the Øresund. A thick ring of ice crystals surrounded it. Was June also looking at it and thinking of me? As I tiptoed upstairs to my room, familiar pictures on the walls and family possessions I passed— touchstones of my childhood—no longer seemed important.

The next morning, I sat down at my bedroom desk to compose a letter asking June if she would go steady with me. Half a wastebasket of crumpled drafts later, I gave up. Better to ask her in person after Christmas vacation. I called Doc.

"So, what is there to do in Denmark when it's too cold to go fishing, Gordon? You never told me this country has no daylight in winter. Talked to Marissa?"

"Bored so soon, Roomie? I called her when I got home, but the butler said she doesn't get back from Switzerland until tomorrow."

"What difference does another day make?"

"Plenty. We're just leaving to spend Christmas in Oslo. Say, Lone Ranger, why don't we swap? You play hide and seek in the snow with my sisters while I'll entertain Marissa in your room. Jerry's makeout sofa is still there, isn't it?"

"Mom would love that, Tonto. Doc, I was wondering … ."

"Sorry, everybody's walking out the front door. Talk to you when we get back. Merry Christmas." He hung up.

I started downstairs, stopped, retraced my steps, and tore each half-written letter to June into very small pieces. No reason for anyone else to look at them, particularly my little brother.

So Doc disappeared into Norway's snowy forests, and my first Christmas in Denmark came and went. As Mom promised, our festivities were Danish. Pa carved the Christmas Eve goose, served with pickled beets and caramelized golden-brown new potatoes. Lissa got the almond in the rice pudding. After dinner, we lit the candles, turned out the lights, and Elena joined us for the traditional dance around the tree. Pa snoozed in his chair.

I had guessed correctly about June's gift—a pair of woolen mittens, blue, with small white and green fish. They fit perfectly. That night I wore them to bed. What was she doing? Had she been to any fancy parties? Was some French university student giving her a private tour of the Louvre? The only thing I was certain of was that, if so, she hadn't gone to bed with him. Still, the thought of her dancing in the arms of some handsome medical intern from the Pasteur Institute made me miserable. In the days ahead, I spent a lot of time wearing her mittens.

Doc phoned when he returned to tell me he'd been out with Marissa. He made it clear he intended to maximize his remaining holiday time with her.

"She's desperate for me," he moaned.

"Are you sure you've got it right as to exactly who needs who? She probably screwed herself halfway to China while you were making snowmen in Oslo."

"You've got it all wrong, Lone Ranger. Man, can she make out. She is the hottest thing I've ever seen. She puts Frankfurt girls to shame."

"Even June?"

The other end of the line went quiet.

"Aw, Andy. You know June isn't like Marissa. She's conservative about things like that. Maybe if she was more like Marissa, you wouldn't be so miserable. Did you ever think of that?"

I had, but it also occurred to me that if June was the type of girl Marissa was, I probably wouldn't hold her in such high esteem, either.

"So, Romeo, how many times have you and Marissa, you know, done it?"

The phone line crackled in my ear.

"She's taking me to some modern ballet on New Year's Eve," Doc replied, ignoring my question. "The dancers are supposed to be nude, with their bodies painted red or white like corpuscles."

"Sounds genuinely Danish."

Listening to Doc talk about Marissa was getting depressing.

"Anything else, Doc? I have things to do."

"Aw, be nice to your faithful companion."

For the next few days, I saw nothing of him, and no letters arrived from June.

On the last afternoon of vacation, he showed up to announce we were going ice skating in Dyrehaven.

"But tomorrow we're flying back to Frankfurt," I fussed. "I have to pack."

"Jeez, Barnes. You sound like my mother." He shoved a pair of skates so old they might have belonged to Hans Christian Andersen at me.

"But I can't ice skate, Doc. What if my feet hurt?"

"Ice skaters live for pain," he replied. "Now stop making excuses and come."

"What are you going to use?" I asked.

"These." He dangled an unblemished, right-off-the-shelf pair in my face. Their blades shimmered like burnished bayonets in the sunlight, and the polished black leathers would have pleased a Parris Island drill instructor. "Real Danish hockey skates. Feel how sharp they are."

"They're flat," I said, after running my finger along the bottom of one of the blades.

"Stop showing your ignorance and get a move on—there are only a couple of hours of daylight left."

Brushing past some evergreens heavy with new snow, we emerged at the edge of one of Dyrehaven's frozen ponds. A group of small boys was playing hockey, while some girls figure skated on center ice. Nearby, older folks dropped wood into a smoking barrel to keep warm. Pulling off my mittens, I sat down on a log to wrestle with the skates.

"Nice mittens," Doc said. "Probably the second pair June ever made."

"I take it you got the first?"

"Makes me feel good to know our arrangement is working so well—shows she's focusing on you and phasing me out," he replied, evading my question. "What gives you that idea, anyway? She wouldn't go to all that trouble if she didn't like you—a lot—which is exactly what both of us want, right?"

"Did it ever occur to you that she may never be mine?"
I asked.

He stopped tightening his skate laces. "Of course she will."

"Doc, it isn't that simple. Yes, she likes me; but you don't realize how much you are still on her mind."

"What are you getting at?"

"Sometimes," I continued, "when she's with us and you laugh about something the two of you did, she doesn't laugh. Her eyes lose their sparkle, and she gets all quiet. It's like she's having a sudden attack of sadness. I'm sure it has to do with you. It's like, like there's things she needs to talk about."

"But we talk to each other every day. We're together in classes, at meals—whenever I see her walking back to the dorm I carry her books ... she's fun."

"Are you sure that's how she sees it?"

"Of course I'm sure. I'm her 'school brother,' nothing more. That's what we agreed on when we broke up last year, and it's been working great ever since."

"Have you asked her if that's how she feels?" I repeated.

"Why should I? If she has a problem, she should be the one to say something." He double-tied his other skate, yanked it tight, and stood.

"Doc, I haven't known June as long as you have, but my gut tells me she's waiting for you to approach her. As long as whatever is bothering her continues, she's your girl—not mine."

He glanced away, staring at the figure skaters slicing the pond's smooth surface with graceful curves. "I thought everything was outstanding between you two. Now you tell me this."

A cheer rose from the kids' hockey game.

"C'mon, Lone Ranger. Time to skate."

"This is typical of you, Doc," I said. "You cut our conversations short whenever sensitive stuff you can't handle comes up, and it really bugs me. This situation isn't going away, and one of these days you're going to have to face her."

But he was already out on the ice.

From the start, I could see Doc was a terrific skater. While I spent more time down than up, he zipped around at top speed, weaving between people, skating backward, and showing off. At one point he raced toward me as fast as he could.

"Watch this!"

I braced for the crash, but he went into a sideways skid, showering me with freezing needles.

"That's my patented hockey stop," he grinned.

"You never answered my question, Tonto," I said, cleaning my glasses. I was determined to get back to our conversation. "If June made you a pair of mittens, why don't you wear them? Level with me."

"I can't talk about it now, Andy—ask me later."

As the sun disappeared, Doc was the last one skating. The wind died, temperatures dropped, and the fire barrel cooled. The pond became a sheet of obsidian as night approached at three in the afternoon. I stood, listening to the slash of his blades across the ice as he went back and forth. Then a whitish-yellow patch appeared at my feet. Moonlight? There was no moon. Car headlights? We were in the middle of Dyerhaven. More colors, glittering all around us.

"Holy cow, Andy. It's an aurora—northern lights. This is amazing!" He headed toward the far shore, skating slowly for the first time since we'd arrived.

Above us, nature covered the sky with a spectacle of green curtains, shimmering against patches of white and purple fog. Then blankets of peach, yellow, green and red appeared and disappeared. I stood watching my best friend skate between heaven and earth as ribbons of color crossing the sky folded him into their pastel reflections on the pond's mirrored surface.

I have no idea how long it lasted—twenty minutes? Thirty? Abruptly it faded, and the once-in-a-lifetime display was over, leaving my mind awash with incomparable colored images.

"Northern lights were never like this in Minnesota," Doc said, pulling off his skates.

"Nature sure gets an A+ for this one," I said, aching because June hadn't shared the unforgettable spectacle with me.

Neither of us spoke as I followed him back to the house.

# *In the Doldrums*

The Navy plane touched down at Rhein-Main the following afternoon. I couldn't wait to tell June about the aurora, but she hadn't returned. I waited downstairs in the lounge, practicing my guitar, until Doc and I went to dinner. About halfway through, she arrived. After an hour of exchanging holiday doings, three trays of gravy-soaked meat, canned sauerkraut, and mashed potatoes were barely touched.

"Not interested in Normand's cuisine?" Doc asked.

"Paris spoiled me," she answered. "Anyway, I'm full."

"C'mon, you hardly ate anything. Andy, I know you're hungry."

"Absolutely. I could use something to get rid of the taste of this stuff."

"Read my mind." He stood up, piled June's tray on top of his, and took her arm with his free hand. "Let's go to the snack bar for some real food—Andy's treat."

She shrugged, and we started toward the door.

"Not so fast, Gordon." The Kreebs pushed back his chair. "I want to speak to you."

"Did you have a nice Christmas, Mr. Kreebert?"

"Don't get smart with me, Mister. I was shocked at the

mess you left in the photo lab just before the holidays." He gurgled a swallow of snot. "Bottles in the wrong place, puddles of dangerous photo chemicals on the basement floor—and that box of printing paper you left open is totally ruined. I've a good mind to charge you for everything."

"Other people use that room, too," said Doc. "Why are you blaming me?"

"Don't try to shift responsibility, young man. Follow me to my office."

"Right now? But we were on our way to the PX. I'll be happy to come later."

"I want to address these issues immediately."

"You two go ahead," said Doc. "I'll catch up in a few minutes."

"Don't count on it." The Kreebs' lips curved into something between a smile and a sneer.

"I love my little music box," June said, as the two of us strolled in the lamplight along the Miquelallee. "O Tannenbaum is one of my favorites. How did you know?"

"I didn't, but it's one of mine, too."

"You're just telling me that to make me feel good."

"I'm not," I replied. "I bet you forgot my present on the train and somebody sat on it."

"If you must know, Mr. Smarty Pants, it's on my desk right now. When I need a study break, I'm going to sit back, listen to 'Tannenbaum,' and think of you. Did you like the mittens?"

"Promise not to laugh?"

"Maybe."

"I slept with them every night."

"Better them than me." She dissolved in laughter.

"Stop. They're the most meaningful gift I ever received. I love them."

Approaching WAC Circle, I took her arm.

"June, I spent my whole vacation thinking about you— what you were doing in Paris, wondering if you were all right, wishing we were together. I missed you so much."

She was silent, as if she could read my mind, knew what I was about to say. I took a breath to steady myself.

"All I could think about was the two of us going steady. I thought ... I mean ... I wanted to ask you before we left for vacation."

Her expression became serious.

"I saw it in your eyes," I bumbled on, "when we were talking, waiting for your taxi."

"Andy, I like you very much, and I know you like me. But I don't want you to get your hopes up about us in that way."

"I ... I don't understand," I said, feeling like I'd been doused with ice water.

"I need to tell you this, so there won't be misunderstandings. I've always felt it's better to be upfront and honest in relationships—especially in our case. I value your friendship, and I don't want you to feel hurt."

"But you're going to hurt me, aren't you?" I broke in. I was shaking inside my baggy duffel coat.

"I'm trying to explain, if you'll let me. First of all, I'm deeply touched—no, flattered—that you want us to be steadies. If I wanted to go steady, I would accept, instantly. Really, I would. Please believe me."

"But?"

"But I don't want to go steady with anyone, right now. I—"

"This is all about you and Doc, isn't it," I said, without thinking.

She recoiled. "He told you about my going steady with him last year?"

"No details, if that's what you mean. I guess it's none of my business."

"You have that right." For a moment she struggled to shift back to her previous train of thought, but the damage had been done.

"June, it hurts me every time I see you going out with all those guys."

"Andy, lots of them want to go out with me. That's just the way it is."

"But I ache. I actually ache."

"Well, you shouldn't," she said firmly. "You should ask other girls for dates. Copper would accept in a minute."

"But I won't be happy with anyone but you."

"Andy, I try to treat everybody fairly. Can't we go out together as best of friends? How about 'special' friends?"

"As far as you're concerned, then, I can never be anything more to you than a friend—is that what you're saying?" my voice rising inadvertently. "That I have no hope of ever being more special than just another friend?"

People stared at us. She took my arm. "Please. You don't need to use that tone of voice."

"I'll use any tone of voice I want. I couldn't wait to get back from Copenhagen to be with you, and now you tell me to stay at arm's length, like … like you told Rex. Or maybe you met somebody else in Paris last week."

"What? What are you talking about? Whatever I've told Rex is between him and me, not you. And if I went out with guys in Paris, that's my business, too. Since you mentioned it, I did meet several cute ones I liked, and all of them behaved better than you. I … oh, forget about the snack bar. I'm not hungry anymore." Whirling around, she headed toward the dormitory.

"Go ahead, stomp off! See if I care."

"Oh, grow up!" she replied, without looking back.

Dazed, I watched the girl I couldn't be without blend into the kaleidoscope of street lamps, headlights, and blinking traffic signals on the busy street. My throat throbbed. Barnes, you dumb bastard, I thought, eyes watering. What have you done? In two minutes everything you've struggled for—worked for all semester, everything you looked forward to—is gone. How is this possible?

Stomach churning, I stepped off the curb toward the PX into the shattering clang of a streetcar bell. An instant before locked wheels screeched past in a shower of sparks, a powerful hand jerked the collar of my coat backward.

"*Mach' keinen Scheiss wegen einem Mädchen*," said a gruff voice, as the iron grip relaxed.

I could barely stand. "*Danke*," I managed, looking up at the stranger whose quick action had saved my life.

A patched military coat, like the padded ones the Commies wore in Korean War movies, was draped over his large frame. A worn German Army cap, graying temples—and it was obvious that, at some point in time, his jaw had taken the full force of a blunt object. Through a rip in one of his boots I saw raw skin. An uncomfortable silence followed. What is he thinking, I wondered, staring down at this American kid—warmly dressed, well fed?

"That was close, cat. If it hadn't been for the big guy, you'd be strawberry jam."

"Jimmy. Am I glad to see you. Can you tell him I'm very, very grateful for pulling me off the tracks?"

In confident German, Jimmy began speaking to the former soldier, who gave me a courteous nod.

"What's he saying?"

"Not sure exactly—something about you arguing with a girl, then you tried to step in front of a streetcar. He says there's no point in killing yourself for a woman. Did you have a fight with June?"

"Who is he?" I asked, avoiding Jimmy's question.

They conversed again.

"His name is Gerhard Asche. He was a sergeant in the Wehrmacht, and taken prisoner by the Russians in April 1945. He was recently released."

"A Russian prisoner? All this time? But the war was over eleven years ago." I stared at this living survivor of hell wandering the streets of Frankfurt, no place to go, no job. How could that be, when he had spent so much time suffering for his country? Could this have happened to Pa if he'd been captured?

"Is there anything I can do, Jimmy? Money? A meal at the snack bar?"

Another exchange and Jimmy smiled. Taking out his Luckies, he lit one for the sergeant and one for himself. Asche took a long drag, exhaling an endless stream of smoke, as though making up for lost rivers of time.

"*Prima,*" he grunted, looking down at the cigarette between his fingers. He said something to Jimmy, who translated before I could ask.

"He says he can't afford American cigs, and asked if I could sell him a pack, cheap."

"I have a better idea," I said.

When Jimmy came down the steps of the PX a few minutes later he gave me a paper bag, which I handed to the former sergeant. Opening the top, he smiled. After shaking hands, he walked away without looking back. As he blended into the sidewalk crowd, he was opening a pack of Luckies.

"Three cartons of cigs, a lighter, a can of lighter fluid, and a pair of heavy wool socks—that's what your life is worth, Barnes. You owe me."

That night after lights out, I told Doc about my stupidity, throwing in the near-death experience for good measure. He shook his head.

"No matter what happens, you somehow manage to screw it up—even suicide."

"Aw, be nice, Doc. This was the last thing I wanted to happen. I'm still not sure how it did. I never felt worse in my life."

"Well, every once in a while these things work themselves out. Then again," he said, mostly to himself, "sometimes they don't."

Quiet settled over the room as we lay in our bunks, each lost in his private world. Were June and I finished? If I'd just listened to her, instead of losing my temper ... if, if, if only. Would Doc be able to help me patch up the mess I'd made? If he couldn't talk to June about serious things, how could he advise me? And, if he didn't say "June, it's over between us," my future with her was doomed. Anyway. I slipped my hands under the pillow, massaging my chapped knuckles with her Christmas mittens.

"Doc," I said, trying to choose my words carefully, "I know it hurts, but could you tell me about the mittens she made for you? You said 'maybe later' when we were ice skating. If it's too personal I'll understand, but since I seem to be doing my best to ruin everything ... I don't know, it might help us both."

"As far as I'm concerned, Andy, there's never a good time to talk about something I've never told anyone before," he answered. "Yes, she made me a pair of mittens last winter. Then we broke up and I never wore them.

That's all there is to it."

"Sorry. I know the pain, believe me. I shouldn't have brought it up, but …."

"But what?"

"I need your advice about what happened with June," I said, unsure what to say next. "How can I make it up to her? I need to apologize. Flowers? A box of candy?"

"You're asking me about apologizing? How would I know? I've never apologized to her."

His tone signaled an end to the conversation. I slipped into fitful sleep, wondering whether my relationship with the nicest girl I had ever known was over.

I was sitting on my bed, guitar across my lap, staring at the wall when Doc returned from washing up before lights out.

"It's been ten days, Doc—ten days. I'm climbing walls. How can I get through to her?"

"Wish I knew, Lone Ranger. But for what it's worth, I don't think she'd be torturing you like this unless you were important to her."

"She's not speaking to me at all—maybe a quick nod or 'Hi' if I'm lucky, and then she continues whatever she's doing. She never says anything unkind—"

"She won't. June's too classy for that."

"The worst part is that she's dating Rex again. Naturally, he goes out of his way to make demeaning comments—things like, 'I can't wait to get her drunk and crawl under the sheets with those marvelous legs.' Sooner or later, Rex and I are going to have it out between us."

"Ignore him. Try hard not to lose your temper. Look what happened when you lost it at WAC Circle. I am worried, though. Last night you were talking about June in your sleep."

"In my sleep? What did I say?"

"Only how much you want to get into her pants, but can't figure out how," Rex said. He was standing in our doorway.

"Butt out, you nosy bastard. I'm talking with Doc."

"I can't believe how naive you are, Barnes. When are you going to learn that the only thing girls are good for is to get as much as you can? Where do their feelings come into it? I'll have to seduce her, that's all. Can't wait to get my .... "

"You egotistical, selfish, son of a—" I jumped up, but he was turning down the hall toward his room.

"Cool it, Andy," warned Doc, grabbing my arm. "You didn't hear anything I said, did you? He knows you're upset. His techniques aren't working on her, so he's striking out. Think of it this way: he's jealous of you."

"Maybe, but that's how he really feels—she's just another conquest. We both know it."

Then, one day after chemistry class, I saw June alone in the hall ahead of me.

"Can I speak with you," I asked. "Please? I promise it won't take long, but I need to apologize. Things can't continue like this between us." For the first time since the fight I sensed that she, too, was unhappy about our situation.

"You have every right to be angry," I continued, "and ...."

"Yes, you owe me an apology. At least it's something. I've been wishing we were back on speaking terms for a long time."

A couple of frosty minutes later, we sat down in an isolated corner of the library. I stared out the window, watching stark branches swaying under gusts from an overcast sky, wondering how to begin.

"I'm so very, very sorry for the way I behaved, June," I finally managed, reaching for hands that remained folded in her lap. "It was rude and stupid, and I'm so ashamed. Please, please forgive me."

"When I got back to my room that night I fell on to my bed and sobbed," she said, quietly. "I didn't want anything to happen to us, Andy. I tried to clarify how I felt about going steady—something important that has caused me a great deal of heartbreak regarding Doc. You never let me explain why I don't think it's a good idea."

"I didn't realize how important it was—is—to you. At the time, after missing you so much over Christmas vacation, going steady was all I could think of. I was being totally selfish, June. I can't stand it anymore. I just want us to be friends again."

"What I am going to tell you is about me and Doc last year, and is strictly between us. Is that completely understood?"

I nodded, unable to think of anything to say.

"Last year I let my heart get the better of me, and went steady with him … this is going to be harder than I thought," she said, struggling to control her emotions. Her countenance reflected pain that, until now, I had never seen on her face.

"Anyway, it didn't last, and I was miserable. I still am. A wonderful friendship that began innocently, with the best of intentions and lots of shared fun, got full of difficult personal problems kids our age shouldn't have to deal with."

"You mean like sex?" I asked, taking a chance.

"That was at the heart of it, yes." She looked out the window at falling snowflakes. "It became a barrier between us. When it was on the verge of getting out of control, I broke away from the relationship. There weren't any temper tantrums like yours—just terrible emptiness."

"I'm sorry, June. I think I know how you felt."

"Do you?"

"Well, I know how I've felt these past weeks—like everything I do is meaningless."

"Andy, the majority of couples I've known who went steady didn't stay together. When things fell apart, they poisoned each other with mean talk and rumors that were uncalled for. When you brought it up after Christmas, that was all I could think of. I didn't want to have that happen to us, and I didn't want to be unhappy again."

"I hope you never are."

She looked at me and her eyes softened. "So that's why I don't want to be tied down right now. I'm trying to be myself, be happy, and stay on equal terms with everybody. It's best this way, really." She reached for her notebooks.

"I'm so glad we're finally talking again," I said, as we stood. "I think both of us feel better—I sure do. Thank you for hearing me out, and for sharing your feelings."

"Just remember why I feel the way I do, okay? And Andy," she added, with her first smile in weeks, "I'm thankful you didn't get hit by that streetcar."

# Doc's Swimming Party

In February, Doc arranged a dorm swimming trip to a German indoor pool in Wiesbaden. It was one of his promises, made early in the school year, when he was trying to get me and Copper together. "I'll reserve one of those big dark Army buses, get box lunches—you two lovebirds will have a fabulous time."

The Kreebs was not interested in being the required chaperone.

"Get lost, Gordon. You don't seriously think I'm going to take a busload of brats to Wiesbaden, do you?"

But Doc kept after him. Things like, "Nice to have it on your resume at evaluation time, Mr. Kreebert, don't you think?" or "Wouldn't Mr. Pulaski be impressed with the extra effort you give to your job—over and above your already heavy workload?"

Then one Saturday morning, Tonto pranced into our room waving a handful of forms.

"The Kreebs couldn't take my bugging him anymore, so he finally caved."

"Are we really going to have a swimming party?" asked Alfie from our doorway.

"Absolutely. Why?"

Alfie glanced around and stared at the floor. "I can't swim, Doc."

"Didn't you ever go to summer camp?" I asked.

"Once, but after I wet my bed they sent me home."

"I think it's time you had your first swimming lesson," said Doc. "I'll arrange everything. You'll like it."

With Miss Maybelle's help, we filled out all the paperwork and The Kreebs signed as "Official in Charge." Doc reserved the Wiesbaden facility and lined up an Army bus from the motor pool. Since we were not expected to return before dinner, he obtained (with a helpful request in writing from Mr. Pulaski) box lunches from Sergeant Normand.

On a cold, overcast Saturday afternoon we piled into the bus—guys in the back, girls scattering toward the front, as usual. In between, couples going steady took seats where they could make out. After The Kreebs's briefing on conduct, to which nobody (except maybe Alfie) paid attention, the bus pulled away from the dorm. The Kreebs sat with Miss Maybelle behind the driver, trying to ignore what was going on behind him. After a while I went forward, passing Copper and June, who were having some sort of serious discussion.

"I don't pay any attention to forecasters," replied The Kreebs, when I asked if he'd heard a weather report. "They're wrong ninety-five percent of the time."

"I never did understand how weathermen could keep their jobs," Miss Maybelle chimed in.

"Andy," Doc called as I retraced my steps. "Send Copper back here, would you? I have to ask my little red squirrel about swimming lessons."

She vacated her seat, leaving June staring out the window, a half-folded letter in her hand.

"Okay if I sit?"

"If you want," she replied, without looking up as I scrunched down beside her.

"I love to swim. How about you?"

"I guess so."

I glanced at the letter. "From Turkey?" She nodded, staring blankly at cars zipping past us on the Autobahn. I tried again. "How's your family?"

She rubbed her cheek and the heel of her hand came away wet.

"Something's happened at home, hasn't it?" I said. "Can I help?"

"My mother." She glanced down at the letter.

I took her hand. "Not an accident, I hope."

"No," she smiled weakly. "But my father says she might have cancer."

"I'm so sorry, June." I touched her arm. "You mentioned she smoked and was coughing a lot. Is it her lungs?"

"Breast tumors. They appear to be spreading, and she will have to go back to the States for tests. Last year I did a research project on cancer for biology class and some researchers suspect smoking plays a role in causing it, so I know enough to be really frightened."

"I'm so sad to find you hit with such awful news, especially when you can't be with her," I replied. "Sometimes having a caring person willing to listen helps."

For the remainder of the trip, June's torment poured out as she told me everything she knew about cancer—the massive operations, treatments that did more harm than good, the grim survival outlook.

"I feel so helpless, Andy. I've pleaded with Mother to stop smoking. I know tobacco has something to do with it

—I know it."

I pulled a mitten out of my coat pocket and dabbed at tears trickling down her face. Her eyes softened.

"Winter's almost over. Surely you don't need to carry those around."

"My mittens go where I go, thank you. Anyway, they're all I have to dry these lovely cheeks."

The bus arrived, and kids jostled as they waited for The Kreebs to let them off. When I stood up, she caught my sleeve.

"Thank you for sitting with me, Andy. You helped a lot."

Heading for the locker room, I hadn't felt so good in months.

Prodding Alfie, I followed him to the pool. Doc was waiting at the shallow end.

"No water wings?"

There was a "whoosh" at our feet as Copper flipped herself onto the tiled edge of the pool like a freckled seal.

"Doc says you don't know how to swim, Alfie. I'll help you get started, if you like."

Alfie's nearsighted eyes flicked from side to side as he inched backward on stiff legs.

"I've changed my mind. I don't want to go swimming today."

"Now, now, none of that," said Doc. "Copper has her Water Safety Instructor's Certificate, YWCA Lifesaving diploma, and Girl Scout merit badge for Underwater Kissing."

She slipped into the pool and gave him a splash, before turning to Alfie with her arms wide. I'd have jumped in a minute.

"C'mon," I said. "Copper will hold you up. You can do it."

Alfie shook his head.

"Are you paralyzed?" asked Doc. "Get in."

I gave our chemistry tutor a shove. He landed on his instructor like a limpet, gripping her so tightly that her breasts half squeezed out of the tank suit clinging to her sleek body like a layer of dark-blue paint.

"I'm jealous," I said, truthfully.

It took all three of us to separate pupil from teacher and calm him down. When Doc and I left, Copper was standing beside him, one arm under his stomach and the other supporting his thighs. Eyes and mouth clamped shut, Alfie clutched the edge of the pool, legs kicking a rooster tail of water as if a barracuda were after him.

Later, Copper gave a diving demonstration from the three-meter board. She belonged to a German swim club and had participated in numerous competitions. When I asked her about it once, she said she wanted to compete in the Olympics. This was not wishful thinking. As I watched her agile body tuck into tight balls, twists, and somersaults, I imagined I was back in time, looking at a teenage Katharine Hepburn.

All the while, Doc kept staring at a platform near the high domed ceiling, accessible only by metal ladders and a precarious catwalk.

"Come," he said, dragging me toward the German lifeguard.

"Oh, no, Gordon. You're not getting me up there on that thing."

"Yes, I am. You know you can't resist the temptation. You don't want people to think that girls are the only ones who can dive, do you?"

"Copper's the best diver either of us has ever seen, and you know it."

"But think how impressed June will be when she sees you climbing up, up, up. Then we tiptoe along that catwalk and—"

"She'll think I'm as batty as you are."

"But it'll be more fun if we break our necks together," Doc pleaded.

"Ja?" said the lifeguard.

Pointing to the platform and speaking a few words in pidgin German, Doc asked what it was for, pantomiming with his fingers. The lifeguard said something about the Wehrmacht, and twisted his head to the side.

"He's saying if you want to break your neck, go ahead, isn't he? For the last time, Doc, I'm not going up there with you and that's final. "

"Are you chickening out on me, Barnes?"

"Call it whatever you like."

He stepped back. "You don't care about impressing June?"

"Doc, you just don't get it, do you? Don't you realize this isn't the way to do it?"

"Okay, Andy, if that's what you think."

"Don't spoil the party by killing yourself," I yelled after him.

Whistle blasts cleared the pool as Doc started to climb, while the rest of us watched from around the pool. Miss Maybelle, followed by The Kreebs, appeared from the office to see what was going on. She froze. The Kreebs, however, went straight to the lifeguard and immediately got into an argument in German, pointing upward and waving his arms. I doubted our supervisor cared what happened to Doc; but facing Pulaski and Army brass about a serious accident (or worse) to a student he was chaperoning was another matter.

"Come down, Gordon, do you hear me? I never gave you permission to go up there."

"But the lifeguard did, Mr. Kreebert, Sir. He's in charge of the pool."

The Kreebs turned purple. "Damn you. I should never have let you talk me into coming."

June looked away, shaking her head. Poor June. She had enough to worry about, already. Doc had no business putting her through this—or any of us, for that matter. But Tonto saw only a feat high above, one crackling with danger he couldn't resist.

Reaching the top, he edged across the catwalk to the metal platform and pushed the gate. It didn't budge. He gave it a shove. There was a collective gasp as it swung open on one hinge. June buried her face in my shoulder, and I wrapped her shaking body close. What she didn't see was the boy she cared so much about, twisting through emptiness, hopelessly grasping for anything to stop his fall. Somehow, he missed both diving boards, hitting the water within inches of the side of the pool. Slowly, his head surfaced. One hand found the tiled edge. He waved. Nobody clapped.

"This event is terminated," The Kreebs bellowed. "When you have dressed, the bus will be waiting outside."

It seemed everyone was anxious to leave—except Doc.

"Aw, Mr. Kreebert. It was an accident. That platform hasn't been used since World War II. Is this really necessary?"

"Yes, Mr. Gordon. And as far as you are concerned, this is only the beginning."

"You really fucked up this time, Gordon," said Rex, back in the locker room.

There were nods of agreement from more than a few naked bodies drying off.

"The Kreebs didn't want to come today," Doc

answered, trying to wriggle out of the guilt I knew he felt. "He used me as an excuse to bag the evening. Why make everybody suffer? He should have sent me to the bus."

"Quit rationalizing," said Rex. "What did you expect—that he was going to pat you on the back and say, 'Man, that was close. I'm sure glad you didn't leave what few brains you have splattered across a diving board on your way down'?"

Except for the clank of locker doors, the next few minutes were unnaturally quiet.

"Hey, Alfie," said Doc, breaking the silence. "Did you like your swimming lessons? Was the teacher I got for you okay?"

Alfie emerged from behind his opened locker door wrapped in a huge towel. A smaller one around his head gave him the appearance of a Hindu spiritual leader with magnified eyes.

"Copper was very helpful. She taught me how to float and dog paddle."

"You mean swim like a guppy, don't you?" Rex sneered.

Alfie moved closer, waiting until Rex was out of earshot. "It was sort of embarrassing."

Doc stopped drying off. "How so? C'mon, you can tell Uncle Doc."

"While she had her arms underneath my stomach and, and was holding my legs up so I could kick, my … it, you know …." The chemistry genius turned beet red.

"It's okay, Alfie. It's nothing to be ashamed about. You're growing up, that's all."

"I'll bet Copper was impressed," I said. "I wish she'd give me swimming lessons."

Night had fallen and, as I suspected, it was snowing when we boarded the bus. I kept right behind June.

"I thought you might like some company on the ride back," I said, removing a dry ham and cheese sandwich from one of Sarge Normand's box lunches on our seat. "Something to eat?"

"No thanks, Andy. I'm not hungry—not after what happened."

"I think we need a break. Want to hear about Denmark? I never finished last fall when we were on the Heidelberg bus."

"Please."

For the rest of the ride, I told her about my family, the village of Taarbaek, my room, Elena, the yard, Taarbaek Harbor, Dyrehaven, Bakken—anything I could think of. She peppered me with questions, which kept her mind off Doc and her mother's situation. At one point the driver hit the brakes and the bus skidded on the slippery highway, throwing us against each other. My arm, which had been on the back of her seat, slid to the front of her shoulder and I pulled her nearer, until her head rested on my neck. She was quiet and, after a few minutes, I realized she was asleep. June finished the trip in my arms.

"Pssst. Wake up, sleepyhead. We're back."

She sat up, rubbing her eyes.

"Thanks for letting me sit with you," I said. "It was the only nice part of the afternoon."

Outside, I adjusted the hood of her coat.

"I really appreciate your company, Andy. You helped me more than you realize." She gave me a kiss, and disappeared inside the girls' dorm. I went back to our room, a dopey grin across my face.

# Hatfield Versus McCoy

My ear was glued to the keyhole of Mr. Pulaski's office door. Inside, The Kreebs was barely able to control his rage.

"You deliberately disobeyed me when I told you to come down. As chaperone, I was in charge of the entire event, and you willfully ignored my authority. You almost killed yourself. You should be expelled."

"I would have checked with you, Mr. Kreebert," Doc replied, "if you had been available. Anyway, a lifeguard is the person in charge of a swimming pool. Isn't that what he's paid for? Since you weren't there, I asked him, and he gave me permission."

Our principal cleared his throat.

"What do you mean Mr. Kreebert wasn't there, Mr. Gordon?"

"He was nowhere in sight, Sir. I have no idea where he was."

Mr. Pulaski asked The Kreebs to remain after the meeting was over.

"You realize your name is number one on The Kreebs's shit list," I warned as we returned to the dorm.

"He can put my name wherever he wants," Doc

213

snorted. "Kreebert only cares about his job. As far as I'm concerned, it's time for revenge."

"Why start a war with that jerk, Doc?"

"Hey, Tarzan," a senior passing us laughed. "Heard you missed a vine at the pool and nearly killed yourself."

"Look," said Doc, ignoring him, "it's duller than nails around here. Isn't a bit of excitement worth it?"

"Don't give me that, Gordon. It was you showing off that caused this mess. You did it for yourself. I think starting a Hatfield versus McCoy feud with The Kreebs is dumb."

"What are you talking about, Barnes? Who the hell are Hatfield and McCoy?"

"They were two quarreling hillbilly families, famous for the length of time their fighting and killing lasted. It started when—"

"Dammit, Andy. I don't need a history lesson. Whose side are you on, anyway?"

"Yours, of course. But why do you always push everything to the limit? Sometimes I feel you're out of control, like you aren't thinking straight. Couldn't the hard feelings between you and Kreebert be patched up with some sort of an apology? It worked when you told me to try it with June."

"Don't mention her in the same sentence," Doc growled. "I told him I was sorry he was upset with me. What more could I say? If anyone needs to apologize, he does."

"You realize that whatever you do is bound to have consequences, don't you?" I said to Doc as we stepped inside our room.

"To hell with consequences. I'm going to get even the first chance I get. And that's a promise I will keep."

"Even if it's a bad one?"

Spinning around he stomped out, slamming the door.

Not long after the swimming fiasco, Asian flu raged through the school, leaving empty desks in every classroom. In short order the dorm was transformed into a fever ward, reeking of barf and diarrhea. Simpering zombies went to the 97th General Hospital, returning with bottles of "GI gin" (an alcoholic cough syrup heavily laced with codeine); handfuls of APCs (horse pills universally referred to as "all-purpose capsules"); and slips signed by Captain Somebody-or-Other, MC, USA, ordering room confinement, fluids, and bed rest. Alfie was sick. Rex lay in his bunk drooling tentacles of Pepto-Bismol and cursing all germs. We didn't see June for a week. Doc and I transported homework assignments for her to Miss Maybelle, and when she gave us the okay we relayed ginger ale floats from the PX Snack Bar. Amazingly, neither Doc nor I got the bug.

"It's because I make you keep a window open at night," he insisted. "The germs freeze before they make it to our mucus membranes."

"It's probably because I made you stop picking your nose, and I never got in the habit, Gordon."

Most of the kitchen crew were sick. Then, one morning at breakfast, we found Sergeant Normand himself standing behind the counter—something he maintained was not in his job description—doling out wagon-wheel waffles with oatmeal plaster.

"Need any help, Sergeant?" Doc asked.

"Are either of yooz sick?" Normand countered.

"We're totally immune," Doc replied.

I forgot about it. Then, at dinner, The Kreebs pulled us aside. Normand was with him.

"Frankly, Gordon, I wouldn't trust you with a dish sponge, but Mr. Pulaski approved the idea of your helping in the kitchen on the condition that you weren't getting sick."

The dorm supervisor gave us a knife-like stare. "Are you?"

"If we were going to get it," my roomie replied, "we would have been in bed with the pukes by now."

"Never mind the graphics. Do whatever Sergeant Normand tells you. Any fooling around and you'll find yourself on restriction into next fall, if you get my drift."

"Absolutely, Mr. Kreebert, sir."

"Have yooz mizerable butts 'eer tomorrow morning at oh-five-hundred hours," ordered Normand.

We sat down to eat.

"Did it ever occur to you, Gordon, that I'm not wildly pleased about being dragged into whatever it is you're up to? Out with it," I demanded.

Doc leaned forward. "This is the chance I've been waiting for, Andy, but I won't know until we start working."

"Chance for what?"

His face glowed with malice. "To get even with The Kreebs. What else?"

"You'll get both of us kicked out of school—that's what else. Ever thought of that?"

"Not going to happen. I won't let it. I see great possibilities here."

At ten minutes to five the next morning, we stood shivering in front of the mess hall. I pulled the hood of my duffel coat over my face in a vain attempt to minimize the smell of rain-soaked cigarette butts from the nearby Weed Pit. Adjusting his chef's hat, the Sarge appeared inside, flipping light switches as he unlocked the door. After handing out paring knives and white aprons, he marched us to the potato vat, where we stopped at an enormous lumpy burlap bag. Ripping it open, the Sarge extracted a spud covered with dirt.

"Scrub, peel, and cut all of zem into small pieces," he ordered, before spinning on his heel and scuttling off.

"This potato smells like shit," I said.

"Probably is. Have you forgotten that in Germany, farmers fertilize potatoes with night soil from those wooden 'honey wagons' you see them using in their fields? Do I need to remind you what night soil actually is?"

"Thanks a lot, Gordon. You got me up before dawn on a rainy Saturday morning so I could scrape human crap off hundreds of potatoes."

A skeleton crew of kitchen staff arrived, and soon the aroma of coffee, sizzling bacon, toast, and eggs overwhelmed the odor of our potatoes. As Doc negotiated some breakfast for us with his friend "Grandma" Helga, Normand appeared. She shuffled away but hid two heaping plates on top of one of the stoves for us.

"What zee 'ell dooz you tink zees iz, Gordon, a picnic?" He clapped his hands several times. "Work. *Vite! Vite!*"

As lunchtime approached, Normand told us to prepare dessert. It was one of his staples—orange Jell-O. It was made the day before, poured into two-by-three-foot flat trays one inch deep, and put in the cold room to harden. I carried one to a table.

"I wants yooz to cuts zeez exactement so," he ordered, slicing perfect one-inch squares of the jiggly stuff with his spatula. "*Cinq* squares in each dish with sauce, eh?" Dropping five pieces into a dessert dish, he dabbed on a spoon of white topping from a large stainless bowl.

Despite pre-dawn rain, the morning turned sunny and mild. Inside the kitchen there was an early hatch of flies— the first since the previous fall. They were most active around the ovens; but a few discovered our dessert trays, and soon we were swatting away squadrons of them.

"This goop would make good flypaper," I said, spooning a couple of black squirmers out of the topping and sticking them under the table like chewing gum. Doc picked up one and examined it. His hand shook with excitement, eyes sparkling like exploding stars.

"This is it, Lone Ranger—payback time."

I had that sinking feeling in the pit of my stomach.

"Andy, do you remember when The Kreebs held up the entire serving line to examine dish after dish of his favorite dessert before he decided which one was the biggest?"

"You mean every time we have Jell-O? What of it?"

"Tonto's prayers have been answered, Kemosabe."

"Yours, maybe—not mine. I know when you're planning something risky. You thrive on that sort of thing."

"That's the way I am. I can't do anything about it."

"I suppose you're right, Doc. It's a flaw in your makeup."

"Stop talking nonsense, Barnes. Are you in or out?"

We continued dishing up desserts, but the work was much more interesting.

"How many flies, Doc?"

"Sprinkle them on top like raisins."

"Too obvious. I don't want to get expelled for a stupid mistake."

"Yeah," he said, rubbing a smudge of white topping from his chin. "It should look more natural, shouldn't it? And Miss Franklin could benefit from some extra protein as well."

Both of us had had run-ins with Miss Maybelle's boss—the unpleasant, overfed, head supervisor of the girls' dorm—whose inflexibility was exceeded only by Stanley Kreebert's.

"But Doc, how do we make sure both of them get the right desserts? We don't want Miss Maybelle to get one; and we can't say, 'Here, Mr. Kreebert. Wouldn't you prefer this bigger dish with more raisins?'"

"Stop worrying. Dig some live ones out of the topping and leave the rest to me."

While I was exhuming specimens, he filled two dishes with extra-large Jell-O squares.

"Drop the flies right in the middle. I'll bury them with topping. When we see Miss Franklin and The Kreebs getting into the serving line, we'll put their desserts somewhere in the back row. The biggest will end up on his tray, and she'll grab the other one—I guarantee it."

Doc's plan almost backfired when, after surveying the entire dessert counter, Lola Franklin took both of them.

"Now Lola," said The Kreebs, picking the biggest off her tray, "let's not be greedy. You know this is my favorite, also."

Throughout the meal, we watched them so closely we almost missed June as she reached for her dessert. Her gaze shifted to the supervisors' table and back to Doc.

"Are you two all right?"

"Their Jell-O …." Doc began.

"I don't want to know," she said, putting hers back on the counter.

A short time later, he nudged me. "Showtime."

It started out well. In an orgy of orange and white foam, Lola Franklin cleaned her dish, including flies.

"Just like a hungry trout," I said as she burped into her napkin.

The Kreebs, however, swallowed several mouthfuls and then choked as he spotted a fly in his topping aimlessly breast-stroking toward the surface. Slowly, he put down his spoon, pointed, and said something to the two women sitting next to him. Miss Maybelle leaned over for a closer look. With increasing alarm, we watched as he dissected the contents of his fortified Jell-O. Abruptly, he stood up, spilling gravy onto his lap.

"Normand, come here right now."

I saw June stop eating and set her tray aside. Silence spread over the mess hall tables.

"Hopefully, he already ate most of them," said Doc, as the chef hurried to their table.

"There eez trouble?"

"There are flies in my Jell-O, that's what," replied the indignant Kreebs. "Look."

"What zee fook?" said the thoroughly confused French chef. He picked out a half-drowned insect, examined, and squished it between his thumb and index finger. There was an animated conversation, a pause, and then all of them looked at us. We pretended to be very busy.

"Oh, shit," said Doc, as the three of them marched toward us. "Let me do the talking."

"What eez zis?" the chef demanded, his thick neck veins throbbing.

"What is what, Sergeant? Can I be of help?" asked Doc.

"*Tu me crois fou? Explique-moi ca, espèce d'imbécile!*" he exploded in his native tongue—something he only did when he was really mad.

"I don't speak French, Sergeant Normand. English, please," said Doc, in a courteous voice.

"Do yoos tink I am an idiot?" said the furious cook.

"What is the meaning of this?" cut in The Kreebs,

jabbing his finger at the flies. "How did these bugs get into my Jell-O?"

"Eewww. That one's still alive," said Miss Maybelle, pointing to The Kreebs's dish. The fly dropped off the edge and he stepped on it.

"I only see two dead ones," said Doc, stirring his finger in The Kreebs's topping. "As for the flies, they've been a pain all morning—flying around the kitchen, landing in the food—it really is unsanitary. You should do something about them, Sergeant Normand. It's a good thing the inspector general isn't here."

The purple drained from Normand's flushed face as visions of an official IG kitchen inspection replaced his rage.

"There's no telling what disgusting stuff they landed on before they got into Mr. Kreebert's dessert," Doc went on. "Andy and I have tried to keep them away from the topping all morning. Sorry if we missed a few."

Miss Franklin looked as if she would barf, but The Kreebs was fuming. Returning to their table, the three of them gathered up their coats and left.

Noticing that everybody was watching, Normand announced, "We will eliminate zeez flies," and hurried to his office like a fiddler crab escaping to its burrow at low tide.

"Phew," exclaimed Doc. "That was close."

We were emptying garbage cans when Sergeant Normand came for our aprons.

Hatfield-McCoy didn't end there. At mail call, Doc got his letters last. If one was from Marissa, Kreebert made handing it over as embarrassing as possible.

"Oooh, here's another lovely perfumed one from Switzerland. I didn't know you liked lavender, Mr. Gordon.

Aren't our Frankfurt girls good enough for you?"

And Doc would reply in kind. After one episode, he pointed to the front of The Kreebs's khakis and said loudly, "Gee, Mr. Kreebert, aren't you going to take those to the cleaners?"

"You know how these gravy stains got there, and they won't come out."

"Are you sure they're from gravy, Mr. Kreebert?"

"How dare you speak to me like that! Consider yourself restricted next weekend."

"House arrest on bread and water, again?"

"Make that two weekends, you insolent snot."

And so it went. I told him I thought it was stupid to provoke Kreebert so often, but it simmered back and forth until the arrival of spring.

# Part 4
# Spring 1957

# June Goes to Denmark

For several weeks Doc did not receive a single letter from Marissa. Easter was approaching, and I knew he couldn't wait to see her.

"What's happening with your Danish Pastry?" I asked, coming into our room after school. "Haven't seen you hunched outside on the football bleachers reading letters from her."

"How would I know?" He was staring out the window, our floor a snow of shredded paper. Then I saw Swiss stamps on the remains of an envelope, and realized it was his collection of her letters.

"Sorry, Doc."

"She says she's not coming back to Copenhagen at Easter—or ever. She can't stand school; her father doesn't understand her; and she's leaving for the Côte d'Azur with Heinz."

"Who's he?"

"How the hell would I know? Some Swiss cheese."

"Jeez," I mumbled, uncertain what to say. "Anything I can do?"

He kicked at the floor, sending fragments of shattered

love fluttering around the room. "I want to be alone, okay?"

"Sure, Doc. Guess I'll head over to the PX."

As I headed toward WAC Circle, my head was spinning. I felt my roommate's pain. Since Thanksgiving, Marissa had been his goddess of perfection, with whom all ultimate desires associated with the opposite sex, real or imagined, were destined to be fulfilled. And now this. Also, Doc's passion for Marissa had been the force behind our Blood Brother Oath, which had been responsible for much of my good fortune with June. I owed this to his beautiful, wild "Danish Contessa." But would their breakup push him into the arms of June again? She was there to lean on, if he needed her, and I had no doubt he would in the coming days. Doc had never 'fessed up to June that their relationship was really over, so how would she react if he tried to come back to her?

As luck would have it, I saw her at the PX checkout counter.

"Hi," I said, as she thanked the clerk and took her purchases. "Feel like a soda or something at the snack bar, my treat?"

She paused. "That would be nice, Andy. I'd like that."

"I can't wait to get home for Easter," I said a few minutes later after the waitress had taken our order.

June looked down at her water glass, slowly moving it in figure eights on the table top. I saw immediately that something was wrong.

"Is it your mother? I know she's been on your mind."

She nodded without looking up.

"I'm here to listen—if you feel like talking."

"I've worried about her for weeks, Andy. My father wrote that Mom is worse, and he's taking her back to the

States for tests and an in-depth diagnosis at Bethesda Naval Medical Center. They'll be gone for the entire month of April."

"Your brother, too?"

"No. He's going to stay in Ankara with the Cardoni family. Major Cardoni is my father's Marine assistant. The plan is for me to spend Easter with them also." She was fighting back tears. "Instead of being with Mom, I'm going to be trapped at the Cardonis', listening to his war stories about drinking fermented coconut milk from Japanese skulls in the South Pacific. If I'm lucky, he might play me a tune on one of his enemy bugles from Korea."

"Sounds kind of interesting, actually."

She pushed back her chair and started to get up, but I reached across and took her arm. "Don't go. I was thinking historically. Listen: I have an idea."

She hesitated, and then sat down as the waitress arrived with our brown cow in a frosty mug. Two straws stood straight up, frozen in beige foam surrounding an iceberg of vanilla. I pushed the drink toward her. "You can have the first sip."

"Well?" she said, toying with one of the straws.

"Why don't you ask your folks if you can spend Easter vacation in Copenhagen with us?" The root beer in her straw drained back into the glass. Silence. I wondered if she thought I was a knight in shining armor or some sex maniac plotting to take advantage of her. "Did I see a flash of hope in those beautiful green eyes?" I smiled.

"It sounds wonderful, Andy, but I'm not sure my parents would let me." She swished the straw back and forth and took a sip. "If only it were possible."

"It's not like you'll be staying with strangers. Your mom and dad undoubtedly have a lot on their minds right now, and it would probably be a relief to know you are staying in a wonderful, safe place with old Navy friends. Your father won't have to make any arrangements except sending a permission letter to Mr. Pulaski, allowing you to fly to Denmark with us."

June took a healthy swallow of root beer. "But would your mother want to have me?"

"Of course she would. I know it. There's a guest room right next to my parents' bedroom, so that's no problem—unless Pa's snoring keeps you awake. The door has a lock on it, so I can't get in. You'll be safe."

"Unless I unlocked it," she giggled.

"June, I know you want to come. You've said how much you'd like to see Copenhagen, and I want to show you how beautiful it is—very, very much. I'll write Mom and tell her about your mother's situation. She'll insist you stay with us. She'll send you an invitation and contact your parents. All you have to do is tell your folks how badly you want to visit Copenhagen."

Later in the week, Mom wrote to say she had written Cora and Butch Everett, promising that June would be "one of the family"; the following week June received Mom's invitation to spend Easter with us. Meanwhile, Mr. Pulaski got a letter from Captain Everett giving his consent. If June was excited, I was ecstatic.

Word spread quickly.

"Why didn't I think of that?" said Rex, upon hearing the news. "I'd take her to the deer park, and even let her carry the blanket."

My biggest concern, however, was Doc. As I had suspected, ever since the snowstorm in our room, he had been spending time with June—a lot.

"Doc, have you heard anything more from Marissa?" I

asked him one night in our room.

"Who?"

"You know, the one who went off to the Mediterranean with the Swiss cheese."

"I hope she screams with pain when he rubs Coppertone on her sunburned fried eggs."

"So," I said, picking my words carefully, "does that mean you two are finished?"

"She can screw Swiss cheeses until she turns into one."

"And June?"

Doc's head appeared over the edge of his mattress.

"Something buggin' you, Roomie?"

"Well, lately, I've seen you with her quite a bit, and since Marissa is out of the picture, it seems like maybe you're getting back together."

"Andy, we signed in blood, remember? No, I'm not moving in on June. But just to be clear, she has always been a comfort to be around when I need her."

"Don't you think she might get the wrong message?"

"No way. And for the record, Lone Ranger, she's not going to stay locked away in your Taarbaek tower over the Easter holidays."

"I'll string barbed wire around it," I answered. "G'night."

"Not quite finished. While we're on the subject of the dear girl, may I give you a piece of sage advice?"

"You will, whether I want it or not, so go ahead. What did I do wrong this time?"

"Nothing. It's what you probably haven't done and need to do—soon."

"Huh?"

"The prom, dodo. When we get back from vacation, it's going to be upon us—fast. The girls are already talking about it. All I'm saying is that you better ask her pronto, before Rex or someone else does. Do you think she's going to turn down invitations while you pull an Andy, and don't get around to asking her until the day before?"

"Point made. Who have you asked?"

"Well, nobody yet, but …."

"But what? I'll ask June when you ask Copper, okay?"

"Just trying to be helpful. G'night."

Classes ended the morning before Good Friday. When our bus arrived at Rhein-Main, I was relieved to see planes taking off, despite low overcast mixed with an ominous buildup of fog. As we boarded the Navy plane, Pa slid back the cockpit side window and waved.

"Get a move on, kids," shouted "Gunner" Fleming, the plane's crew chief. "The captain wants wheels up, before we get socked in for the rest of the day."

We piled into the plane and within minutes were roaring down the runway for an immediate takeoff. I had intended to sit with June, but she was with a bunch of girls in back. During the flight female conversation was, as Doc had foreseen, focused on one thing: the prom. His warning about asking June promptly flickered through my mind, but there would be plenty of opportunities while we were together during the week ahead.

Wheels screeched on Kastrup's runway, and the plane taxied to a stop near the military hangar, where a cluster of happy families waited. Mother gave June a big hug, repeating several times how glad she was to see her again "after all these years." Aage nodded toward my guest and waggled his bushy eyebrows in approval as he put our suitcases into the Ford. We walked through customs without stopping.

"Aren't they going to stamp my passport?" June asked.

The inspector on duty, a friend of Aage's, came out of his office and made a show of writing something inside the green booklet with embossed gold lettering she handed to him.

"What did he put in your passport?" I asked as Aage led the way to the Embassy Ford.

"'Danish Customs hopes you enjoy your stay in our wonderful country,'" she read.

"June, dear," Mom said, "Why don't you sit in front so you can see the sights of Copenhagen better? It is such a beautiful city. I'm sure Aage would be delighted to give you a quick tour on the ride home."

"What is not to like about Denmark?" said Aage, pleased at this green light to showcase the city he loved.

"That would be wonderful, Mrs. Barnes. Thank you," June replied with a big smile, revealing excitement and happiness accentuated by the dimples I adored.

"Andy can sit in back with me," Mom added, "to give you a little breathing room."

Ignoring Mom, I scrunched into the front seat next to June.

After dropping Pa at the Embassy on tree-lined Østerbrogade, we maneuvered through bicycles and traffic as Aage pointed out the sights.

"Here is the statue of Hans Christian Andersen. You know of him?"

"Oh yes. Everybody does."

"There is Tivoli. You have heard of Tivoli Gardens? "

"Of course," she smiled.

June marveled at Copenhagen's relaxed beauty. Whenever she commented on how happy or carefree the Danes were, Aage beamed. We passed the royal residence at Amalienborg Palace; Rosenborg Castle ("where the royal jewels are kept"); The Citadel ("a very old fort"); and "the park by the water where The Little Mermaid sits." All the while Aage hummed the song "Wonderful, Wonderful Copenhagen," repeating the first stanza—the only part he knew—over and over. Mom leaned forward.

"Aage, could you please turn off the radio?"

"But this car has no radio, Mrs. Barnes. Oh. Now I understand. The radio is me."

Then we were heading north on the Strandvejen, racing along the Øresund's harbor-studded coast past Hellerup, Charlottenlund, Klampenborg, and home.

"It's absolutely gorgeous," June exclaimed as she followed Mom inside the front door of our house. "I adore old houses." She ran her smooth hand over the rough twists of the frayed two-inch hawser along the staircase banister. "I can tell this is the home of a naval officer, Mrs. Barnes."

"That horrible rope is my husband's sole contribution to decorating this otherwise lovely house," Mom replied as the two of them shared a laugh. Carrying June's suitcase, Elena led the way to the second-floor guest room overlooking the Øresund.

"This view is incredible," said June, moving to the opened window, where curtains fluttered in a lazy breeze off the water. She shivered.

"Is it too chilly, dear?" asked Mom.

"Maybe a little. We're not used to sea breezes in Frankfurt."

Elena closed it, giving me a wink as she left the room.

"June, dear, your towels are behind the door in the bathroom across the hall; if you need anything, let me or Elena know. Why don't you take a few minutes to unpack and relax before we have a late lunch? You must be starving."

After a meal of open-faced sandwiches followed by my favorite shredded carrot and apple salad, June asked to see the kitchen. Pointing to a bunch of small potatoes, Elena shoved a peeler at me as the two of them began a lengthy discussion about Danish food. Mom appeared eventually, inquiring if June would like to see the rest of the house.

"More than anything, Mrs. Barnes. Thank you."

For the next hour she got the grand tour.

"The high ceilings, these spacious rooms with views of the water from almost every window, the old wood floors, the roses, Taarbaek village—I adore this place so much." Mom went on and on, but for once I didn't get bored. After years of experience sizing up acquaintances and new friends every time we moved, she knew how to make people feel comfortable. She also genuinely enjoyed young people, and I was delighted to see the two of them getting along well. June had not seemed so stress-free and cheerful in weeks. Then, as we arrived at Mom's now sizable collection of Royal Copenhagen, Pa's ship's clock chimed.

"Goodness," she exclaimed. "I didn't realize how late it is. I have to be at a tea for the new Army attaché's wife in forty-five minutes. Andy will have to take over."

"Before you go," June said, "I want to thank you again for inviting me to spend Easter with you. It's like being home. Please let me know if I can help with anything."

"It's wonderful having you stay with us after all these years," replied Mom, giving her a hug. "You have grown into such a lovely person. I'm looking forward to knowing you."

At last. I had June all to myself.

"Would you like to see my room?" I asked, starting up the narrow staircase.

Stepping inside, she walked straight across to the

French doors and onto the balcony.

"It's so beautiful, Andy—the garden, the water—is that Sweden in the distance?"

"Yup. That's the port city of Malmo on the horizon."

"I thought you were exaggerating, but everything you said about this place is true."

"When the roses are in bloom, it's spectacular," I replied, pointing to rows of bare bushes below. "And that's our dock."

Stepping inside, she spied my bird book and binoculars on the table.

"I didn't know you were a bird-watcher," she said, picking up the binocs.

"I'm not. Mom gave them to me for my birthday, hoping to get me interested." June turned toward my favorite window facing Bellevue Beach. It was a mild afternoon, and the grassy hillside I spent most of my time examining with the binocs she was holding was dotted with nude bodies enjoying the afternoon sun.

"Uh, I use them on the balcony over here, for, um, for looking at sailboats on the Øresund." I pointed behind her toward Sweden. She paid no attention.

"Rex said something about this beach being quite popular. Oh. I see. These birds are all female and don't have any feathers." She turned around. "Why, Andy. I haven't seen you blush this much since we were getting to know each other last fall."

I led her across the backyard to the dock. It was almost ready to use, except for railings and areas of unfastened planks.

"Let's walk out to the end," I said, taking her hand and peering down at the water. She looked at the scattered tools and lumber lying around.

"What are you doing?"

"Looking for cod around the pilings. I thought maybe we might do some fishing."

"Are you sure it's safe? I have no intention of falling in." She let go of my hand and moved to the middle of the four-foot-wide structure.

"Everything's fine. Besides, it's not very deep. We could —" Waving my arms for balance as loose boards tipped, I splashed into the Øresund where I stood, spitting mouthfuls of icy water, looking up at the girl I most wanted to impress in this world.

"Andy! Are you all right?" Laughing hysterically, she hid her face in her hands.

Trembling, I pulled my body onto the sea wall and squished toward the house, followed by her laughter. At dinner, she described the whole sorry episode in minute detail, to the amusement of all but one.

# *Spring Vacation in Copenhagen*

I slept late the next morning, savoring the comfort of a real bed. At breakfast, Elena told us the dock would be ready by midafternoon.

"That's great, Elena." I began mentally planning our day. First, we would walk to Taarbaek village and see the harbor. After lunch, a spin on Pa's tandem bicycle through Dyrehaven. Returning, it would be time to go fishing. Then, after dinner, we'd watch Copenhagen's lights twinkle in the distance as we sat inside the gazebo making out. I would ask her to go to the prom with me. This was going to be a perfect day.

The phone rang. Alexander Graham Bell would have felt at home using this vintage contraption of exposed wires, magnets, and a hand crank to ring the operator. A braided cord linked it to a small hole in the wall. Where it went from there was known only to the Danish National Telephone Company and generations of mice. I picked up the receiver.

"What do you want, Doc?"

"Let me speak with June."

"Why?"

"Look, Lone Ranger: if you think just because she's

staying in the same house with you, it means you can hog her for rest of the week, think again. Now put her on."

I covered the speaker with my hand. "It's Doc. I was about to tell you what there is for us to do today. Call him back."

"Let me have the phone."

I handed it over.

"Hi, Doc."

After several minutes of laughter, punctuated by "Oooh, that would be wonderful. Yes, by all means. When?" she hung up.

"Now what?" I said, spilling my orange juice as I shoved my plate aside.

"Is something the matter?" she asked, with a touch of innocence.

"Well, I thought today I could show you Taarbaek Harbor, and we could take a bike ride in Dyrehaven, then maybe go fishing together."

I was rewarded with an affectionate look.

"I'm not sure about the bike ride or fishing, but I'd love to have you show me Taarbaek. Maybe we could go after I get back."

"From where?"

"Doc is going to drive over in his VW to take me sightseeing."

"His VW? It belongs to his father."

"He didn't know what your plans were," she teased, "but said there might be room in the back, if you want to come."

I wadded up my napkin and tossed it on the table. "Sounds great."

Within an hour the little car, its convertible top down, chugged into the driveway. Rex whipped open the door and waved June toward the rear seat.

"Welcome to Holt Tours, Beautiful. You will be sitting next to me today. Our driver will be Mr. "Eyes-on-the-Road" Gordon, who will point out a few sights here and there on the remote chance you get exhausted making love in the backseat."

I could see Doc, sitting behind the wheel, enjoying Rex's presentation.

"June, don't—" I stammered.

"What about Andy?" she asked. "Won't he be jealous if I spend the whole day making out with you, assuming two can even fit back there?"

"He can play with himself in the front. When he gets bored, he can help 'Eyes-on-the-Road' navigate."

"I think I'm bored already," said June. "I have a better idea: I'll sit with Doc so I won't miss anything, and you can make out with Andy."

"The hell he will."

"Get in the back, Andy," Doc ordered, motioning June into the passenger seat beside him. "You're safe—I don't think Rex is that horny."

"Where are we going?" she asked. "You mentioned an aquarium."

"That's in Charlottenlund, the next town over," I said.

"But we can't spend today indoors—it's too beautiful outside," June exclaimed.

She was right. The morning shouted to the world that spring had finally conquered Copenhagen's long winter. Beech tree branches displayed hints of pale green; the air temperature hovered around 68 degrees Fahrenheit; and low clouds resembling marshmallows dotted a sky the color of smoky sapphires.

"In that case," responded our chauffeur, "let's take a

scenic drive and show our visitor why we love Denmark. I know a beautiful shortcut through the woods. We'll see lots of deer, too."

"That sounds wonderful, Doc. Can I take pictures of them?"

"As many as you like."

The car turned onto a dirt service road toward Bakken. I leaned as far forward as I could from the cramped back seat. "Doc, you know cars aren't allowed inside Dyrehaven."

"Are we doing something illegal?" she asked, alarmed.

"These roads are for horse-drawn carriages," I said. "We'll probably end up handcuffed to each other in a Danish jail. It won't be as bad as the ones in Turkey, though."

"If you don't stop right now, Frederick Gordon, Andy and I will have a great time together for the rest of the vacation."

"Straight ahead, Doc. Go as far as you want into Dyrehaven," I chimed in from the rear seat.

"You win, June," he grinned. "Let's take the shore road to Helsingør and visit Kronborg."

Her eyes widened. "Hamlet's Castle?"

"The one and only."

"That would be fabulous."

After stopping at Doc's house to clear the trip with his mother and get a picnic lunch prepared by Brynne—the Gordons' equivalent of Elena—we headed north along the coast.

"I don't know about the rest of you," said Doc, when we were about halfway there, "but I'm getting hungry. What say we stop for lunch?"

Braking to let a family of ducks cross the road, he

pulled off at a small beach with a couple of wooden rowboats turned over on the sand. Rex started to open the lunch basket, but snapped it shut.

"This stuff smells like Andy's feet."

"It does smell like unwashed socks," June giggled, wrinkling her nose. "Open the box, Andy, and let's find out what it is."

I withdrew a container of soft, almost runny cheese.

Rex clamped his nose.

"It's cheese," I said. "I can't remember what it's called, but I think it's considered a Danish delicacy. Mom told me about it. She was at a dinner party, and everything went fine until this delicious-looking pie appeared for dessert. I think this must be the same stuff."

"What happened?" June asked.

"She had to leave the table when the first piece was served."

Rex gagged. "For God's sake, Barnes, chuck the stinking cheese."

"But what will I tell Brynne?" asked Doc. "That we thought the picnic lunch was great, but her special cheese smelled like Andy's feet so we threw it out?"

"I want to try it," said June.

While Doc opened four bottles of Majami—carbonated lemonade produced by the Tuborg Brewery—she dribbled the soft cheese over pieces of bread.

"Now, on the count of three." We each took a bite.

"This is yummy," I exclaimed, licking my lips.

"Best cheese I ever ate," said Doc. "Another, please?" She fixed several more and passed them around.

We sat on an overturned skiff, eating and talking. There was no wind, and the warm sun felt good on my winter-white face. A couple of bees arrived to sample our opened pop bottles. Eventually, the incoming tide told us it was time to go, and we left in a good mood—even Rex.

Arriving at Helsingør, Doc parked the car and we walked to Kronborg. Built hundreds of years ago to strategically command the entrance to the Øresund, its high walls and pointed spires stood out against a now-hazy sky. A pair of swans snoozed on the placid waters of the castle moat, paying no attention to children tossing bread at them.

"Why can't those ducks make an honest living eating that green scum in the water instead of getting fat on handouts?" asked Rex.

"It's watercress," said June, "and those children with the swans would make a marvelous picture." Taking her camera, she walked back and forth along the shore, composing snapshots.

"Did you get some good ones?" I asked, when she returned several minutes later.

"The one I took was superb."

"Only one?" asked Doc. "The object is to take several, then pick out the best."

"That's wasteful," she replied, advancing the film in her boxy little Brownie Hawkeye. "I don't like paying to develop pictures I'm going to throw away."

"Kee-rist," said Rex. "The joint will be closed before we get there."

It was—almost. We missed the last tour, but the ticket lady gave us some literature and sent us off to see as much as possible. If June was embarrassed by all the horny paintings on the ceilings of the royal bed chambers, she didn't show it. We saw the tapestries, many of which were hundreds of years old, and the ballroom with its gigantic fireplace.

"I think the guard wants people to leave," I said, sorry to miss the ship models in the maritime room and the statue of Hans Christian Andersen's legendary Holger Danske dozing in the castle cellar. As we returned to the car, fog was twisting over the gray waters of the Kattagat.

"Looks like rain on the way," I said as we put up the convertible top and squeezed in.

"I'm so glad we came today," said June. "I'll never forget this afternoon—or Brynne's delicious lunch."

I wasn't surprised waking up the next morning to a raw Easter Sunday. When I asked June if she'd like to go fishing after breakfast, she gave Mom a desperate look.

"I was counting on our guest to help with the Easter decorations, dear."

"I'd love to," June said, immediately.

Mom could be very annoying at times.

Out of self-respect, I collected my fishing gear and headed for the dock. After forty minutes of fruitless casts into a northerly gale, I succumbed to the weather gods. Back inside, I found June on the sofa, reading to Lissa.

"No fish?" she smiled.

"Andy only catches cold when he goes fishing," my sister exclaimed, sticking out her tongue at me. She ran off before I could grab her with my ice-cold hands.

"So what have you been doing besides reading?" I asked.

"While you were out there freezing, I helped your mother make flower arrangements and set the table. See?"

Inside the dining room, the table was a spectacle of Open Lace Royal Copenhagen place settings—the ones Mom used only for special occasions—accented with matching blue and white candles.

"I'm going to soak in the tub," I said. "Want to join me?"

She extended her arm. "Go."

Easter dinner was delicious, especially Elena's *rødgrød med fløde*—red pudding with cream—a traditional Danish dessert. By evening the rain had let up, so I asked if June would like to go to a movie.

"What's playing?"

"Three Coins in the Fountain. Have you seen it?"

"No, but it sounds like fun. Give me a few minutes to get ready."

"You'll like the Bellevue Theatre," said Mom. "It's old, but elegant inside."

The previews had started as we made our way down the dimly lit aisle, its rows of large soft seats—perfect for making out—almost empty. I picked two seats near the back.

"Why are there so few people? Because it's Easter?"

"Probably."

I knew the real reason; but this was the first chance I'd had to be alone with June in intimate surroundings since we arrived, and I was determined not to waste it. I put my arm across the back of her seat, and she didn't object when, a bit later, I gently squeezed her closer to me. As Jean Peters and her two roommates were emptying their pocket money into the Trevi Fountain, my hand inched further down until it came to rest on the front of June's sweater. It was there only a couple of seconds before she guided it back to her shoulder again.

"Down, boy. When I'm at a movie, I want to concentrate and not be distracted."

I started to remove my arm, but she pulled it back and snuggled closer.

"Oh, come on, Andy. Don't be offended. I'm flattered by your interest—really. But don't you think it's better to go slowly about these things? After all, I want you to have something to look forward to."

"If this is the best I can do, so be it."

When the movie was over, we waited under the theater portico for a heavy shower to subside.

"I'm sorry you didn't enjoy the evening," she said, gazing at the pelting rain.

"What are you talking about? I thought it was great."

"You fell asleep on my shoulder. You're the first date I ever had who got so bored he fell asleep in the middle of the movie."

"I was pretending, so you'd let my head slump on your shoulder. It was nice."

"You were so bored you fell asleep," she repeated.

"I did not. Ask me something. Go ahead."

"All right. Tell me what happened to Clifton Webb."

"He got a fatal disease, but married her anyway. All three of the girls found boyfriends, lost them, got back together again, and ultimately married them, right?"

"Yes. But I know you were asleep. How can you remember the rest of the movie?"

"I have a confession to make," I replied, wrapping my arms around her.

She raised her eyebrows. "Let's hear it, Lover Boy."

"Three Coins in the Fountain has been the only movie at the Bellevue since Thanksgiving. This is the third time I've seen it."

"Why, you sneak. You set me up."

Her eyes closed, and she didn't resist as I leaned toward parted lips.

For the rest of our vacation, Doc and Rex kept June constantly busy. I gave up hope of ever having her to myself and cursed Marissa for going to the French Riviera. The Four Musketeers (as Doc called us) scoured downtown Copenhagen, visiting stores and tea shops. June particularly liked the Glyptotek museum, with its sculptures and paintings by Danish and French impressionists.

"My feet hurt," I said after we'd been standing around for hours while she examined every Renoir and Degas.

"Those two have the right idea," commented Rex, pointing to Auguste Rodin's statue of two naked lovers wrapped in each other's arms.

"I guess this place has some redeeming qualities after all," commented Doc.

"The trouble is," Rex went on, "this guy, Rodent, screwed it all up."

"What do you mean?" asked June. "This is one of the most famous pieces of sculpture in the world. And by the way, Rex, his name is Rodin—not Rodent."

"Well, I don't think he went far enough," Rex continued. "I mean, if he had given his models a bit more time before he chipped them out of that chunk of rock, he could have had a statue of two people … you know … actually doing it."

"You're positively hopeless," June exclaimed, whacking him with her museum brochure. "All of you. You only have one thing on your minds."

# Heart to Heart

The week flew by, and every day something occupied the times I tried to be alone with my special house guest. Then, the day before vacation ended, June and I were finishing breakfast on the patio. I put down my toast.

"What is it, Andy?"

"Could we spend this morning together—just the two of us? I want to show you the statue of The Little Mermaid. You'll like it. We can be back by lunchtime, if you want. Please?"

Her eyes lingered on mine, then wandered to the phone in its pantry niche. By now, I despised that octopus of magnets and wires—it had ruined my vacation. As if on cue, it rang.

"Hi, Doc. Why did I know it was going to be you?" She listened a minute and laughed. "That sounds wonderful, but not this morning. How about sometime this afternoon, after Andy and I get back? No, you and Rex can't come. No, Doc. Sorry. That's a secret," she laughed. "No. None of your business." She put her hand over the phone. "He says he'll expect a full account of everything that happened as soon as we get back."

"Tell him to drop dead and hang up. We have to hurry."

I took our dishes into the kitchen while she ran upstairs to get fixed up—something I never thought she needed to do.

We barely made the S-train at the Klampenborg station, leaping into the last silver car seconds before its automatic doors whirred shut. As the train quickly accelerated, we lurched onto comfortable seats next to a window in an empty compartment. June's cheeks were pink from sun and salt air, which, I noticed for the first time, had frizzed her hair a bit. Shivering, she pulled her blue wool coat tighter. The style was all the rage that year—double breasted, with two rows of buttons between wide lapels. She shook again.

"How can you be cold? You're wrapped up like an Eskimo." Then I realized temperature had nothing to do with it. "You're thinking about something, aren't you?"

She stared out the window at unseen scenery flashing by.

"My mother; a bunch of things."

"Pa swears that Bethesda Naval Med is the finest hospital anywhere. The Navy doctors have the newest equipment and will know the best way to treat her. Your dad will be there, and that's a big comfort, too. Don't worry, she'll come through."

"Why is it when I'm with you, I feel you understand me?" she answered, studying my face. Her voice dropped to a whisper. "Even when you make me mad, I care about you. You're the only person I've ever met I've felt this way about."

I struggled for a reply. She had never said anything like this before.

"I don't have the experience with girls that Doc and Rex have, but right now, all I know is that it's painful to see how much you're hurting. It's about Doc, isn't it?"

"He doesn't communicate, Andy. He never has. He always ends up kidding around. And I know he's writing to somebody, a Danish Countess. Rex told me," she added, seeing the look on my face. "I didn't believe him, but when Doc refused to talk about it, I knew it was true...." She wiped a meandering tear with the back of her hand. "Why can't he tell me it's over between us?"

"I, I don't think he can," I said, softly.

"Why not?" The pent-up anger in her voice caught me off guard.

"I'm not sure, June. But I think it has to do with not wanting to hurt you."

"Doesn't he know that's exactly what he's doing? Can't he tell?" She looked away.

"I've told him a number of times it's better to be honest and to tell you how he feels. He knows. But he seems to have this fear of saying it to your face. Too embarrassing, maybe? Afraid he might cry? Too brutal? If he found a way that wouldn't be painful for both of you ... I wish I knew, June."

Crying softly, she pressed her head against the front of my jacket. I kissed her forehead, and the words tumbled out.

"I'm envious that he still shares your heart, sweet June. We both love him. Next to you, Doc's the best friend I ever had. I just wish I were as important in your life as he is. Right now, the only thing I can think of is a poem by ... by one of those women poets we had to read in English class: 'Pity me that the heart is slow to learn what the swift mind beholds at every turn.' I don't remember the rest."

Her arms were around my neck so tightly I could barely breathe.

"That was Edna St. Vincent Millay," she whispered in my ear. "And yes, Andy, you are more important to me than," she paused, "even Doc."

I couldn't believe what I heard her saying—words I had longed for all year. For several minutes we sat wrapped together, cheeks damp, our bodies rocking with the motion of the train.

Then, at the sight of her reflection in the window, she straightened up.

"Boy, am I a mess."

"Now that you mention it, you do sort of look like a red-eyed raccoon—but a beautiful one," I added, quickly. "Seriously, it's so important we can trust each other with our feelings. They shouldn't get trapped inside."

Hellerup Station came and went as we sat, lost in the quiet of our thoughts. Whatever future we had during the remaining weeks of school hinged on Doc's taking the initiative: he had to tell her their relationship was finished in a way he felt did not hurt her.

She broke the silence.

"We need to talk about Doc so we can figure this out. Normally, I wouldn't think of telling anyone about my feelings toward someone else, or of asking you to do it, either. But for both of us—for whatever time we have left together—we must be on the same track here."

There was no turning back.

"Sometimes," I began, "I feel I know him really well—that's usually when we're having fun—which is often."

I told her about the time he took me to ride the elevator in the I.G. Farben Building.

"He said I had to get down on my hands and knees because it continues past the top floor and flips over when it starts down again—in other words, the ceiling becomes the elevator floor on the way down. Of course, no such thing happened. I was on my hands and knees crawling around when it stopped at the top floor again, and a bunch of high-ranking Army officers in dress uniforms got in. Talk about embarrassing!"

When we stopped laughing, I told her about several other episodes, including the time Doc bet me "movie tickets and burgers at the PX snack bar" that he could make the always-inquisitive Germans in downtown Frankfurt look at nothing.

"What?" June gave me a quizzical look.

"It's true, June. We were arguing about how they stare at us in town, and I said it was because we were Americans. He said it wasn't, the Germans would look at anything, and he would prove it. 'I can get them to look at nothing,' he insisted. You have to remember this was sometime last fall, before I knew him as well as I do now," I added.

"So what happened?" she asked.

"I should have known better. Like an idiot I said, 'You're on, Doc,' and we took a tram downtown to a busy street corner with crowded sidewalks. He stops, looks up, and points excitedly at the roof of a building. 'Look up,' he orders, shaking my shoulder, 'and point.' 'But Doc,' I said, 'there aren't even pigeons up there.' 'You're getting smarter,' he replies."

"So who paid for the movie, Andy?"

"I did, of course. Within five minutes there were at least fifty people standing there, pointing up at the roof. The traffic slowed down. We watched from across the street until a police car arrived."

We shared another laugh at my expense.

"I've never known anyone in such good physical shape," I mused, thinking of Doc climbing up and down the ropes in the gym, arm over arm, four times without stopping. "He's got more energy than he knows what to do with, and maybe that's why he pushes himself to the limit. Like when we went ice skating during Christmas on that pond in Dyrehaven I told you about. He raced around the whole time, only slowing down after dark when everybody was gone and the northern lights illuminated the ice. It was like he was inside pastel curtains God put there especially for him."

"There are times when I don't understand him at all, like the swimming pool incident," June shuddered. "Those risky things he does scare me, Andy. Did you know Doc had been to that pool the year before?"

"Yeah. Now that I think of it, he probably organized the trip just so he could jump off that stupid platform."

"When he started up those ladders, I felt sick to my stomach. I knew something bad was going to happen—I could feel it. Why did he go up there? Why?"

"It wasn't solely to show off," I replied, "although that was part of it. I think it was the danger. Like the platform was an unfinished challenge left over from last year—it was there, so he had to do it. He wanted me to go with him. I told him 'no way,' and I tried to talk him out of it. But his mind was made up. When he gets like that, he reminds me of a Siamese cat I had in Newport. It would sit on the porch and stare at the street for the longest time, then run straight across without stopping."

"What happened to—no, don't answer that."

"I'll give you another example." I recounted the story of the storm on the Øresund with Inge and Kirsten, and how Doc badgered the girls into staying out after the race.

"I'm not sure I want to hear the rest of this, either," she interrupted.

"I'll stop if you want, but it's a good example of how he craves situations where he can test himself—even if he has to set them up."

She nodded, so I continued—about how he climbed up the slippery mast, risking his life to fix the halyard. "So what does he do at the top? He starts goofing off and almost falls. If he'd hit the deck, or gone overboard, that would have been it—end of story. I'll never forget that night."

"It sounds like that trip was almost the end of the story for all of you." She pulled her coat tighter around her neck. "It certainly shows Doc at his mixed-up worst, which brings me back to our central question—why does he crave doing those things?"

I couldn't think of anything more to say. Our conversation had produced no conclusions, no plan regarding Doc. But something had changed—our feelings toward each other—how I felt about expressing myself to this amazing girl next to me. It was as if I'd been doing it all my life. Being together seemed natural. The train slowed.

"Hey, Østerport Station coming up. Let's go see The Little Mermaid."

"I'd love that."

We stepped off the train into a fragile—but new and wonderful—relationship. If I hadn't lost my temper that night at WAC Circle, would it have happened earlier?

We approached The Little Mermaid, Denmark's best-loved and most famous statue. She sits alone at the edge of Copenhagen's harbor, lost in sadness. June raised her camera, then lowered it.

"Out of film?"

"I don't need a picture, Andy. She's timeless. I want to

remember her sitting on her rock by the sea, pensive, beautiful."

"Do you know the story?"

"I remember she fell in love with a prince and it ended unhappily."

"Yeah. His old man made him marry some princess, so The Little Mermaid died of a broken heart. Anyway, millions of people around the world still love her."

On the return trip neither of us said much. She snuggled close as the train hissed in and out of the familiar stations. How to get Doc to have a serious talk with her kept turning over in my mind. Time was running out for all three of us.

When we arrived at the house, the red Beetle was parked in the driveway.

"Looks like they've been here a while," I said, putting my hand on its cold engine cover.

"A little waiting will do them good," she replied, kissing my ear as I pushed open the front door for her.

In the kitchen, Rex was pestering Elena, as usual. Doc stood at the sink, making a mess of skinning an otherwise nice piece of salmon. Elena gave an exaggerated sigh of relief as her tormentors immediately surrounded June. Rex made a point of subtly pushing me aside as he stepped between us, but his latest slight didn't bother me.

On our last day in Copenhagen, Doc and Rex didn't show up. After a morning of packing, we took an afternoon tandem bike ride through Dyrehaven. The beech trees were greener than when we'd arrived, and early wildflowers added scattered patches of yellow and purple to the forest's palette. New spring fawns, fuzzy coats dotted with white spots, frolicked or nursed from their mothers. At one point we observed a flock of jackdaws making life miserable for a hawk perched on a dead branch.

That evening after dinner, the two of us walked out to the end of the dock. Moonlight shimmered on riffled patches of breeze across the surface of the Øresund, reminding me of glittering schools of tiny ivory fish. In the distance, the lights of Copenhagen winked in the fading dusk. June rubbed her arms.

"It's cooler than I thought," she said, resting her head on my neck. "I should have worn a warmer sweater."

"Let's go inside," I said, opening the gazebo door. As we sat down on the wicker bench, I draped my jacket over her shoulders.

"I'm going to miss this wonderful place and your family," she said.

"I'll miss not having you here. Your cheery face made every day special. When I first asked you that day in the snack bar, I was afraid you'd turn me down."

She smiled. "For the chance to visit Copenhagen, I decided you were worth the risk. It was good for me to be doing fun, interesting things—instead of spending ten horrible days with the Cardonis in Ankara, worrying about Mother."

"There were times when I knew you were mentally with her; but I'm glad Copenhagen helped make things easier. It was great that you and Mom got along so well. She likes you a lot—we all do."

"Your mother made me feel like I was family. Everyone has been so nice."

I squeezed her shoulder. "Because of you, I'll never forget this Easter—despite the fact that Doc and Rex practically lived here."

"Don't underestimate yourself, Andy. I know it wasn't

great for you to watch me enjoying myself with them. But it's not often a girl gets to have three handsome escorts every day for ten days. Maybe we didn't get to spend much time together, but in a way I'm glad. Otherwise, we might have ended up not doing much else, if you know what I mean."

I certainly did, but before I could respond she continued.

"I want you to know that even without Doc and Rex, I would still have had a wonderful time with you alone."

I leaned toward her. "June, can I … I mean, would you mind if … I wondered if …." Finally, I heard myself say, "Thank you."

She looked down, shaking her head. Her curly hair swished against my cheek as she took my face in both hands. Then warm lips pressed against mine in an unhurried kiss. I took her in my arms, gently pressing the small of her back. My jacket fell from her shoulders, her body relaxed, and we swayed ever so slightly in the shadows of that bright night. I don't remember how many times we kissed, each with tenderness I had never known. She did not stop my hand as it wandered, caressing gently. The wavelets lapping against the dock, the soft wind filtering around the gazebo—even the beauty of the moon's endless light—all ebbed from my consciousness. There was only June.

Her hand brushed my face, fingers coming to rest on my lips. "I think it's time to go back," she whispered, easing her cheek away.

"Do we have to?"

"Yes."

Slowly, we stood. I opened the gazebo door as she

straightened her dress and fluffed her hair. A channel marker's lonely bell echoed across the Øresund in the darkness.

# Piece of Cake

The next morning, our departure cast a shadow over the breakfast table. Finishing his ham and eggs, Pa glanced at his watch.

"I have a meeting today, so Major McManus will be flying you back to Rhein-Main."

"Who's he?" I asked.

"The new assistant air attaché. Mac is one of the finest pilots in the Air Force. Before he went to Korea, he flew the Independence."

June looked at him, her eyes blank.

"President Truman's personal plane," Pa said, smiling at her.

After breakfast we took a last walk out to the dock, where wind-whipped flecks of foam from whitecaps raced across the water. June reached for my hand.

"Andy, I want to thank you for being so tolerant this past week."

"Thank you for last night," I replied, kissing her. It just happened. Her body tensed, relaxed, and I felt her arms around my neck.

"Come, you two," called Mom from the house. "I'm afraid it's time to leave."

I slipped my arm around her waist, and we turned our backs on the Øresund.

While I carried down June's suitcase, the phone rang.

"For you, Captain Barnes," called Elena.

"What is it, dear?" asked Mom, alert to his somber face when he returned.

"That was Mac at the airport. He doesn't like the weather report and wants to leave as soon as possible. Time to go, kids."

While Aage loaded our luggage, Elena put a small packet into June's hands. "Some recipes to remember Denmark," she smiled. The two of them embraced.

"It's been wonderful having you," snuffled Mom, hugging June. "I wish you could stay longer. Give my love to your parents and tell Cora she will be in my prayers."

At the plane, pandemonium reigned. The whole Gordon family was there. Doc's little sisters shrieked as he chased them around miscellaneous luggage, which Chief Fleming was stowing in the back of the aircraft as quickly as he could. Somebody's dog raised its leg on somebody's suitcase. Off to one side, General Holt was browbeating Rex about how important it was to get good grades so he could enter the Air Force Academy. Saying goodbye to Pa and Aage, June and I followed one of the other girls aboard. Handing Chief Fleming the coat hanger with her red prom gown, she begged him to put it where it wouldn't wrinkle. That's when I remembered: I'd completely forgotten to ask June to the prom. We sat down, picking the two forwardmost seats overlooking the portside engine. Through our window we watched Doc cavorting with his sisters. Flipping the littlest one onto his shoulders, he danced around while the others clamored for their turns.

"C'mon, Gordon," the chief yelled, drumming his fingers against the plane's aluminum skin. "If we're going to get to Frankfurt before the storm front, we have to leave right now, son."

After hugging each little girl and his mother, Doc trotted up the boarding ladder and sat down in the aisle seat behind us.

"Mind if we swap seats?" he asked Rex, leaning over him to rap the window. "I want to wave to my sisters."

"Yes, I do mind," Rex started to say, but Doc paid no attention. "Ouch. Get off, you oaf. Haven't you seen enough of them this past week?"

The engines whined into life and the prop outside our window became a whirring, yellow-edged circle. Abruptly, a belch of flame spurted from its engine cowling. The whole plane shook, and a puff of heavy smoke engulfed everybody outside.

"What was that?" June exclaimed, clutching my arm.

"I don't know," I answered. "Do you, Doc?"

He shrugged. "A backfire? Sometimes they do that when they start."

Chief Fleming peered intently through our window at the engine—now responding with its customary, throaty roar—before disappearing into the cockpit.

Twisting around, I saw Doc, his nose pressed against Rex's window, waving to his oldest sister. She stood in front of her three siblings, shielding them from the prop wash, trying to hold her dress down with one hand and blow him a kiss with the other. As blond hair streamed across her face, I saw her lips form soundless words: "Bye, Doc."

"Bye, Chippy," I heard him say.

The plane turned, taxied out, and waited for a big

Scandinavian Airlines DC-7 on its final approach. Major Mac kept revving the port engine, testing it. Then we were rolling down the runway, smoothly picking up speed. The tail rose and the old seagull lifted into its element. June and I looked down at the spot where the still waving families were. In a second or two, they were gone.

Reaching its cruising altitude of 9,000 feet, the plane bounced in unstable air from cumulus clouds that became raggedy, tall, and numerous. Later, as we crossed into Germany, purple-black thunderheads appeared across the sky like sinister clusters of Portuguese man o' wars. Chief Fleming emerged from the cockpit with a handful of sick bags.

"Everybody is to stay strapped in their seats at all times —major's orders." He extended one to June, but she shook her head.

"I've never been airsick," I said. "Have you?"

"Let's talk about something else."

"June, I've wanted to ask you this for a long time."

"What is it?"

"I mean, um, would you go to the prom with me?"

She stiffened with an expression that couldn't conceal frustration. Instead of the big smile and immediate "yes" I'd hoped for, I got an uncomfortable pause.

"There's no one I'd love to go to the prom with more than you, Andy," she finally said. "Especially after all the wonderful times we've had this past week. Please believe me. But I can't. You're too late. I've already been asked, and I accepted."

I stared straight ahead. Barnes, you dumb, stupid ... you should have listened to Doc and asked her weeks ago, when he warned you about how important the prom was.

"Why didn't you ask me before anyone else?" she asked,

exasperation in her voice.

"You know how I am—I put things off until the last minute. I thought of it several times, but I forgot. I'm really sorry, June."

Her eyes flashed. "That's not good enough, when it comes to inviting a girl to the prom. The sooner she knows, the better. People have been asking me for—"

"You must have known you're the only person I wanted to go with. When we were flying up from Frankfurt, I told myself, 'I'll wait and ask her this week when we're together.' You knew I'd ask you, eventually. Couldn't you keep a waiting list, or something?"

I shrank into my seat, knowing before I'd finished that this was not the thing to say.

"I can't believe you," she shot back. "You expect me to keep a list of prospective dates for the biggest dance of the year, so they can twiddle their thumbs while you make up your mind? What about their feelings? What am I supposed to say, 'Sorry, but if Andy Barnes doesn't ask me, I'll be happy to go with you'?"

"No, of course not. That wouldn't be right. I'm not making sense, am I?"

"That's the first sane thing you've said during this whole idiotic conversation. I wasn't happy about it either, but I had to accept the first person who asked me. There is a code of ethics involved. Do you understand?"

I nodded, unable to think of a reply. "Who is it?"

"Technically, that's not your business. This time, however, I'm going to tell you, rather than let you find out from the individual concerned or others, who would probably tell you in ways that would make you angry at me all over again—maybe more than you are right now."

"I'm not mad at you, June; I'm mad at myself—furious.

It's my fault, not yours."

She closed her hand over mine. "I'm going to the prom with Rex."

My body tightened. "Not him. June—you can't."

"Yes, I can, and I intend to see that he has a good time. That's my part of the bargain."

The wing dipped, skittering luggage across the floor behind us. She grabbed my arm.

"What bargain?" I snapped back, unable to think straight. "He doesn't care about you. As far as girls go, he's only interested in one thing. I know. That's all he brags about in the dorm."

"I'm sure you all think about that."

"Not the way he does," I spit out.

"Calm down. I don't want us to fight again."

"Me either," I stammered. "But I'm worried about … I don't want anything to happen to you, you know, with him."

She twisted slightly, making sure no one could hear, and lowered her voice. "Nothing is going to happen—I promise you, so don't worry. I understand how you must feel, but after this week, I know Rex better than you think."

The plane took a hard bounce, and her fingers dug into my arm.

"You and I are solid individuals—Doc also—though Doc is Doc," she said with a half-smile. "We have loving families, and parents that allowed us to develop self-confidence and taught us how to enjoy growing up."

"What are you getting at?"

"Just this: there are kids like Rex who aren't as fortunate as we've been."

"So, you accepted because you feel sorry for him? Rex

is so brittle, you were afraid he'd break into pieces if you didn't—" Fortunately, I caught myself. I knew I was one step away from undoing every good thing that had happened during the previous week. "I'm sorry. I have no right to go on like this. I know you can take care of yourself. And you're right about Rex, I guess. I've never cared much for him, but I suppose he must have a good side."

"That's better. His background is completely opposite from yours. He's an only child, so he never had siblings around to teach him he wasn't the center of the universe."

"They do have a way of doing that, don't they?" I said, mostly to myself.

Her eyes softened, as she repressed a smile.

"This whole vacation he never once invited us over to see his house or meet his folks. In fact, I don't remember him even mentioning them. Today at the airport, his father was chewing him out like some lowly recruit. The two of them have a miserable relationship. Do you think Rex would ever have asked General Holt about inviting me for Easter vacation? If he had, we both know what the answer would have been. Rex covers up his insecurities by being the way he is. In any case, that's how I see it. Just remember, Andy," she concluded, "that although I feel sorry for Rex, I'm not attracted to him, so try to be tolerant."

"I think you've sized him up pretty well," I admitted. "Until now, I only saw him as an adversary; but you've helped me see that he has another side."

The plane jolted upward, and June's grip on my arm tightened.

"If I come to the prom," I asked, "can I at least have one dance?"

Her lips flirted with a smile.

"I would be furious if you didn't dance with—"

A brilliant flash, instantaneously accompanied by a crash of the loudest thunder I had ever heard. A sizzling noise, wisps of smoke, and the cabin went black. We were falling. It was as if a giant hand had thrown us toward earth. My eardrums popped, and everything not tied down smashed against the ceiling at the same time. The harsh, tearing sound of metal ripping apart, a rush of bitterly cold air, screams, a bone-jarring "thud" that pressed us into our seats. Then we were lifting upward, as if inside a powerful elevator. Hail clattered against the fuselage like machine gun bullets. Thankfully, we were all tightly strapped in, so nobody was hurt.

In the eerie glow of the cabin's emergency lights, I turned to see Doc staring at the boarding ladder. It was sticking halfway through the ceiling at an angle, as though angry storm gods outside had harpooned the old R4D. We looked at each other, then at the ladder again, saying nothing. He was wired into this crisis, living for the moment of its conclusion, good or bad, while the rest of us were too terrified to think straight. I heard vomiting. June clapped her hands over her ears and stared straight ahead, her face the color of beach sand. Chief Fleming emerged from the cockpit and groped his way aft to the ladder. With a tremendous yank it came free, crashing on top of him. He sucked in his breath as blood spewed from his forehead. Staggering past us toward the cockpit, he left a trail of bloody handprints on each seat back he grasped for support. More barfing somewhere behind us. June's fingernails dug into my shirt-sleeve.

Then, outside our window came a grinding noise, followed by a high-pitched whine and violent shuddering.

When we looked the prop was spinning freely, like a wayward, three-bladed windmill.

"What the hell's that?" said Rex.

"Looks like the port engine's out," Doc replied. It was the same one Major Mac had been revving as we waited for takeoff at Kastrup Airport. The wing dipped and the plane rolled to the left, thrusting me against June. She was pressing her rigid body as far away from the window as possible. The nose tipped downward, and I felt power to our remaining engine decrease.

"He's trying to maintain airspeed, so the ailerons and rudder will work well enough to get us level again," Doc continued, as if narrating some airplane disaster movie. There was no sign of panic in his voice.

"Jesus, Doc," said Rex. "Listening to you, you'd think we were in a friggin' laboratory."

For the first time in months I laughed at a Rex comment. Then the nose came up as Major Mac added partial power to the starboard engine, and little by little we returned to level flight.

Chief Fleming leaned over us as he studied the port engine through our window. Blood oozed from gauze pads on his forehead, held in place by twists of black electrical tape.

"Okay," he yelled in the direction of the cockpit. "Hit it."

A powerful explosion. Pieces of metal sprayed against the fuselage as parts of the engine vanished, leaving a river of dark liquid spreading over the wing.

"Shit!" uttered the chief, under his breath. "Cut it! Cut it!" He ran forward into the cockpit, slamming the door.

Outside, tongues of blue flickered into uneven spasms of orange yellow. June recoiled.

"Is that glow what I think it is?" Her voice was flat, expressionless. Across the wing, trails of oil from the remains of the engine burst into flame—only a few feet from our window. We were on fire.

"I love you, June," I blurted out. "I always will."

There was a "whoosh" sound, like compressed air escaping, and the flames became streams of smoke.

"We'll get down in one piece," I said, forcing myself to sound upbeat. "Major Mac is the best pilot in Copenhagen, remember?"

She made no reply, but I knew things were better, because her grip on my forearm loosened.

Nearing Frankfurt, occasional filtered glimpses of sunlight poked through the storm as its violence decreased. We were not out of danger, but at least our stricken aircraft was still flying. At one point, Alfie announced, "I didn't even wet my pants."

"Oh, shut up, Guppy," said Rex.

"You certainly would have been forgiven if you had," Doc replied, giving our chemistry tutor a thumbs-up.

"June, I feel really bad for almost messing up everything, just when things were starting to work for us," I said. "I'm sorry for being such a jerk."

She took my hand. "I only get angry at people who are very important to me. Otherwise, I wouldn't have said any of those things to you."

"There was something I wanted to give you," I said, "before all this happened."

Checking to make sure Chief Fleming wasn't in sight, I unsnapped my seatbelt and half stood, reaching into the pocket of my Levis.

"What's the matter with you?" June exclaimed. "Sit down."

I plopped back, clicking the seatbelt on the second try.

"For you," I said, putting a crushed package into her hand.

"I never expected—thank you. Do you want me to open it now or later?" she smiled.

"Whenever you wish."

Demolishing the wrappings, June carefully removed the inner tissue paper, exposing a tiny sterling silver charm.

"It's The Little Mermaid sitting on her rock, and the rock is a tiny bell," she exclaimed, jingling it next to her ear. "It's beautiful, Andy. I don't know what to say."

"You don't have to say anything. I'm glad you're happy with it."

"I love it. When did you get this?"

"While you were biking with Doc and Rex, I told Mother how much you liked The Little Mermaid, and she said, 'June must have a charm bracelet. Why don't you get her one of those Royal Copenhagen Little Mermaid charms?' Then she told me about a jewelry shop downtown that carried them, and gave me some extra money, just in case. So, I went back and got it for you. Something to remember Copenhagen by," I said, almost to myself.

"You know, Andy, your sensitivity is a special gift, and now that I've stayed with your family, I can see where it comes from. There's only one problem."

"What's that?"

"I don't have a charm bracelet."

"What, exactly, is a charm bracelet? I never heard of them until the other day."

"Lots of girls like to collect charms from places they've been, and put them on a bracelet to wear. Believe it or not, no one ever gave me a charm until now."

I made a mental note to find her a bracelet in downtown Frankfurt.

As the flaps lowered and main gear whirred into place, Chief Fleming appeared again.

"In a couple of minutes, we'll be making an emergency landing. Our remaining engine is performing normally, and the plane is under control, so everything should be fine. But just in case, I want everybody tightly strapped in and prepared to exit the aircraft quickly, if necessary. Don't worry," he added, as an afterthought.

"I know he means well," June whispered, "but the way that man says things upsets me."

We began our final approach. Treetops rushed past, followed by grass marking the edge of safety. Firetrucks and a couple of ambulances swept by our window as the tarmac reached up to receive us. A bump, another, and Pa's battered R4D was on the ground. We clapped and cheered, and there was plenty of hugging. I held June until we were as entwined as humanly possible, considering we were strapped in and separated by an armrest.

The plane lost speed and Major McManus braked. Sirens caught up with us and asbestos-suited men--white ghosts waving red fire extinguishers--sprayed foam over the port engine. Medics rushed aboard. Spying the chief's bloody forehead, they plastered it with bandages. We could hear him cussing as they dragged him to a waiting ambulance. Men in overalls cleaned barf off our suitcases before loading them onto a blue Air Force bus. As I helped June off the plane, she took my arm.

"Now you have to get yourself a date for the prom, Mr. Barnes."

I knew she meant it innocently enough, but my immediate reaction was another flash of anger for not asking her before Rex did. I couldn't see myself with anyone but June.

Major Mac appeared, and we gave him a prolonged round of applause.

"That was the best piece of flying I've ever seen," said Doc, summing up how we all felt. "You should get a medal."

"Piece of cake," he smiled, putting his hand on my roommate's shoulder.

# *Spring Fever*

The Frankfurt spring of 1957 was a sparkle of clear, damp mornings, warm days, and trees sporting umbrellas of new green. Bulb gardens flashed rainbows of color, and birds greeted us with early-morning song. None of this was conducive to studying.

"I hope you had a superb Easter vacation," said Miss McCafferty as she brought our first English class to order. "I trust you are recharged and ready to work for our remaining four weeks."

I stared at the Stars and Stripes outside, wrapping and unwrapping around its white flagpole. I was sitting in the gazebo with June, looking at slivers of moonlight on the Øresund.

"Now that Andy is alert," Miss McCafferty continued, without looking at me, "it is time for the highlight of the year, your Junior English Research Paper."

I'd heard seniors talking about this miserable thing—the JERP—and more than a few of us wished Miss McCafferty's appendix would rupture, necessitating a substitute.

"As a special treat," she continued, "I have decided to

let you choose your topic—either instructional, or about your life."

June chose breast cancer as her topic. Doc chose to write his autobiography. He submitted a meticulous outline starting with birth, which our teacher approved after considerable editorial surgery. At the last possible moment, I turned in a proposal about Mozart. "Wolfgang," it began, "was a composer." Miss McCafferty requested I stay after class.

"Tell me, Andy, besides June Everett, what are you most interested in?"

My face turned tomato red as I stood in front of her, unable to speak.

"I … June … how?" I stammered.

"Apologies, Andy, but long before vacation you were spending most of my class staring across the room at her. Teachers do notice these things," she added, her eyes twinkling. "Now, think a minute, and then answer my question. What are you most interested in?"

"Bass fishing, ma'am."

"Fishing it is, then. I know nothing about it, so you can enlighten me. Get to work."

I decided to write a manual on how to catch largemouth black bass. Having spent the previous two years catching several hundred of them in Florida, I could write it from memory. Besides, there was nothing in the school library on the subject, probably because bass didn't exist in Europe. I figured this would make my bibliography easier.

Academics, however, paled in significance to the forthcoming prom. It was on everyone's mind, especially June's.

"Who have you asked?" she inquired, after school a few days later.

"I'm working on it."

"You said that yesterday. You must ask someone now. Your date needs time to get ready."

"For some reason I fail to understand, it's important to you that I get a date. Every day you want to know the same thing."

"Andy, lots of sweet girls who haven't been asked would love to go with you."

"If I can't take you, I won't have a good time."

I shrank before eyes of glittering kryptonite.

"When are you going to stop feeling sorry for yourself? You're the one responsible for the fact that we aren't going to the prom together. I'm glad I'm going with Rex, if only to teach you a lesson about how to make the best of things that don't turn out the way you want them to. Life is like that."

She walked off, leaving me to pick up the pieces of what had been, up to then, a nice day. I knew she was right, and it made me angry at myself all over again.

"Have a great time with Rex," I yelled after her, "because I'm not going to be there to see you with him."

June started to turn around, but then continued.

That night after study hours, Rex stood behind me in the snack bar line.

"Since we got back from Copenhagen, she's warmed up to my charms a lot, Barnes," he crowed, as I paid Alfie for my sandwich.

"Who are you talking about, Holt? The dorm cleaning lady?"

"My beautiful date for the prom—June Everett, of course. I think you know her?"

Saying nothing, I headed back to my room. Rex followed. "We won't stay at the dance long. I've made reservations at a nightclub downtown, overlooking the river. Very romantic place."

"How nice." I took a bite of the puffy white bread cemented together with peanut butter and grape jelly, and kept walking.

"First I'll get her drunk, then we'll go to a hotel for some exquisite pussy."

"Knock it off, Rex. We both know that's not going to happen."

As I turned away, he gave me a shove, hard. Spinning around, I flattened my sandwich in his face. Throwing a half-eaten Clark bar aside, he lunged. As I grabbed his collar with both hands I slipped (Alfie told me later it was on the sandwich) and fell backward. Rex's momentum flipped him over my head, where he landed on his back.

"OOOW," he yelped. "My wrist. I can't move my hand," he cried, getting up carefully. "It's broken, damn you."

"You started it, you jerk!."

"What's going on here?"

Spectators froze as The Kreebs strode toward us. He smiled.

"A fight, is it? Fighting in the dorm is punishable by expulsion. Did Barnes do this to you, Holt? Speak up."

Rex gave me an "I could fix you good" look, and I held my breath.

"We were fooling around and I slipped," he answered, grimacing as The Kreebs reached for his wrist. "Don't touch it. Something's broken. I need a doctor."

"Yes," said Kreebert, quickly letting go. "It does appear serious. I must fill out an accident report. Then I'll write a permission slip for you and an escort to go to the hospital."

"I'll see that he gets there and back safely," volunteered

Doc, who arrived too late to witness the fight.

Rex nodded, and the two of them trailed The Kreebs downstairs. I went back to our room.

Several hours later, Doc returned and climbed into his bunk.

"The X-rays showed a definite break. His forearm's in a cast, but he'll be okay."

"Serves him right."

"I can't believe you," said June, pulling me aside the next day. "When are you going to grow up? Do you have any idea how embarrassing it is to have two otherwise sensible men throwing jelly sandwiches at each other because I'm going to the prom with one of them? Between classes today, I overheard several girls giggling about 'The Jelly Queen incident.'"

I hadn't seen her so mad since our fight at WAC Circle. For a moment I thought she was going to slap me.

"It wasn't my fault, June. Rex started it. I tried to walk away, and he shoved me from behind. It's the truth. Ask anyone who was there."

"I don't want to hear anything more about it, from you or anyone. Is that clear?" she replied, loud enough to turn heads of passersby. She stormed off like a departing thundercloud, leaving me to wonder when lightning bolts would next strike.

That night during study hours, Doc and I were working on our JERPs. He picked up several of my crumpled title pages, flattening them on our desk.

"'How to Catch Largemouth Black Bass. Bass on a Fly Rod. Live Shrimp for Lunkers.' Are you planning to publish this in Field & Stream Magazine?"

"Oh, shut up."

"What's bugging you, Lone Ranger?"

"Nothing. Everything's fine, just fine."

He wadded up "Live Shrimp for Lunkers" and threw it at me. "Don't gimme that. After all these months, I can tell when something's bothering you. Let me see. It can't be Rex—you busted his arm like it was a potato chip. The prom? I know you and June had another row about it. No. Nothing out of the ordinary on that score. But it is June, isn't it?"

"Mind your own business or—"

"Or what? You'll bust me up like you did Rex?" He shook his head. "How do you manage to keep messing up with her? Do you like being miserable?"

"Of course not. I'm mad at myself, because I didn't follow your advice and missed my chance to take her to the prom. There. Are you happy?" I squeezed one of my title pages into a tight ball and threw it at the closet.

"Have you thought about pitching for the Red Sox?"

"Please, Gordon. I'm not in the mood for your humor." I buried my face in my hands.

"So, Lone Ranger, what can I do to get you out of this funk? When Doc Gordon makes up his mind something's going to happen, it happens, remember?"

"No, I don't remember. What are you talking about?"

"I'm serious. Since you can't, I'll have to solve your problem—for all our sakes."

"Okay, Mr. Fix-It. How about one dance with June at the prom? Can you manage that? Just one dance would do it. I need something to hope for."

He frowned. "Jeez, Andy. Why don't you ask her?"

"I did, on the plane. She almost agreed, but everything got interrupted when we nearly crashed. Now she's furious because I'm not taking anybody else to the prom. To make matters worse, there are these dance book things.

"Dance books? What are those?"

"I only heard about them the other day, when Rex was bragging about the one he has for June. As I understand it, even if I was there and wanted to dance with her, I couldn't do it unless he puts my name in this stupid book he has."

"Fat chance of that happening," Doc replied, shaking his head.

"June means a lot to you, doesn't she?" he asked.

I stared down at the pencil in my hand. "I've never known anyone like her, Doc. She's smart, easy to talk to, down to earth, fun, understanding, beautiful ... she's really, really nice, and I want to be with her so badly." Removing my glasses, I rubbed my eyes.

"Did it ever occur to you that you're in love—big time?"

"Yes, dammit, it did. And for that matter, you're the reason she refused to go steady with me, when I tried to ask her in January ...."

Too late. Why didn't I keep my mouth shut? I started scratching a doodle on the desktop as Doc watched, saying nothing. I thought of the breakfast table in Copenhagen the time I narrowly escaped  infuriating Pa when I protested his order to swab the seagull shit off the dock at dawn.

"Andy, what have you told June about me?" he asked, slowly, breaking the silence.

"I didn't tell her anything about Marissa, if that's what you mean—nothing. But she already knows."

"She knows? How is that possible? If you didn't tell her, who ...."

"You did, Doc. She brought it up, and then told me she knew it was true when you wouldn't talk about it. That's why you still need to clear up loose ends with her."

Looking tired and confused, my roommate sank into his desk chair.

"You keep saying that. But if she knows about Marissa, that means she knows it's over between us, doesn't it? As far as I'm concerned, you have a clear shot at her."

"Not exactly," I replied, choosing my words carefully. "Over Easter you were at my house every day. You couldn't keep away from her. For former steadies, you two are still deeply close. And I know for a fact that June feels your relationship won't be finished until you tell her it is."

"To her face? She wants me to tell her, flat out, there's another woman in my life, and our friendship is finished? Done? Kaput?"

My patience frayed. "Doc, you've been hurting her for a long time because you won't talk about it. Why can't you sit down with someone you care for and have a meaningful discussion—without kidding around? I'll tell you another thing, too: unless you do, forget about my ever being the substitute in her life you were hoping for when we made our blood brothers deal last fall. You should probably tell her about that arrangement, too. And while we're on the subject, what about telling me why you two broke up last year? Oh, never mind. Now it's so late it doesn't make any difference, anyway."

He stood by the window watching a bunch of moths attracted to our ceiling light shredding themselves against the screen.

"You're right, Andy. What the hell—it's over and done with; what difference does it make?" He turned back to me. "You already know we first got acquainted at Copper's square dance and hit it off right away. It was like I never had so much fun with anyone in my life. We got really close that fall, and after the Halloween dance, I pressured her to go steady. Eventually, she agreed."

"And that turned out to be a not-so-good idea?"

"Everything changed. Instead of having fun, we got more and more involved. By Thanksgiving vacation we were spending most of our time making out."

Then I understood why June got so upset when I kept pressing the subject of going steady. Why didn't I listen when she tried to explain her feelings at WAC Circle that evening?

"One night," Doc continued, "I took her ice skating at Rhein-Main. We caught the last bus back and, after a couple of stops, we were the only ones left for the rest of the trip. We were way in the back and got into it, so much that she got upset and begged me to stop. It wasn't easy, but I did."

"Is that when you broke up?"

"No, but it was the beginning of the end. Things got more and more shaky—it was like there was a cloud of gloom over us. I realized I wanted more than she could give, and I saw that all I was doing was hurting her. I couldn't stand doing that, and still can't." He slumped into his chair.

"And the mittens?"

"The day before Christmas vacation, we exchanged presents: she gave me mittens she had somehow found time to knit, and I gave her one of those German music boxes—like the one you gave her. I accidentally broke the spring, and it felt like something between us had snapped. We started to laugh: then she cried. We both knew it was over. Instead of admitting it, however, we agreed to continue like 'brother and sister.'"

"But you seem on such good terms this year," I said.

"The two of you must have talked it out at some point."

"Oh, we managed to patch things up, respect each other's feelings, stuff like that. But I never—as you figured out—told her I was losing interest. To be honest, I didn't know if I was or not—until I met Marissa. Meanwhile, June began dating everybody under the sun—even you."

"Not quite, Doc. After you met Marissa you wanted to tell June but couldn't figure a way that wouldn't hurt her, so you hit upon your blood brother plan—which has come back to haunt you."

He looked puzzled.

"Now you not only feel the pressure of your guilty conscience, but you have me pushing you to tell her. Only you can release her, but you still can't figure out how to do it painlessly, can you, Tonto? Well? Am I right?"

"I can't talk about it anymore right now. I'm thinking, okay?"

He interlocked his fingers behind his neck, twisting from side to side, as he tried to understand why he must open his feelings to her, and how to do it without hurting her. At that moment, with time running out and the semester almost over, I loved Doc for caring so much about June and me, and felt saddened for all three of us.

A few days before the prom, The Kreebs surprised us at mail call.

"And what's this? Why, it's a letter from Geneva written in lovely handwriting addressed to Doc Gordon." He rubbed the last letter in his hand, a thin blue envelope with slanted red stripes on the edges, under his nose, inhaling a moist sniff. "Lavender again. I'll bet it's from that special girl who used to write you. If I remember, she stopped some time ago."

Doc snatched it out of his hand and stuffed it into his

pocket. I caught up with him later, on the way to dinner.

"I told you you'd be hooked if Marissa wrote again. What's up?"

"It's the craziest thing, Andy. Apparently, she and Adolph, or whatever his name is, went to the Riviera—that town where all the film stars go."

"Cannes?"

"That's the place. Anyway, while they were toasting their buns on the beach, this lost mutt befriends them. Turns out it belongs to the horny girlfriend of some over-the-hill Italian movie star, who insists on taking them to dinner. Adolph disappears with the slinky chick, leaving Marissa to fend off this guy old enough to be her father."

"What then?"

"She escaped, and has promised to make it up to me."

"I'm sure she knows exactly how," I replied. We continued along the well-used path behind the gym toward the mess hall. I hadn't seen Doc so cheerful in weeks.

"Andy," he said, making certain nobody was nearby, "Can you keep a secret?"

I stuck the palm of my hand with its "blood brother" scar in his face.

"Marissa is eighteen," he began, "and I won't be seventeen until right after school is out."

"Okay, she's older than you. So what?"

"For some unknown reason, it's a big deal—at least with her. Whenever we've been together, we've made out like bandits, but that's as far as it's gone. We never actually … you know. To make up for how she's treated me," he continued, "she's promised a genuine Danish birthday present this summer. It'll be close, though, because my family is supposed to return to the States about then. Dad's orders are due any time; I just hope it's not before

Marissa and I can—"

This took several seconds to register. I assumed they had already been as intimate as it was possible to get, so finding out that this fundamental life experience was yet to come amazed me.

"You mean you're actually a virgin like me, panting for your first screw, and now you and Marissa are going to—"

"Yes, dammit. Don't be so dense."

# The Prom

Later, back in our room, I pressed him about the prom.

"Why don't you invite Marissa? I know there isn't much time left, but I'll bet she'd be more than willing to come if you asked her."

"You mean pull an 'Andy,' like you did with June at Easter?" He paused, turning serious. "You're probably right, and I think it's a great idea, but the logistics are too complicated—finding her a place to stay, transportation, expense, not enough time—it wouldn't work."

"Just a thought, Roomie. Only trying to cheer you up. Anyway, will you or will you not be at the prom?"

"I'm going. The dance committee wants me to be the official photographer."

"Doc, I just had a brainstorm: do you need an assistant? Then I wouldn't need a date and could still get my dance with June. How about it?"

He walked over to the window and waved to somebody on the patio below. "How does that work, Lone Ranger— the dance card business you mentioned a few days ago? From what you said, I gather that Rex is the one in charge of it, not June, correct?"

"I guess so," I replied. "Why?"

"Well, assuming he has any say in the matter you don't seriously think he's going to let you dance with her, do you?"

Until now, this hadn't occurred to me. I watched my Roomie pace back and forth, muttering to himself. "I wonder ... maybe ... I could ... yeah, it might work. It just might."

"Doc?" I clapped my hands a couple of times. "We were talking about me getting a dance with June at the prom. It would have to be a waltz, because that is all I know how to do. And, we were also talking about my going to the prom as your assistant, remember?"

"We were—I am. Waltz, huh? Brain cells at work. Yes. Being my assistant would be fine with me, but I'll have to run it by Copper's prom committee. There's another possibility, too."

"What's that?"

"I know they're looking for entertainment at intermission. I'll tell them you will bring your guitar and sing a couple of songs. After hearing your bell-clear baritone high notes, how could June possibly be mad at you for not having a date?"

"Well, I mean, what would they want me to sing?"

"Does it matter? Try 'Footprints on the Dashboard Upside Down,' for all I care. If you don't go, there's zero possibility of dancing a waltz with her, right? Think fishing —you must cast a line in the water to catch a fish, remember? It worked for you last fall, didn't it?"

The next day, I attempted to patch things up with June.

"Copper has asked me to sing at the prom during intermission. When I told her I do most of my singing in the shower, she said, 'Wear clothes.'"

"I heard," June replied, without looking at me as she

struggled with a piece of overcooked bratwurst on her plate.

"Aw, you're not still mad, are you?"

"What do you think?"

"But I'll be at the prom. We can have our dance. I love to waltz; do you?"

"Yes, but it will never happen if Rex has his way—that I can tell you. He's in charge of the dance card, not me."

"If you were to put in a good word—possibly? Well, maybe?"

June reached across the table, putting her hand on mine.

"Andy, that's something you and Rex have to work out. I've done as much as I can with this, and you know how I feel. If there's any chance for us to get our dance, it's up to you. Please talk to him, for both our sakes."

That night after study hours, I swallowed my pride and knocked on Rex's door. Pushing it open, I found him shuffling messy rows of lined note cards on his desk. The cement cast on his wrist clunked awkwardly. A library book about the Army Air Force in World War II was opened to pictures of bombed-out German cities.

"Hi, Rex. Working on your JERP?"

He turned, eyes burning.

"I'm not stupid, Barnes, so spare me the 'Sorry, Rex, can I sign your cast?' crap. You're sniffing around for a dance with June at the prom, you sonovabitch. You've been working on her all year, but I'm the one she agreed to go with—me, not you. And why is that, Barnes? Tell me."

I was unprepared for anything like this. His revenge was total.

"All right, I'll say it for you: you didn't ask her soon enough, did you? Not smart, Barnes." He pulled a white booklet held together with a trace of gold ribbon from a drawer. "In case you're not aware, this is her program. There are places for the names of six guys—six—who want a dance, see?" He shook it back and forth in front of my face with his good arm. "I guarantee yours won't be one of them. Now bug off."

Our dance was dead in the water. How could I tell her this was my best effort?

"Didn't you hear me, Barnes? Get the fuck out of here."

"I'm … I'm sorry you feel this way, Rex. It's only one dance—one. Won't you give me a chance? There must be something I can do to get on your list. Could I help arrange those research cards? Doing it one-handed is pretty slow. Maybe if I did some of your actual research, too?"

He fanned his face with the booklet, curving his lips into a cunning smile.

"How about doing the whole JERP? That might be worth it. The topic is bombing Germany during the war—right up your alley."

"Are you just trying to humiliate me some more?"

"You're the one begging for a dance with my date, Barnes."

"But how would I get two JERPS done by Miss McCafferty's deadline?"

"That's your problem."

"Look, Rex: I could be a big help writing your cards and organizing them, especially considering your hand, and all. That would save lots of time, and then we could both finish."

"You heard my offer. Take it or leave it."

My mind raced. I might have been able to do both, but the school year would be over in a few weeks. No, it's not right, I decided. I'm not going to waste time doing Rex's JERP for him. What if Miss McCafferty found out? What would June think? How would I feel about myself? Rex knew he had lost her. As far as the prom went, however, so had I.

"No dice, Rex. I'll help with your research, but I won't write your paper—even for June."

"I tried," I told her, the next morning at breakfast. "I really did, but his mind was made up."

"What happened, Andy?"

"I went to his room, and he knew exactly why I was there. He took out your dance card and guaranteed my name wouldn't be on it."

Doc set his breakfast tray down on our table and slid into a chair. Tonto had grilled me the night before, so I didn't want to rehash the specifics of Rex's conditions. June knew he hated my guts, so why burden her with negatives about the person she was obligated to spend the prom with? She was committed to making the best of it, and it wasn't right for me to make it harder for her. No, last night was strictly between Rex and me—the culmination of a year of rivalry over the wonderful girl sitting across from me.

"I wanted to waltz with you so badly," I choked, trying to hold back the lump in my throat, "but it'll never happen now."

Saying nothing, Doc shook his head as June reached across and enclosed my hands in hers.

The prom was held in the Palmengarten, in downtown Frankfurt. Above the room an old chandelier that had somehow survived the war hovered like an ornate UFO. There was no mistaking the Hoagy Carmichael "Stardust" theme: long strings of silver and gold paper stars—

representing hours of work by Copper's prom committee —twisted and glittered on strings of different lengths from thick wooden ceiling beams. Round tables with wooden armchairs ringed the periphery of the oak dance floor. Above each table, two or three white and gold helium-filled balloons, tethered to a small vase of fresh flowers, dodged back and forth in confused currents of air. Doc selected one of the tables and began unpacking his camera bag.

"Having another June-Rex attack?" he asked, attaching the flash unit to the side of his Leica. "Stop looking so gloomy—you're here. You're near her." He slid a handful of bulbs over the varnished tabletop. "Put these in your pocket and go stash your guitar backstage. Then make yourself useful. We have work to do."

On stage, a six-piece German band was tuning up. I asked their leader about intermission.

"Are you making announcements?" he replied, in fluent English.

"No, sir. I'm supposed to sing, but I've never done it on a stage before."

"Surely you have sung somewhere," he replied, detecting my anxiety.

"Mostly by myself," I smiled, "in my dorm room, small groups in our lounge, buses going to basketball games."

"I will announce intermission and adjust the microphone before we leave, so step up to it and try to relax. Put your soul into every word. You'll be fine."

"I'll try, sir," I replied, far from confident. "Thank you."

Doc and I got busy. I never knew girls could look so gorgeous. Copper's green strapless gown was stunning. June was wearing a multi-layered opalescent chiffon dress in soft blue that came to just below her knees. Sequins sparkled on its bodice, which covered one shoulder, leaving the other bare and sensual. Around her neck she wore a thin silver chain with a small opal pendant—an heirloom from her mother—with matching earrings. Other girls had obviously been to hairdressers, but June's naturally curly hair needed no help in that regard. Before I could say hello, Doc hustled me away to take faculty pictures.

"The camera can't do much for Miss Franklin, but I want a good shot of Miss Maybelle."

Eventually, we made our way back to June's table.

"Hi, Andy. I'm looking forward to hearing you sing at intermission."

"You look beautiful, June. I think you're the prettiest...."

"Stick to your pictures and leave my date alone, Barnes," snapped Rex.

"Will I be able to dance with you?" I asked June, ignoring him.

Rex took her prom booklet from his pocket. "It's already filled, so I'd say you have about as much chance as a snowball in hell of dancing with her tonight."

She looked away.

"C'mon," said Doc.

As he dragged me off, I turned. "Bye, June. I hope you have a wonderful evening."

Time passed with dizzying speed. Doc took dozens of pictures, while I recorded personal information and juggled hot flashbulbs. Sooner than expected, the music stopped, and the bandleader announced intermission.

Doc nudged me. "You better get going. Break a leg."

"Thanks, Roomie."

As I started toward the stage, June blew me a kiss and I

returned an uncertain wave. Opening my guitar case, I broke into a cold sweat. There were more people out there than I could count. My performance had to be perfect, but how? I'd never done anything perfect in my life; was I going to make a complete ass of myself?

Then Copper was at the microphone. "And now I'd like to present ...."

Ducking my head underneath the red-and-blue embroidered guitar strap—the one from Chile Mom had sent from Taarbaek for good luck—I walked onto the stage. I felt woozy.

Copper put her hand over the mike. "Are you okay?" she whispered. "What's wrong? Your fingers are white."

"They won't move, Copper. What if my voice cracks? What if I forget the words? I'll get booed off the stage."

"Stop panicking and relax, Andy. Pretend you're singing to someone you love. She's out there in the audience—or have you forgotten?"

I stepped to the microphone.

"I thought this song was appropriate," I began, "because the year is almost over and many of us will be moving this summer. The title is ... of the song I would like to sing is ... is ...." The room fell silent. "Copper," I croaked, strangling the mike for support, "I can't remember the title—something about God."

"Never mind," she said, as the room rocked with laughter. "Sing it anyway."

At that point, I no longer cared what happened. I played the introductory chords and began to sing. I couldn't see June—or anybody—because the stage lights blinded me. It didn't matter; I was singing to her and my voice did everything perfectly—even the high notes. When it was over, I was surprised at the applause.

"I just remembered the title of that song," I said to the audience, when the noise had died down: "'May the Good Lord Bless and Keep You.'"

"We already figured that out," somebody yelled, and the room erupted in more laughter.

"Well done, Roomie," cried Doc. "At last I'm proud to be seen with you."

The musicians returned, and soon the room shook with a mixture of traditional Big Band, rock and roll, and slow, intimate pieces—the "vertical intercourse ones," according to Doc.

"It would be a good idea if you asked your friends in the band to play a waltz for dance program number six," he said, "and tell them to make it long."

"A waltz?"

"Just do it, okay?"

"Sure," I answered, wondering what he was up to.

I arrived at the stage as dancers were disentangling themselves from "Unchained Melody."

"You did very well, my friend," said the bandleader. "Are you here to ask for a job?"

"No, Maestro," I grinned. "But your advice made all the difference."

"What can I do for you?"

"I was wondering if you could please play a long waltz for dance program number six, the last one on the card. It's very important."

"You mean a medley of popular ones—like 'Tennessee Waltz'?"

"What about Strauss—maybe 'Roses from the South'?"

After conversing with his musicians, he returned. "You will have it."

Doc put me back to work scribbling photo information.

Occasionally I caught glimpses of June dancing with Rex or some other baboon he'd fixed her up with. Dance five came and went; but at dance number six I was surprised to see him appear out of nowhere, June in tow. He took out her dance program.

"Number six, Doc Gordon—last one I have to sit out tonight."

After making a show of putting her hand in Doc's, he rummaged around in his pockets. "Can I borrow a pencil, Gordon?"

Doc nodded toward me.

Rex grabbed the one in my hand and crossed out number six. "Too bad, Barnes," he leered. "Have a nice dance, June."

As Rex disappeared into the crowd, the band began to play "Roses from the South." Doc's eyes met hers.

"Darn," he said, "I wait all night for a dance with you and, of all things, they play a waltz. I don't know how to waltz. Roomie, could you be a pal and do the honors with this lovely girl?"

Leaning down, he kissed her forehead. "Time to let go," he said quietly. "We both know Andy is the right person for you."

"I've known for a long time," she whispered, putting her arms around his neck and pressing the side of her face against his chest.

At long last, he had released June without the pain of hurting her.

They eased apart and he straightened up. "You better get out there. The two of you are on your own, now."

On the dance floor, she put her arm on my shoulder, as I placed my right hand against the small of her back. The music began, and June's body swirled in graceful circles as we dipped, twirled, and laced back and forth. Since most of our classmates preferred Elvis, we had the floor mostly to ourselves. I caught a glimpse of Rex arguing furiously at Doc, who didn't seem to be paying much attention. He had a huge smile on his face.

"Everybody's watching," June said, at one point.

"Let them." I whispered. "This is heaven."

When the music ended, we were surprised to receive applause. I took June's hand and bowed, while she curtsied.

"We don't want to forget the band," she said, so we walked over to the stage, shook their hands, and thanked them. Doc was delighted.

"I got some great shots of you two strutting your stuff," he beamed, "and a spectacular one of June as you gave her one of those big twirls."

"I'd like to buy it," she said.

"Not a chance, my dear. You and Andy get whichever ones you want."

She wiped a tear away before it could damage the wispy blush of makeup on her cheek, then gave Doc his second embrace of the evening. He stood there—leather camera bag slung over his shoulder, flashbulbs in one hand, camera in the other—caught by surprise. Rising on her tiptoes, she kissed him.

"Thank you, Doc."

We walked back to June's table, where I returned her to a smoldering Rex.

"Thank you, June, for the most marvelous dance of my life," I said, giving her a kiss. "And thank you, Rex. That was very thoughtful of you."

"Thank Doc," he spat out, glaring at me through angry eyes.

"We already have."

# The Final Weeks

The approaching end of the school year held no forthcoming summer vacation pleasures for me. The girl I loved would soon be a memory. How could letters substitute for holding her? For the happiness in her laughter? And I knew from experience that, sooner or later, letters eventually stopped. Neither of us wanted to talk about our forthcoming separation—it was like discussing our funerals. I preferred to imagine time spinning backward: June and I square-dancing; holding each other in the gazebo that moonlit night; gliding across the dance floor at the prom. I quit looking at the calendar, but the days slipped by as the relentless countdown to our last goodbye continued.

For reasons known only to the Pentagon, Colonel Gordon's orders were delayed. All Doc could tell me was that he was going to spend the summer on his grandparents' farm in Georgia. Then, one afternoon in our room after mail call, he ripped open the letter in his hand and let out a whoop.

"Andy, we're going to Randolph AFB in San Antonio, Texas, the first week of July!"

"What's great about that? Do tumbleweeds and coral

snakes turn you on?"

"Who cares where we're going? Think, Roomie, think. What was the most critical thing about Dad's orders? What have I been most worried about, all this time?"

"You didn't want to leave Copenhagen before your birthday."

"Yes? Yes? Come on, I know you can do it. How old am I going to be?"

"Seventeen. You're not leaving Copenhagen until after your seventeenth birthday. That means Marissa can give you your … present."

He vaulted onto the top of our desk and began doing a Cossack dance.

"Stop acting like a partridge in heat."

"It's Happy Birthday in Denmark! Happy birthday to me, happy birthday to me, happy …."

"Jeez, Doc. If you'd quit rupturing my eardrums, I'll tell you what I'm going to get you for your birthday present. It comes in a little foil package."

He froze with one leg in the air and fixed me with a long look of genuine affection. Then, hopping down, Tonto rummaged through several bureau drawers.

"Put out your hand."

I looked down at the white scar on my palm and hesitated.

"No, I'm not going to stab it again," he said.

Then Doc closed my fingers around a tarnished but genuine 1882 American silver dollar.

"You're the best friend I ever had, Andy. I'm going to miss you, Blood Brother."

"Thanks for being my roommate," I choked. "I'll never forget you."

During our year together, I had learned a lot from Doc.

In his happy, adventurous, energetic, sometimes dangerous way, he had pulled me out of my shell, daring me to challenge the unknown. He had guided me through dorm life's countless ups and downs, giving me confidence to face whatever the future might have in store. From him I had learned the importance of friendship, no matter how short it might be; how to laugh at myself; and when certain risks were acceptable, and when they were not. Most of all, as my "advisor on matters of love," he had paved the way for my mystifying, at times bewildering, tangled, and ultimately successful relationship with June, who had altered my life even deeper than he had. And yes, Doc, you always kept your promises. At that moment, I felt closer to him than to any guy I'd ever known.

The last week of classes, June and I were sitting on the bleachers after school. Like Doc, she had been in limbo regarding her father's orders from Washington.

"Dad's been assigned to the Pentagon. We'll be leaving Ankara shortly after I return from school," she said, as we watched several track team members—including Doc— jogging on the red cinder lanes around the athletic field. He waved as they passed.

"Mom will be able to continue cancer treatments at Bethesda Naval Medical Center."

"That's good news," I said, "but where will you live? How long until I can write?"

She stroked my hand. "I wish I knew. We'll probably rent an apartment near Bethesda until the folks find a house—you know the drill. I want to finish my senior year at my old school, Sidwell Friends. Maybe you could write me there."

"You wouldn't get it until school starts in September. I can't go that long without hearing from you—I'll go crazy.

You know the Taarbaek address, so you'll have to write me first. Promise you will, June, and please, please write often."

"Don't worry. Of course I'll write first. That's a given, okay?"

"Do you remember on the plane when we almost crashed ... and you were squeezing my arm so hard it hurt, and I said—"

"You said 'I love you. I always will.' A girl doesn't forget those words." Sensitive fingers brushed my cheek as misty eyes met mine.

I sank my face into her curly hair. "I meant it," I said.

She stroked the back of my neck. "I know you did, and I know you do now. I love you too, my sweet Andy."

I wrapped my arms around her, and we nestled closer.

"I want you to have something to remember me by," I said, wrenching a small package from my pocket. "You can't open it until sometime when you are thinking of a friend in Copenhagen who loves you. It's to go with The Little Mermaid."

Our lips touched.

"Thank you for sharing so much of yourself with me this year, Andy."

"I've never been so miserable about saying goodbye to anybody, anywhere," I replied, looking away. I was about to lose it, and I didn't want her to see me in tears. "I don't know which is worse—the pain of losing you, or the hopelessness of our situation. I've never experienced anything like this before, June."

I pressed my face against the front of her sweater. She shifted position and looked at me.

"Andy, have you ever wondered what it would have been like if our fathers were never in the Navy, and we lived our whole lives in one place?"

"Hard to imagine," I answered, staring at traffic rumbling past the football field on the Miquelallee. A crow cawed in the distance. "I'm not in a mood for games."

She leaned away. "C'mon, let's try."

"You mean, like, if we lived down the street from each other in some small town?"

"Exactly. You and I meet one morning walking to elementary school. There's this big dog that barks and lunges as I pass his fence, and he jumps out. I'm terrified."

"I hit his nose with my Donald Duck lunch box, and we run for it. Something like that?"

"Same schools every year," she continued. "Teachers who know our parents; glee club; school plays …."

"Hanging out at the only drugstore, sipping cherry Cokes with two straws," I added, beginning to come around. "I pick you up on our way to the junior prom in my first car—a Chevy jalopy I bought with money saved from my summer lifeguard job …."

"We watch the Fourth of July parade from our favorite spot on Main Street."

"The one with the town's only police car, followed by the fire engine and the selectmen waving American flags from their Model T?"

She clapped her hands. "Exactly. The band is playing. Here comes the Historical Society float, the one with a big bunch of bananas and pretty girls throwing handfuls of Tootsie Rolls and Pez candy to scrabbling kids jumping into the road."

"And the whole thing is over in ten minutes," I added, laughing.

"That night we share a blanket at the harbor, surrounded by half the town, everyone oohing and clapping at fireworks bursting overhead …."

"You mean a single skyrocket shooting off every five minutes, don't you? And then, after half an hour of swatting mosquitoes, the grand finale: six of them at once."

By this time, it was hard to tell if we were laughing or crying. She reached for the edge of her skirt and wiped her eyes, serious again. "We would have grown up with friends who didn't vanish. Don't you wish sometimes that we might have shared experiences like those?"

"If you were the person I shared them with, absolutely. But I've never understood what it means to have permanent roots—a life without moving anywhere, traveling, new places, new friends …. The only person I know who has lived in one place like that is my grandmother, in Tacoma, Washington. Her street hasn't changed at all. Neither has her life, compared with our Navy lifestyle. I'm not even sixteen, but I've lived in one territory and five states; been across the country three times; made four long ocean trips, including through the Panama Canal twice; and not just traveled in, but lived in three foreign countries. I mean, how many teenagers back home have done stuff like that?"

"Ours is a pretty exclusive club, isn't it?" she said.

"When I was eleven," I went on, "Pa was the exec of an aircraft carrier based at Quonset Point, Rhode Island. He took me out of school to go on a ten-day cruise. A real aircraft carrier. Imagine. I saw planes taking off and landing, a couple of crashes, gunnery practice. For a kid to do something like that was incredible."

I lapsed into silence, feeling foolish after this outburst. Weren't June's experiences equally unique?

"I never took a cruise on one of my Dad's submarines,"

she mused, "but you have a point. Perhaps being in one place all the time would have been a bit dull. We would have had a lot more time to enjoy our friends, though."

"And each other."

We watched Doc and the track team practicing relays. I felt the warm pulse of her temple against my cheek. If only these moments could last forever ....

"We don't have a place like that to go back to, do we?" she almost whispered. "Anyway, I suppose it doesn't matter. Being over here has made me see the world differently. I'm definitely not the same, but I'm not sure how different I am, either."

"More broad-minded, maybe?"

"Perhaps," she smiled. "But for you and me—and the rest of us—life in small-town America, and all that goes with it, was never meant to be, was it?"

"Does that bother you, June? I can't see it rattling that logical mind of yours."

"Maybe a little. When we go back to the States, we'll never be the same as our new friends who have not experienced the world as we have. Sometimes I wonder if I'll stand out like a sore thumb because Frankfurt has given me such a broader perspective on things."

"It's so unfair!" I spat out, unable to contain my frustrations. "Here we sit, forty miles from the Iron Curtain, waiting to get run over by 'Russky T-34' tanks, or whatever that crazy major called them last fall. We aren't draftees, but the military controls our lives. It does what it wants with us, whenever it wants. We're just 'Military Brats.' Our feelings don't matter. We might as well be slaves."

"Shh," she soothed, a playful smile brightening her face. "Not slaves. How about 'Uncle Sam's Kids?' Does that describe us better?"

"If you like. You know what I mean. Nothing can make up for your being gone."

"But we have no choice. Our fathers' careers will continue to determine our futures until we go to college and eventually choose careers of our own. That's the way it works for us."

"I only know one thing, June: I don't want to lose you —not in the years ahead, not ever."

Her arms closed around me, and for a few brief minutes, I forgot the calendar.

# The Last Day

Doc intended no malice when he dumped the wastebasket full of water on me while I was still in bed that morning. Normally I would have taken it in stride. I might even have seen some humor in it. Isn't the end of school cause to do nutty things and celebrate? But these were not normal circumstances, and his prank was past the point of amusement. My world was collapsing. Exams and parting with June were all I had left. It was a matter of hours. When we spoke our final words, she would see the tears I was holding back. Then I'd be crying like a baby over a situation neither of us could do anything about. That's why my roommate's cheery "Reveille, Lone Ranger. Wake up. Now." pushed me over the edge.

"Damn you, Gordon! I'm totally sopped. Everything's sopped."

"I'm just keeping my promise to get you up every morning, remember?" he said, as I stripped off my pajamas and bedclothes.

"I know one promise you made and never kept," I growled.

"You're just making that up. If not, what is it?"

"In that taxi driving across town last fall, remember? We

crossed the Main River Bridge and you said you'd take me kayaking there. You never did, did you? Now the year's over, and there's no way you can do it." I grabbed my towel and headed for the showers.

Wispy clouds lacing the sky that morning foretold a hot, hazy day. During breakfast Doc tried to make amends. If he hoped for support from June, she stayed out of it.

"Please, Lone Ranger, let's not end the year like this."

I ignored him. After exhausting pleas for mercy, he picked up his barely touched tray and left.

"Andy," she said, setting her bowl of Wheaties aside. "Doc's your closest friend …."

"No, you are."

Her expression softened. "Look at me. He's miserable about this. I can tell. It isn't worth ruining what little time is left by being angry. Can't you show a little compassion?"

I said nothing, but the look in her eyes melted me. This was important for her.

"You can be very irritating at times, and you didn't get cold water poured over you either," I said at last, unable to prevent a sheepish smile. "Want to go to the PX after breakfast?"

"I need to study for finals—and so do you, I might add."

"Aw, June. Please?"

"Tell you what. If I get enough done today, you can take me to the Teen Club End-of-Year dance tonight. It should be fun. How's that?"

"You win." I stood.

"And Andy," she smiled, "make up with Doc in the meantime, okay?"

When I returned to our room, Doc was making my bed. Everything was dry, blankets drum tight.

"If you drop that silver dollar I gave you on this bed, Andy, I guarantee it will bounce."

It did.

"Whose mattress did you swipe, Gordon?"

"I didn't. I flipped yours over."

Shaking my head, I turned toward the door. June's words at breakfast came to mind, but my anguish over goodbyes overrode common sense. Doc's remorse made it worse.

"Please Andy. If you'll be my friend again, before I leave Copenhagen in a couple of weeks, I'll get Marissa to fix you up with one of her gorgeous Danish sisters—even though you are underage for such things."

"Marissa is an only child, or have you forgotten, Gordon? And if you don't know by this time that June is the only girl I'll ever want," I turned toward the door, "then something's wrong with you."

At lunch, he pulled up a chair.

"Andy. I've been thinking."

I glanced at June. She was looking straight at me.

"What is it, Gordon?"

"This afternoon would be the ideal time to spend a couple of hours on the river. It'll relax us—get our minds off finals. It's perfect weather. You don't want to spend it studying, do you? I'll get a bunch of us; we'll rent boats, get some exercise and sunburn, and be back in time for dinner. It's our last chance to have some fun before everybody leaves."

"What about The Kreebs? Doesn't boating require parental permission?"

"You know there's no time for that. Don't you see? We spell it out for him in the sign-out book, then do it. He'll be furious. I can see his bloodshot eyes bulging right now.

It's perfect." Shaking her head, June went back to picking at her sausage, potatoes, gravy, and canned spinach.

"What happens when we get back?"

"What can he do to us? Absolutely nothing. Exams start tomorrow. If he restricts us, so what?"

"Who cares if Barnes can't make up his mind?" Rex broke in. "I'll go with you, Doc." He glanced at June. "How about you, beautiful?"

"Sorry, guys. I have to study this afternoon."

"This is the first halfway decent suggestion you've had today, Doc," I said.

June smiled as she folded her paper napkin, dropping it on her barely touched tray.

"What time and where?" asked Jimmy.

Doc glanced at his watch. "WAC Circle. One-thirty should be about right."

"Meet you there," he replied.

When we signed out that afternoon, most of us put "downtown Frankfurt" as our destination; Doc, however, printed "Kayaking, Main River" in bold letters beside his name.

"Wish I could see The Kreebs's expression when he reads this," he joked.

In high spirits, we trooped to WAC Circle and caught the streetcar for Offenbach.

Thirty minutes later, we got off at the Main River and followed Doc a quarter-mile to the boat rental place. It was dead calm, and I could feel my pale arms, face, and neck starting to cook in the sun. Walking down the gangplank to a large float, I looked at the rental kayaks while Jimmy negotiated in German with the boat people.

"Are you sure these pieces of junk will float, Doc? I asked. "None of them have been painted since the Franco-

Prussian War, and there's probably rot in some of those skuzzy green waterlines. The plywood deck on the one you're getting is coming apart. Take this one—it looks better."

"Stop fussing, Lone Ranger. It's fine. This'll be a great afternoon. Admit it."

"Any life jackets?" I asked, looking around. There were none, but we were young and indestructible, and probably wouldn't have worn them anyway. We paid for three hours of paddling time, and I started to get into a single boat. Doc grabbed my arm.

"Uh-uh, Lone Ranger—over here." He motioned toward the two-seater bobbing at his feet. "You come with me."

I took a step and stopped. I wanted to get into Doc's boat. We had done so much together, had so many good times. And he was right: this was our last chance at what promised to be a fun afternoon. One step, and Doc would understand I wasn't angry with him anymore. I could get even with him once we were underway. I smiled, thinking of Tonto stuck in the stern seat, getting drenched with my paddle after paddle of water. He would appreciate this sort of reconciliation. June would be pleased because I had taken her advice, and Doc and I would be friends again. And yet ... that night on the stormy Øresund ... my oath never to get in a boat with him again ....

Waving his casted arm in my face, Rex pushed me aside. "I'll go with you, Doc. With this piece of cement, I need someone with muscles." He climbed into the bow seat and fumbled for his paddle. Shrugging, Doc swung down behind him. Jimmy got into the bow seat of the other double, the rest of us in singles, and our group shoved off. Splashing and ramming each other at flank speed, Admiral

Gordon's flotilla headed upstream to play in the waters below Offenbach Dam.

After the war, destroyed dams for navigation and electric power were rebuilt at key topographical intervals along the Main and other German rivers. The one at Offenbach stretched from shore to shore, with water flowing over its top, down twelve or fifteen feet of concrete wall to the river below. On one side of it was a lock that was raised or lowered for barges to pass through by filling or emptying the chamber. When the water was expelled, it transformed the river's otherwise tranquil surface downstream into several minutes of tumbling waves.

For a short time, we splashed water and rammed into each other, goofing off. Then a barge departed the lock.

"Follow us!" bellowed Doc. His boat peeled into the now fast-moving current, riding the froth downstream for a hundred yards or so before returning via an eddy that circled upstream along the shoreline. Doc was right: "running the rapids," savoring the cool spray against our sunburned backs, was fun. After ten minutes, the waters below the dam flattened out again.

"What now?" someone shouted.

"We do it again when another barge comes along," Doc yelled. "There are lots of them."

So we floated around, waiting. Doc's boat turned into the eddy where I sat, resting my paddle across my kayak's flimsy cockpit coamings. "This is boring," he said, twisting his paddle over and over in his hands. "Andy, let's go over to the dam. I want to stick my hand through the falling water and touch the wall."

It sounded bizarre, but I was used to Doc's quirky impulses. I had no idea I would remember the next few minutes for the rest of my life. Shielding the sun from my eyes for a better look, I studied the imposing structure. A continuous thin sheet of water slipped from the top and down its concrete wall, disappearing into a line of foam where it touched the river. I shivered, without knowing why.

"I can't tell for sure, Doc, but it seems like there's more water coming over the top than there was before. I don't think it's a good idea."

"C'mon, Lone Ranger. A quick touch and we'll be out again."

"It doesn't look right. I'll race you over to the far shore and back, okay?"

Jimmy's boat bumped mine as it pulled into the eddy behind us.

"Jimmy," cried Doc. "Let's go over to the dam. It's not far."

"Nah, I don't wanna get wet."

"You're already wet, you weenie," said Rex.

Jimmy shook his head.

"Doc, I'm sure there's more water spilling over the top of that thing than there was a few minutes ago," I repeated, louder this time.

He wavered. Then Rex shoved my kayak away in disgust, nearly losing his paddle in the process. "You're scared, Barnes, you chicken. C'mon, Doc. Let's ram that wall."

A vision of the two of them at Bakken that night, dropping from sight as their roller coaster dove into the first steep abyss, flashed through my mind.

"Please, Doc. Look at the top, will you? There's more water. Listen to me—just this once."

I watched, powerless, as their boat headed forward. He

twisted around, the old familiar grin on his wet, sunburned face.

"Come on, Lone Ranger. It's fun."

Our eyes met, his filled with excitement, mine with fear. He turned away, leaning into each stroke with every ounce of power his muscular frame could provide. Bucking waves and current, Doc and Rex inched closer to the brown curtain of falling water at the dam. I lost sight of their boat as my friends seemed suspended in swirling foam. A desperate burst of back-paddling. My body turned to ice as I realized there wasn't a thing any of us could do. What I was seeing could only end one way: Doc wasn't going to get out of this one. The nightmare situation June and I had tried to understand on the train was happening in front of me. This wasn't real. It was all a bad dream.

"They're sinking!" someone yelled.

Throwing his paddle away, Rex stood and jumped. Holding his cast above the waves, he struggled to tread water. The river swallowed him.

"Harder, Doc! Back-paddle! Harder!" Jimmy yelled. "More!"

For an instant, I thought Tonto might win his battle against the odds. Then his swamped boat bounced forward, picking up speed. The bow splintered against the dam and the stern, where he sat gripping its sides, rose out of the water. He stood.

"Don't!" I screamed. "Stay with the boat. It's your only chance!"

But Tonto jumped. His arms were useless as relentless suction forced him toward the dam. And then, he too, vanished.

Digging my paddle into the eddy, I clawed great scoops of water heading toward where I'd last seen him.

"I'm not moving. What the hell's wrong?" I screamed.

"They're gone, Andy," said a steady voice behind me. "It's over." Jimmy's hand was clamped on the stern of my boat.

"Leggo, damn you!" I brought my paddle down across his wrist. Hard. He did not let go. "Please, Jimmy. For God's sake. They'll come up. I have to get over there."

"There's nothing any of us can do. I just lost two friends; I'm not going to lose another."

As Jimmy spoke, Doc's kayak, which had been rolling over and over at the base of the dam, plunged out of sight. His paddle skittered past us in the current. My eyes darted over an empty surface. I couldn't swallow. I half expected Doc to pop up, grinning, from the brown water next to my boat. That's it. It's one of his jokes. He's playing tricks on us. But it was no trick. What was left of their splintered kayak pierced the surface and fell back, pinwheeling aimlessly downstream. Numb with shock, I watched it pass a few feet away as the double-bladed paddle in my hands chattered against the gunwales of my boat. By now, the other kayaks were all in the eddy, five pairs of eyes searching the surface for any sign of hope.

A crowd formed above us along the pedestrian bridge crossing the river. Jimmy was yelling to them for help. After a time, the water over the dam ceased. By then, the whole place was full of sirens, flashing lights, and radio chatter from military police jeeps. I lost track of Jimmy and the others as American MPs recorded our individual statements, which were rechecked by English-speaking German police. I had difficulty explaining that two friends drowned because one of them wanted to touch the wall of the dam. Eventually, an MP drove me back to school in his jeep. Later, I overheard Mr Pulaski say that a barge with Navy divers had arrived.

# *Aftermath*

Since I was from Copenhagen and Doc's roommate, I was given the third degree in Pulaski's office by Army and school officials. How did it happen? Regulation 72-982004 Paragraph 41 (c) says parental permission is required to go boating … Why were you breaking the rules? The Kreebs was more aggressive than ever. Sticking the opened dorm sign-out book in my face, he jabbed his finger at Doc's name.

"What is this signature supposed to mean?" His voice was velvet soft, his eyes volcanic slits. "You knew that kayaking was against the rules, but you did it anyway. You wanted me to know you were breaking dorm rules. You wanted it to look like I wasn't doing my job, didn't you? Well, I hope you're satisfied. Two boys are dead because of your stupidity. Whose idea was it? Answer me."

"Ask Doc," I replied, looking away.

"That will do, Stanley," said Mr. Pulaski, putting his hand on my shoulder. "Why don't you see if any dorm kids need support?" Although deeply shaken, he was the only one in the room who showed any empathy or sense of loss. Everyone else was worried about his job. The worst part was when Mr. Pulaski answered the telephone and, after listening for several minutes, handed the receiver to me.

"The general wants you to describe what happened," he said as I put it next to my ear.

I wished I hadn't. Thinking he was still talking to Pulaski, the man on the other end of the line cursed a blue streak at him as I listened. His tone changed when he realized he was screaming at a fifteen-year-old kid. Other than the fuming Kreebs's dispatch to the dorm to help kids deal with news of their loss, there was no further reference to any kind of counseling. If so, nobody told me about it. I learned that to the Army—in those days, anyway—grief was a private thing: you dealt with it as best you could. If you had problems, that's what chaplains were for. When I was finally told I could return to the dorm, my adolescence remained in Pulaski's office.

I didn't bother signing in. The Kreebs's teapot was whistling behind his closed door as I started up the stairs. Except for Harry Belafonte singing "Sylvie" on someone's record player, the dorm was unnaturally quiet. Our room was the same, only very, very empty. My inspection-perfect bed still smelled like damp chicken feathers from Doc's bucket of water that morning. Adrift, I placed his hockey skates inside his footlocker, next to the black and gold Frankfurt High track letter he had received at the annual school athletic dinner.

"Andy, I don't know if I should ask, but there are these bad rumors going around and I wondered if you could—"

Standing in the doorway, Alfie removed his glasses and passed a hand over his eyes. Awkwardly, I stood up, unsure what to do. The boy who had gotten us through chemistry and saved me in geometry that year was taller and less chubby, no longer "the Guppy kid with a turkey feather in his Tyrolean hat." Should I give him a hug? Did he want one?

"It's true, Alfie. Doc's gone. Both of them."

I put my arms around him and felt his quiet sobs through my dirty T-shirt. Then it hit me: Alfie's crying, but I am not. Shouldn't I be crying, too? He pulled away, wiping his eyes.

"I need to know what happened, Andy. The rumors are driving me crazy. Please tell me."

Not now, I thought. God, not now. But the friend in front of me was suffering. Sinking onto the edge of the bed, I repeated what I had told so many others.

"Thank you for the truth," he said, when I finished. "I can deal with the truth, but not all the stupid talk. I learned a lot being around Doc this year."

"So did I, Alfie."

A few minutes later, I heard Mozart's Requiem—the music of God—coming from Alfie's room. I lay on my bed, staring up at Doc's mattress springs.

Outside, a creamy, peach-hued dusk was bringing the evening of an unimaginable day to a close. June. I needed June. Then I remembered about the end-of-semester party I was supposed to take her to. As I approached the Teen Club, small groups of kids—some in tears, some laughing in shock—were leaving. It was surreal. Then I saw her running toward me. We stood where we met—near the theater entrance—holding each other tightly, not moving, not speaking. A soldier on his way to the movie whistled. Another said, "Get it while you can, kid." His buddies laughed.

"I couldn't get to them, June."

"I heard Jimmy held your boat. That's probably why you're still here," she answered, choking back sobs. Taking my hand, she steered us toward the Grüneburgpark, a botanical garden a block or two behind the dorm. It consisted of an occasional bench on sandy paths rambling in and out of small, new bushes and trees planted there to replace old ones reduced to matchsticks during the war.

"We need a long walk," she said, taking my sunburned hand. "If you want to talk, I'm here to listen. If you want me to hold you, I will. Or we can just be quiet together."

"I feel like I'm sobbing my guts out, but nothing's happening. How is it possible to hurt so much without tears?"

"In time, they will come," she replied, wiping her eyes. "Besides, I have enough for both of us right now."

Darkness fell as we wandered along paths with no beginning or end. The rapture we had shared so tenderly in the gazebo the month before had vanished, replaced by the crushing pain of our shared losses. I told her all that had happened, but my words felt hollow. She listened and held me. At times her chest heaved against my sweat-stained T-shirt as we sought solace in each other.

It was well after hours when we got back. She pressed her cheek against mine.

"Always remember, I love you, Andy."

I started to say, "I love you, too, June. I always will," but no words came out.

A long embrace, the click of the door to her dorm closing, and June was gone.

I stayed awake for hours, eventually falling into troubled sleep. At dawn I took a shower, dressed, and started putting more of Doc's stuff into his footlocker. Crisp footsteps stopped outside the door. Several sharp raps followed.

"Wake up, Andy."

I threw myself into Pa's embrace.

"I flew Colonel Gordon and the general to Rhein-Main late last night. I'm afraid this is going to be a hard day for all of us, Son—especially you—so I think some breakfast is in order. I know a small German place with plenty of privacy that should suit."

My food remained untouched as I told Pa everything I could remember. When I started to repeat things, he reached across the table and put his hand on mine, something he had never done. It was callused and rough, and I wanted to cry. I couldn't.

"You're probably thinking I'm trying to smooth things over by what I'm going to tell you, but I want you to know I do understand how you feel." Then he shocked me by recounting how he had witnessed the loss of three of his closest friends in the Pacific—one shot down, one in an exploding plane, and the third in a fiery crash landing on their aircraft carrier. He sat, hands folded around his coffee cup, unlocking each terrible experience from its protective compartment in his memory. His sharp hazel eyes looked past me, lost in a cruel period of history that he, like so many others, had played a role in shaping.

I listened silently, probably the only person to ever hear him talk like this—certainly in our family. As he spoke, I began to understand that the rows of ribbons on his uniform (which I'd taken for granted all these years) represented more than bravery, battles, or jobs well done. His grim words were tempered by the hollow reality that pain kindles in a person's makeup over time. And yet they were strangely comforting, because they told me I wasn't alone in this misery of personal loss: my dad knew what it was like, too.

"I'm truly sorry this terrible experience has happened to

you so early in life," he finished, staring at his coffee. "I often remember the men I just told you about."

"Pa," I said, unsure how to show him I appreciated his love. "I know you were unhappy when I didn't go on that Danmark cruise, and my geometry grades haven't been as good as we both wanted; but thank you for making me come to Frankfurt."

The scar on the corner of his lip tipped upward slightly. Refilling his cup, he stirred in two heaping spoons of sugar, added a generous amount of cream, and pushed it across the table to me.

"You're a bit young for real Navy coffee, but I think you could use this."

Returning to school, we joined Colonel Gordon and General Holt in Mr. Pulaski's office.

"Where's Jimmy?" I asked. "Shouldn't the others be here to help answer questions?"

Pa and Colonel Gordon looked uncomfortable as General Holt cleared his throat.

"I have read all the official statements from those who witnessed the accident, including James Smith's. I'm only interested in what you have to say."

I looked at Pa, but his eyes told me there was no other alternative. So I recounted events again.

As I spoke, the general kept interrupting. "Why did you go? Of all places, why the river? Why weren't you studying for exams? Why did you break school rules to go kayaking?"

After a while, I stopped trying to respond. A secretary entered, telling Mr. Pulaski that divers had found Doc and Rex, and their bodies were awaiting identification.

"I'll do it, if that's okay with you two," Pa said, after an uneasy silence.

Colonel Gordon wiped the corner of one eye. "Thanks, Barney."

The general nodded.

While Pa was at the morgue, I searched the school for June. I found her hunched over a desk in the midst of a two-hour exam, filling a second blue book. How can she concentrate like that, after all that's happened? I know she's hurting as much as I am, yet she's able to make herself answer those questions. I was about to tap the glass of the classroom door but stopped. If she saw me, it would wreck her concentration. I knew how important these exams were to her. Flattening my hand against the glass, I took a long look. I'll always love you, June. Slowly, I turned toward Pulaski's office.

Through the closed door, I heard Pa conversing with the principal and guidance counselor. I was to leave on the Navy plane the next day, eventually taking my exams under supervision at the Copenhagen American School. At least I'll be able to see June before we leave, I sighed with relief.

Then General Holt spoke, his voice hard and official. "Never mind flying back tomorrow. I want to return immediately, understood?"

"Yes, sir," I heard Pa answer.

Then Mr. Slimbaugh cleared his throat. "Er, Captain Barnes?"

"Yes?" I could tell Pa was annoyed. Although he never said anything to me, I knew from numerous conferences that he did not care much for Mr. Slimbaugh.

"Um, before you go, there is one other thing, Captain Barnes. I am concerned that something is seriously wrong with your son."

I pressed my ear against the door.

"What do you mean?" My father's voice was sharp.

"Well," said Mr. Slimbaugh, "um, in my professional career, I have never seen a boy of fifteen experience something like this without exhibiting visible emotion. In these situations, crying is the norm, and Andy has shown no signs of grief at all. This is very odd indeed, and I think —"

"You think what?"

"I, um ... I think your son should be seen by a psychiatrist. I know a good one at the 97th General Hospital."

"He's in shock, you goddamn idiot!" Pa exploded. "Don't you have enough degrees to tell that? Men in my squadrons—survivors who returned from seeing their buddies blown to bits in the skies over the Pacific and Korea—responded to the fact that they were alive and their friends weren't the same way my son is doing. How many other situations of this kind involving school-age kids have you had experience with?"

"Well, ah, none," said the badly shaken guidance counselor.

"You may go, Silas," said Mr. Pulaski. "Thank you."

The door opened, and a frazzled Slimbaugh stepped quickly past me without a word.

"Well, gentlemen," said General Holt, "I think we're finished. As soon as I collect a few of Rex's things for his mother, I'd like to leave for Rhein-Main."

Chairs scraped as the meeting broke up. Pa was the last one to leave.

"I have to say goodbye to June, Pa," I said frantically. "It's my last chance, but she's taking an exam. Can't we stay long enough for me to say goodbye? I'll probably never see her again."

He squeezed my shoulder, massaging it for a second or

two. "Believe me, Andy, if I were calling the shots, I'd say of course. But General Holt is the senior officer present. However abrupt, he gave the equivalent of a direct order. Under the circumstances, it would not be wise to ask special favors—he wouldn't understand. Personally, I'm very sorry about your not being able to connect with June. I know she means a lot to you."

"But what difference does a couple of hours make? One hour? General Holt took up my morning when I could have been with her. Why don't I ask him when he's in Rex's room? Then he'd have a little more time to pack …."

"Andy, you can't do that," Pa said firmly. "General Holt is in grief, and probably angry that you are alive and his son isn't. I'm sorry, but no."

In Copenhagen, the general did not invite me to speak to Rex's mother; but the Gordons were waiting with hugs. Doc's mother was warm and comforting—even though I knew her grief far surpassed mine. I don't know how she managed, other than recognizing that she was a military wife. Long ago she had lost Doc's father, and now her only son. As we sat together in the living room, I tried to recount the good times we'd had together, and tell her how much his friendship had meant to me. It was hard having his youngest sisters asking where he was. Chippy, however, understood everything. I wished there were something I could have said to make her feel better.

As I was about to leave, Mrs. Gordon took my arm. "Andy, Doc would have wanted you to have these." She handed me his hockey skates. I still treasure them.

Marissa was not at the memorial service, but I didn't care. I remember sitting like a hollowed-out stone while a minister droned on and on. For all I knew, Doc was skating in and out of pastel clouds somewhere in the flashes of the aurora, laughing at us. Why couldn't I cry? Was Slimbaugh right? Was something wrong with me? What Doc said that first day we met—when he was talking about his father's death in the war—kept turning over in my mind: "Losing someone you love is part of life. Sooner or later, it happens to all of us. The important thing is how you deal with it."

Now it had happened to me, but I felt only emptiness and gnawing guilt. I should have been paddling with him that day. Why had I hesitated when he ordered me into his kayak? Was it his prank before breakfast? Or my vow never to get into a boat with him again, after we nearly sank that night on the Øresund? If I had been in his kayak, could I have stopped him from paddling to the wall? Would I have tried? I sensed the danger—if I had thought to grab his boat in the eddy as Jimmy held mine ... if he had stayed with the boat when it swamped ... if they had been with the wreck when it resurfaced—so many whys, what-ifs, if-onlys. What the hell did it all mean?

The Gordons left Copenhagen for the States a week after what would have been Doc's seventeenth birthday. One month after his death, I turned sixteen. We had known each other little more than a year.

# The Important Thing Is
# How You Deal with It

I wasted the summer of 1957. My heart was not in Denmark, but with June. God, how I missed her. Eventually, the letters came; nearly a month passed before I got the first one, but it arrived on my birthday. She had written it on the plane to Ankara three weeks before, after opening my going-away present—the one I told her not to open until sometime when she was thinking of a friend in Copenhagen who loved her. There were dried tears on the paper. She said every time she looked at her new charm bracelet, or heard the Little Mermaid bell ring, or listened to Tannenbaum when she raised the top of her music box, she thought of how special I was, and how much she loved and missed me.

I spent that afternoon in the gazebo, reading and rereading her letter—precious words that made my existence bearable. If I could have received one present to last the rest of my life, those two sheets of tissue-thin, blue airmail paper were it. I told her so in my reply.

The gazebo, with its memories of kissing her in the moonlight, became my sacred spot—the place I went to open, read, and answer each of her letters that summer. Sitting inside, listening to the Øresund lapping at the seawall, I could feel her presence; she was not thousands of miles away but there with me, teasing, cheering me with her humor, steadying me with her common sense. What was missing was the warmth of her touch.

There were times that summer, when I couldn't get my mind off Doc. Kirsten and Inge invited me to sail with them, and I went a couple of times; but the memories of our trip the previous summer hung over the boat like suffocating fog. I started building a complicated flying model of a P-38 Lightning in my room, working on it day after day. When I took a break on my balcony to look at boats sailing by on the Øresund, my eyes strayed to Doc's bullet hole in the gazebo roof.

At night, I often met Jimmy at Bakken, until his father unexpectedly was transferred back to Fort Something-or-Other in the Midwest. Decades later, I found him among the 57,939 names on the wall of the Vietnam Memorial in D.C. I went to a kiosk for a soft pack of Luckies to put below his name, but the kid behind the counter said he didn't have any. I left Camels and tears instead.

Elena, too, left my life that summer. I had forgotten about the friction regarding Mom's rigid dress code and Elena's opened-buttons approach to housework, so her departure came as a surprise. When I found her packing in her room, I was frantic.

"Please don't leave, Elena. I'll convince Mom to change her mind about the buttons."

She closed her travel case and hugged me, burying my face in her bosoms. "I love all of you very much—especially you. But it is not your mother's decision. I choose to go. How I wear my clothes is my business. It is principle."

"But you are like my big sister. I need you."

She took my face in her hands. "Listen to me, Little One. This blackness will pass for you. Doc would not want you to stay in your room, sad for him. He would want you to remember him by enjoying Denmark. I know it is hard now, but try to do that for him—and for me—when I am gone." She kissed me, and her red-blond locks brushed my forehead for the last time. Mom replaced her with Leena, who never shaved her legs. Curt referred to her as "Hairy Leena." She buttoned the starchy blue uniform collar so tightly she could hardly talk.

That summer, I developed an appreciation of Mozart's music, thanks to Alfie. He lived on the other side of Copenhagen and called one day to ask if I wanted to come over and listen to "Wolfgang" with him. I went numerous times. It was therapy. Best of all, the boy genius promised to help me with physics in the fall.

In September, I returned to Frankfurt High as a senior. Many friends were gone, including Copper. Like so many other kids I knew growing up, she followed her family into the revolving doors of her father's career military rotation system, stepped through, and disappeared. For years I skimmed sports pages for her name in connection with diving competitions, but I found nothing.

Significant changes had occurred at the school. Sergeant Normand was missing, transferred to Fort Dix, where he presumably rejoiced in poisoning luckless draftees instead of students. Mr. Slimbaugh, too, was gone. I did not miss either one. So was Miss Franklin—permanently—from a heart attack. For once the government did something right and promoted Miss Maybelle to the position of head supervisor of the girls' dorm. She became a surrogate mom for many of us guys as well. Because of The

Kreebs's exceptional concern for students under his care, he was now Director of Dependents' Dormitories for Germany, with a fancy office in Heidelberg. His replacement was an older gentleman named Lorenzo Batallini—a definite improvement. His assistant was Robin J. Nelson, a former football star from UCLA. In two days they were known as Batman and Robin.

I was assigned a newly painted single room complete with all-new furniture. Gone were the metal beds with wretched wire springs, replaced by wooden ones with foam mattresses. Doc's "vomit green" walls were now light-beige, framed with white woodwork. Even the curtains had been replaced. Most incredibly, however, was that when I went to wash my first load of clothes, I found a modern washing machine. I smiled at the thought of the two of us swishing our stuff around its fungus-lined tub with the busted baseball bat. Apparently, the screaming general on the telephone that day had decided the dorm needed a makeover.

As my senior year progressed, I began to feel a meaningful part of Frankfurt High. New faces filled desks of departed classmates. Some would become close friends for life. Remarkably, Mr. Pulaski and I got along quite well. My grades improved—especially in physics—until Alfie's dad was transferred on short notice to Japan, taking my tutor to the other side of the world. I participated in activities and even made the football team. The fact that I was totally deficient in killer instinct meant that I spent most of the season on the bench, but I didn't mind. It was therapy.

Memories, however, lingered everywhere. I drilled a hole in Doc's silver dollar and wore it around my neck. One overcast afternoon in October the dormitory was officially dedicated to him and Rex. The bronze plaque on the girls' side said Gordon Hall. Doc would have liked that. His dad flew all the way from Texas to be there. Afterward, Colonel Gordon took me to dinner at the Officers' Club. It was the last contact I had with Doc's family.

Every day I talked to my framed picture of June, twirling during our waltz, the one Doc had taken at the prom. But her touch, laughter, and the swish of her skirt as she walked beside me at school were irreplaceable. I lived for her Friday letters—regular as clockwork each week—a page or two of cherished words in familiar handwriting that I read more than any textbook. I wrote twice for every time she wrote me, until she got mad and told me to spend less time writing and more time studying. Her parents found a house in Silver Spring, Maryland, and she had no difficulty fitting into Sidwell Friends School again. Teachers and classmates remembered her from ninth grade, and soon she was as popular as she had been at Frankfurt: honor society president, student council, chairman of the social committee, president of the science club. Sadly, her mother lost her fight with cancer. I tried to help June through this difficult period, but my letters weren't the same as being with her. That would have made all the difference.

After Christmas she wrote that she had received an early acceptance to Wheaton College near Boston, where she would be a biology/pre-med major. When I told Mr. Glover, our new guidance counselor, that I wanted to go to Wheaton, he laughed.

"Wheaton is an excellent all-girls school—like Wellesley or Holyoke. I don't think you would qualify. Aside from the gender issue, your grades aren't high enough. Have you given any thought to enlisting in the Army?" I went to college instead, eventually ending up with a doctorate in history from American University in Washington D.C.

At the prom that year, I played my guitar and sang two songs, dedicating "Scarlet Ribbons" to June and "Sylvie" to Doc. It had always been his favorite.

On June 1, 1958, the anniversary of Doc's death, I signed out for the afternoon. The weather was a carbon copy of what it had been the year before—hot, hazy, calm. At the river, I rented a kayak from the same place and paddled upstream. Silhouettes of Doc, Rex, Jimmy, and the others laughed and cursed as phantom paddles splashed in the foam. At the dam, water poured over the spillway and the dancing waves again gripped my boat, shaking it into the eddy.

Doc, Doc … Why did I trust you so completely, and how did we become such close friends? You were my mentor, my charismatic companion—so persuasive, at ease with girls, teachers; a pal like no other, with crazy humor and a quick mind that got us into, and out of, so many unnecessary tight spots … Was this the side of you that attracted me? Or was it your willingness to be the risk taker I never was, could never be? We were total opposites—my cautious nature, constantly tested by your ceaseless energy, your urge for adventure and chancing the unexpected, against which you measured yourself. That was the part of you I loved—and feared—most. If you had lived, we would have been lifelong friends. I can see you as a hell-for-leather Air Force pilot like the real dad you never knew; or perhaps a daring combat photographer in Vietnam, living on the edge between life and death, striving for that elusive Pulitzer Prize-winning photograph.

I fixed on Tonto's jackknife scar across my palm, and exploded into a flood of memories: our blood brothers oath; the shaving contest; the Wiesbaden swimming trip; the Jell-O incident; Easter in Copenhagen; Doc's farewell to June at the prom; the Main River ... "C'mon, it's fun!" you waved, and seconds later, you were sitting alone, waiting, hands on the gunwales of that disintegrating piece of crap as it was being sucked those last few feet toward the Offenbach Dam. Did you know that this time you were not going to make it? You weren't book smart like June, or street smart like Jimmy, nor interested in history and fishing like me. No, Doc, you were the funny, magnetic, loyal friend who celebrated life like no other kid I knew while I was growing up. Lone Ranger should have been with you in that kayak, not Rex. Did you save my life that morning with your wastebasket of cold water? That thought still haunts me.

Taking Doc's silver dollar from around my neck, I threw it far out into the current next to the cement wall where I'd last seen him.

"Bye, Tonto."

And the tears finally came.

*Epilogue*

# *Winter: 1995*

Ignoring the *Betreten verboten* sign, we ducked through a gap in the fence, putting traffic noise from the Miquelallee behind us. Inside, the oval track around the football field was recognizable only by scattered patches of faded reddish cinders. Behind the empty school building, coughs from wrecking equipment coming to life in the bitter early-morning cold signaled we were trespassing on prized real estate in this once war-ravaged city. Soon, Frankfurt American High School would be gone.

The solid gray quilt above us foretold heavy snow, soon. My wife tightened her parka hood and I took her hand. Cautiously, we picked our way through vegetation, shriveled in winter's nakedness, across grounds where spring flowers once lent a cheerful backdrop to our youthful comings and goings. It was the dormitory I yearned to see, if only to reassure myself that once it had played a brief but formative role in my life. The heavy glass patio doors—the ones we'd yanked open so many times every day—were chained. I started counting second-floor windows on the boys' side, looking for Room 15, but her tug on my sleeve diverted me to the girls' half of the building.

"There, near the entrance at eye level—his plaque."

I'd watched German workmen install it before the dedication ceremonies. Now, after decades of neglect, the date was scarcely visible: June 1, 1957.

The Little Mermaid, tiny silver guitar, shark's tooth, and various other charms on her bracelet jingled as she put her arm around my waist. We stood in silence looking at Doc's name engraved on his bronze plaque, green and discolored by the years.

"It's been a long time since the three of us were here," she said.

Her silver hair, still curly as ever, was prettier than the day we'd first met in this place, only a few steps from where we now stood. Gently, I squeezed her close. Leaves rustled around our shoes as an icy puff of wind scattered the first flakes of snow across the flat stones of the dormitory patio.

# Author's Notes

Although this work is fictional, some scenes are based on real-life events, including the final one, which had a formative effect on the person I was during my time in Frankfurt and has never been forgotten. While much did happen as depicted in this novel, I have combined characters, added or subtracted scenes, invented dialog and such as necessary to tell a good story, while still trying my best to be true to the times as they were back then and the people I knew, lived with, and loved.

I have been fortunate to benefit from excellent mentors and supporters essential to give this story life. To these knowledgeable people of goodwill, who guided me over the years, I cannot possibly express my deepest gratitude and heartfelt thanks to them for helping on this project. I came to depend on them for advice as they willingly gave of their time to read, proof, and comment. Their cumulative interest, suggestions, and encouragement added a special quality to Uncle Sam's Kids and made writing it a special event in my life. Pat, my wonderful wife of 55 years and the inspiration for the character of June, is responsible for making things happen and keeping the wind in my sails. And without my son Ray's extensive writing savvy and publishing experience, USK would still be my imagined goal. My grandchild, Ash, read the manuscript 3 times between the ages of 12 and 18, furnishing feedback unhindered by the cobwebs of age. I particularly wish to thank Dina Harris Walker, who reread the manuscript many times, providing advice and encouragement I could not have gotten from anyone else. Others who kept me going include Anna Nielson, Mort Inger and Daryl Forth of Cape Cod; Raquel Pidal and Julie Lipkin, my professional readers; Inger and Aage Rasmussen of Copenhagen, Denmark--old friends and my Danish readers; Dr. Thomas Huber, Ph.D., my authority on all things German; CPT John A. Fitch, USA (ret) for his flying expertise and all things army; and Ethan Canin, Ben Shattuck, and the Cuttyhunk Island Writer's Retreat "Hunkers 4 Lyfe" Class of 2018—the most pleasant, productive, and useful seminar I have ever experienced. Lastly, I want to extend best wishes to Uncle Sam's kids, former students of Frankfurt High School when I was there, and extend special thanks to my classmate, Zonetta Fain Glenn, for reading several drafts and relating her remembrances of the school, as it was between 1956-58.

Made in the USA
Middletown, DE
01 February 2021